Murder Gets Even

by
John Molino

ISBN 1722497718

EAN 978-1722497712

For Eileen

Murder Gets Even

by
John Molino

At times alone, but more often in pairs or groups of three or four, the crows came to rest in the welcoming arms of the dormant trees. In a tree line that easily stretched a quarter mile, they appeared to select the branches of a small cluster of white oaks, red maples, and loblolly pines that formed a semicircle of sorts around a space near the train tracks.

They kept arriving. The nearly leafless trees now lost their skeletal profile, ripe with the black-feathered blossoms that were hundreds of crows.

And they kept arriving. Were there a thousand by now? Who knew? There were too many to count.

When a light breeze passes from west to east, it chases the fallen leaves and causes them to scrape across the railroad tracks and the concrete of Backlick Run. The spillway soon joins with Holmes Run to form Cameron Run, a 3-mile stream that feeds Hunting Creek and, not long thereafter, the Potomac River. Only when the leaves come to a halt, waiting for the next gust to move them further along, do you realize that the birds—the thousands of birds—make no sound. Nothing. Where is the annoying cawing that so characterizes crows everywhere? Not a feather ruffles.

In silent tribute, they perched. A fallen comrade. A dead crow on a bed of leaves, already beginning its journey, returning to the earth. A victim. A crow, like so many of the species' population, which had not lived to adulthood. What better homage to a lifetime of flight and survival than a moment of stillness and silence?

Just when it seemed the calm would last forever, the crows—husbands and wives, young and old—simultaneously (or so it seemed) sprang from their individual perches and flew to the south. On a silent command, the black cloud, alive now as though a creature possessed, banked to the west and gradually dissolved as the birds embarked on their separate routes.

Cameron Station Military Installation
Alexandria, Virginia
Summer 1970

1

Colonel Fleming Andrews sat at his desk, puffing his pipe, in the office of the commander of Cameron Station, a 164-acre U.S. Army installation in Alexandria, Virginia. While its primary role was as an administrative headquarters for the worldwide movement of personnel and equipment, the base also hosted a commissary (the military's name for a grocery store) and a military exchange where area military personnel (active duty, reserve, National Guard, and retired) and their families could shop for clothing, and other items commonly found in a department store. As a community in the shadow of the monuments of Washington, DC, and a stone's throw from the Pentagon, there were many in the local area who enjoyed this privilege.

Despite the military police at the front and rear gates, Cameron Station was much less a fort and more a small city within the city of Alexandria. Like any community, it had certain overhead obligations and bills to pay. Buildings, roads, and law and order had to be maintained, trash picked up, the electricity kept on, etc.

Andrews didn't know much about moving people or equipment around the world. He was not a logistician. He had been a military policeman his entire career. He entered the Army after graduation from West Point and served in domestic assignments, as well as in Germany and in Korea after that conflict reached a stalemate and the gunfire ceased. Though he never saw actual combat, a tour of duty in Vietnam helped secure the colonel's eagles he wore on his shoulders.

At his promotion ceremony just over two years ago, Andrews expressed a sense of humility and gratitude to the many soldiers with whom he had served who helped make his promotion a reality. Not only did Andrews not mean what he said, most of the people at the ceremony knew he was just saying what was expected and that he could not have been more insincere. Fleming Andrews had a large and delusional ego.

"Do you think the asshole thinks we believe him?" one junior officer turned to another and asked under his breath.

"No. But he's never given a shit what we think anyway. If they had fragged pencil pushers in 'Nam, he wouldn't be here today and we wouldn't have to be here like potted plants to fill the room."

"I hear you, man. I'm just here for a piece of the cake."

Throughout its history, the U.S. Army has had many stellar performers with the demonstrated potential for increased responsibility. In the late 1960s and early 1970s, the Army was large enough to include lesser men and a few near scoundrels (like Fleming Andrews) who willfully used people to gain personal advantage without a second thought.

Soon after his latest promotion, he was assigned to Cameron Station. Like most "bird colonels," Andrews kept telling himself he remained competitive for promotion to brigadier general, although it was highly unusual for an installation commander to receive the coveted star of a general officer. Troop leaders in the field usually got that recognition. If Andrews were totally honest with himself, he would know the odds were even more remote for the commander of an installation the relatively small size of Cameron Station. In fact, no one who had held the job before him had ever been promoted beyond their current rank. Some transferred in the same rank; most retired after three years in the position. Being honest with himself was not, after all, a Fleming Andrews attribute.

Nonetheless, this was his city. He was the commanding

officer. While he often referred to himself as the "Mayor of Cameron Station," he really thought of himself as the royal leader of a small kingdom. Ironically, though he was responsible for the buildings on Cameron Station, he had no control over what went on inside most of them. Andrews hated the fact that there were three officers working everyday within the confines of the base who actually outranked him.

These multi-starred generals ran their respective agencies, which were referred to as tenant organizations on Cameron Station. Fleming Andrews' role was to ensure the installation functioned efficiently so more significant work could go on within the buildings. This arrangement also allowed the senior generals to be unconcerned with the "housekeeping" requirements of the base.

Occasionally, Andrews lamented this fact to a West Point classmate, who was no longer in the Army, when they spoke on the phone. "These guys shit, and it's my job to make sure the toilets flush. You tell me which is more important. They wouldn't know what to do if the things they take for granted suddenly disappeared."

Self-deprecation was not easy for him. He found great comfort in the fact that, as the commander of Cameron Station, he was able to enjoy the few perks of the position. And Fleming Andrews was all about the perks. Opportunities to engage with local civic leaders were frequent. Most were pleasant, social, and superficial. Right up his alley.

He would gladly speak to the Rotary or be grand marshal for some parade. He even enjoyed the periodic town hall meetings where locals would invariably complain about the traffic in and out of the base during the morning and afternoon rush hours.

He knew he could get away with a promise to look into any issue that surfaced at the meetings, with no real intent to do anything about them. This was the beauty of the standard three-year assignment, in Andrews' opinion. Once he was there too long to blame things on his predecessor, he could treat most issues with benign neglect until the situation resolved itself, was forgotten, or simply outlived his tenure in the job.

After almost every encounter with the community, a nonplussed Colonel Fleming Andrews would routinely remark to a staff member, "They bitched about the traffic again, but not one of them complained about the soldiers' money spent outside the gate in their businesses or the jobs I provide on post for local civilians."

In mid-June, Andrews would celebrate his second anniversary as the Cameron Station commander. He told his West Point buddy, "At this point in my tenure, I can kick an issue so far into the future, I ought to be kicking field goals for the goddamn Redskins. I can promise these sons-of-bitches anything without worrying about delivering."

Who knows, Andrews thought, echoing the dreams of so many Army contemporaries equally uncompetitive for promotion, *this time next year I could be pinning on my first star.*

Andrews insisted he have access to virtually every locked door or secured area on Cameron Station. There were exceptions, of course; certain classified documents, areas cleared for discussions at the top secret level, ammunition and weapons, medical supplies, etc. But Andrews contented himself with the knowledge that, as the one man responsible for all of Cameron Station, his key ring was larger than anyone else's on the installation.

Every week, he would spend an hour or two being driven from location to location, stopping for announced and unannounced visits throughout the base during and after regular duty hours. He did it because he could. The actual stops at the fort's gas station, the Recreation Services office, or the commissary were less exciting to Andrews than the fact that he had the authority to make the visits.

Among his favorite places was the rail yard at the back end of the installation. His regular driver on these excursions, Henry Washington, took Andrews there early in his tenure as part of a detailed tour of the base. For Andrews, he might just as well have been a child given a life-sized train set to which he and few others had access.

As rail yards go, Cameron Station's was modest, but it was his—the man with the biggest key ring on Cameron Station—and he would visit it frequently when making his inspection rides.

Soon after summer began, Andrews climbed into the back seat of the Chevy Blazer. As he did, he lit his pipe, newly packed with tobacco.

"Where're you taking me today, Mr. Henry?" Andrews asked the man who was sitting behind the wheel.

Henry Washington had worked for the U.S. Army as a civilian employee since 1943. He tried to enlist the year prior, but the Army had little interest in black men and no interest in volunteers who had feet as flat as his. He got a job with the Cameron Station Facilities Engineer as a general handyman. Over the years, he had a handful of jobs and, for the last 15 years, had been a driver in the motor pool, working for the Post Engineer who was assigned to the staff of the installation commander. Andrews was the eighth Cameron Station commander Henry Washington had served under, and the fourth with whom he had considerable interaction as his primary driver. Among the jokes about Colonel Andrews was that he was so self-absorbed, after nearly two years, he still didn't realize that the man he called "Mr. Henry" was really named Mr. Washington—Henry Washington.

When asked about it, Henry Washington would only shake his head and say, "What can I say? That's Colonel Andrews." In fact, Washington had too much respect for the rank to correct a colonel, but enough disregard for Andrews to allow him to continue to embarrass himself unknowingly.

Washington's lack of a high school diploma belied his native intelligence. Every newly assigned installation engineer might assume Henry Washington to be the most expendable man on the staff, but, within a few months, each considered him a valuable member of the team.

"It's been a while since we inspected the train yard, Colonel. I thought you might want to walk through the area today."

Andrews almost always got in the car knowing where he wanted to go. He would usually ask Washington the question and routinely say, "Maybe next time." Today, their thoughts on a destination aligned.

"Great idea. I love that part of the post. It's a key resource that is relatively unknown to most who live and work here. It's an important part of the war effort, but you've heard me say that a hundred times. Haven't you?"

"Not a lot of activity there, Colonel. That's for sure. When they park a train, it can stay for a while. I'll bet there are some boxcars that have been there since last winter."

While Andrews grossly overstated the rail yard's strategic importance, Washington only slightly understated the activity level. Cameron Station was the home of three active train tracks supporting commercial cargo movement, as well as an occasional train carrying military supplies. Routinely, boxcars would be detached from the trains and would sit empty in the yard, be coupled to another train, or get reloaded with additional supplies. Now, once a month for no more than a day or two, the yard was a fairly busy place. The Army had consolidated certain logistics activities; so, the yard came alive less frequently, but in a more concentrated way when it did. On rare occasions, when the yard was very busy, Andrews, in his capacity as a mere observer, found it a wonder to behold.

The seemingly incoherent, unrelated movement of boxcars was all part of a larger plan, incomprehensible to the casual observer. When the yard was quiet, especially at night, it had the air of a graveyard with oversized tombstones resting on a web of tracks and switches.

A narrow gate, when unlocked, provided access for an individual on foot. Next to it, another gate was large enough to accommodate large trucks. Across the yard, two other gates allowed access to the active tracks.

"If you don't mind using the narrow gate, Colonel, I'll leave the vehicle outside the yard," Washington said. "If the big gate ain't held open, it slides closed by itself. It don't lock, o'course, but damn near looks it."

"The American railroad system is a national treasure," Andrews said. "And this is my piece of it."

"Indeed it is, Colonel. Indeed it is."

"Why don't you walk with me, Mr. Henry?"

"Colonel, if it's all the same to you, I'll stay here with the vehicle, like I usually do."

"Suit yourself. Doesn't the smell bother you—being parked by the dumpster?"

"Not usually. They empty it every Monday morning. Every now and then, the yard boss finds a dead animal on the tracks or in the area. These guys will toss the carcass in the dumpster. When that happens, it can be a might rich here, but it's fine most days."

"Well, they should call Animal Control instead of throwing a carcass in the dumpster. Even a small rodent can stink bad for a few days."

"That's true," Washington said. "But the trash company ain't ever complained…to my knowledge."

As he walked through the gate, Andrews' attention was drawn to the rhythmic click-clack from across the yard beyond the distant fences. A commercial cargo train of at least 100 cars moved at a reduced speed to a destination known only to the man operating the engine.

Andrews usually walked throughout the yard with his hands behind his back, puffing on a pipe clenched in his teeth. Except for the passing cargo train, there was no activity today. He stepped over tracks and between boxcars. Here, Andrews was the master of all he surveyed. As a result, even though there wasn't much to inspect and seldom anyone with whom to speak, it was no surprise that the visits to the rail yard invariably kept Andrews out of the office longer than other inspection tours.

The visit complete, Andrews was about to exit through the narrow gate to rejoin the vehicle outside, but he stopped and stood, looking up into the tall trees that nearly surrounded the area.

Washington stepped out of the Blazer, with a hand on the open door.

"Somethin' wrong, Colonel?"

"I'm watching one of those trees. It's as though it's pulsating…you know…like a heartbeat. I think it's because of all the black birds perched in it. Look through the leaves, Mr. Henry. Can you see them? There are more birds still arriving."

Washington shot Andrews a quick glance that silently said, *I know what the word pulsating means, asshole*, but instead, he said, "It's not just that tree, Colonel. There's half dozen of 'em…all bunched together and I'd bet they's a thousand crows."

"What the hell are they doing?"

"Prob'bly grievin', is my guess."

"Did you say *grieving*? Are you serious?"

"As a heart attack. Crows are smart animals. Real

smart and kinda social. They mates for life. When a crow dies—and lots of 'em dies young—its circle of crows comes together to say goodbye. I bet you if we went to the area right 'neath that group of trees, we'd find a dead crow."

"Maybe, but I bet we would get shit on by a thousand fucking birds," Andrews said.

"That's pretty funny, Colonel. You know, I also heard that they remember faces and, if they get pissed at you, they never forget," Washington said.

"How do you know so much about crows, anyway?"

"I sees 'em all the time here on post; so, I read up on 'em at the library. They might crap on us, Colonel, but I doubt they'd crap on the dead crow...too much respect."

Andrews continued to look at the trees.

"I'll be damned. How long do they stay?"

"Not sure, 'zactly. Not very long. Pays their respects and then flies off, I imagine."

Henry Washington climbed back behind the Blazer's steering wheel while Andrews lingered a minute longer. As he turned to walk through the gate, a cloud of crows lifted in unison from the trees they had populated for the funeral rite of their fallen friend. They rose together and, on some silent command, swooped down toward the spot where Andrews was now frozen in his steps, his mouth open and his pipe in his hand.

The blanket of crows glided across the face of the sun, briefly casting Andrews in a slight shadow. He could swear he felt the temperature around him drop as the ominous cloud seemed to come directly at him. For a split second, he felt a level of anxiety he had never before experienced. The birds formed a dark, angry face. It was the face of a dragon. He was sure of it.

He saw two piercing eyes looking both at him and

through him. Pupils were aflame. At that brief moment, he felt genuine fear. He sensed that the dragon formed by the birds would attack him, grab him in its talons and rip him apart. When the birds banked again, abandoning the assault, the image dissolved instantly. He flinched slightly at the movement.

Andrews sensed the air around him return to its previous temperature. He felt perspiration beading on his forehead and running down the center of his back. He composed himself by tapping his now unlit pipe against the palm of his left hand to shake out the remaining tobacco, wondering if Henry Washington noticed his nervousness.

Washington had noticed, of course, but he wouldn't mention it.

"That's the damnedest thing ever, Mr. Henry."

"Yes, sir. Been observin' that behavior for years. A bunch that big is called a murder."

The word got Andrews' attention, but he thought he had heard wrong. "What's it called?" he said.

"Yeah, Colonel, you heard me right. A bunch of crows ain't called a flock. They's technically called a murder."

"After that demonstration, I can see why."

2

They drove back to headquarters.

"Thank you, Mr. Henry. I'll see you next time."

"For sure, Colonel." Washington touched the bill of his cap as Andrews exited the car and closed the door.

It was nearly 4:00 in the afternoon. Andrews prepared to put in a final hour at his desk before going home. There were always papers to sign, administrative actions to decide, and reports to be filed. Department of the Army regulations routinely required select administrative actions receive the installation commander's consideration and, usually, bear his signature.

Generally, though, Andrews occupied himself during the final hour of each day by smoking one last bowl of tobacco in one of his pipes, deciding what could wait until tomorrow (nearly everything), discussing the day's events with his Command Sergeant Major, the most senior noncommissioned officer on Cameron Station, and previewing the next day's calendar with Laura Bennett, the longtime secretary to many of the installation's commanders.

"It's been a good week, Laura. What's in store for Monday?"

Before she could answer him, Sergeant Major Ed Rodriguez appeared behind her, placing a hand on her shoulder.

"Excuse me, Laura. Colonel, I'm taking off for the day. My mother-in-law is visiting and I promised my wife I'd swing by the commissary for a few things and get home early. I've got the monthly senior NCO meeting on

Monday morning. I'll give you any highlights after the meeting."

For as long as the United States has had an Army, the relationship between a commander and the unit's senior noncommissioned officer has been very special. When it works, it is as though the two people have one mind, synchronized to lead a singularly productive organization that exceeds expectations regardless of the unit's mission. When it doesn't work, mediocrity is about as good as it gets.

Andrews and Rodriguez were on a course for almost certain mediocrity. Sergeant Major Rodriguez had been at Cameron Station about 18 months, arriving 6 months into Andrews' tenure. He gave the colonel every benefit of the doubt, but it didn't take long for Rodriguez to have seen enough of Andrews to know that he was a man on an ego trip who was willing (if not eager) to cut corners, however discretely, to enhance his own image.

Sergeant Major Rodriguez tolerated Colonel Andrews. As their relationship evolved, they essentially worked independent of each other. They would meet during routine staff meetings, seldom enjoying the one-on-one professional intimacy so many good commanders nurtured with their most senior NCOs. Rodriguez rarely confronted Andrews directly, but did all he could to protect the integrity of other members of the organization as they interacted with and followed the directives of this flawed commander.

For his part, Andrews respected, but, in some ways, was intimidated by Sergeant Major Rodriguez. They worked together because they had to work together. Rodriguez's very high standards of conduct helped keep Andrews from going too far over any lines or from violating any laws. Andrews often saw regulations as being far more directive in nature for others than they were for him. He was in many ways jealous of Rodriguez. The respectful treatment he received from every officer he encountered and his rapport with fellow senior NCOs, as well as junior enlisted soldiers, was well-earned and genuine.

The tension between Andrews and his sergeant major was real, but in an odd way, it reduced the chances of a direct confrontation. Rodriguez was too professional and Colonel Andrews' character was too weak. Together, they would not fail; neither would they excel.

"No problem, Sergeant Major," Andrews said. "Although, if my mother-in-law was in town, I'd probably work late." Andrews followed this comment with the obligatory laugh at his own weak joke—the standard practice of people who have virtually no sense of humor. Both Rodriguez and Laura Bennett gave him the insincere and perfunctory chuckle. The sergeant major turned to leave, but not before he wished both of them a good weekend.

"Okay, Laura, where were we?"

"You have a fairly light day on Monday, Colonel. Ed Anderson from the mayor's office will be in at 10:00 to talk to you about the plans for the Fourth of July parade next Saturday. Susan Braswell from Public Affairs will sit in on the meeting."

"That's great." Andrews' enthusiasm was, for once, sincere. He was going to be the Grand Marshal of the parade through Old Town Alexandria in just over a week. There was nothing he liked more than hearing about how he would be featured in a parade. The icing on the cake for the meeting was that he would engineer it so that he sat at the table directly across from (and staring down the blouse of) Susan Braswell of the Cameron Station Public Affairs Office. Braswell was a slim, attractive, 30-something brunette with a great figure and breasts that were the center of Andrews' attention whenever he and they were in the same room.

Ten minutes into her initial meeting with the newly arrived Colonel Fleming Andrews, they drew conclusions about each other that had not varied over the last two years. After that introductory session, when a colleague asked her about the new commander, Braswell told her, "If someone told him that I had one eye in the middle of my forehead, he would have no way of refuting it because he never looked at my face."

For his part, Andrews came away from the meeting convinced Susan Braswell wanted nothing less than to have sex with him on the spot.

"You don't have any other appointments on the calendar," Laura Bennett said. "By the way, sir, do you remember Marie Garrett, last year's summer intern?"

"Sure. Nice girl." Truth was that Andrews had only a vague recall of the skinny, high school sophomore who did minor administrative work around the office the previous year. Marie was part of an Army program to gainfully employ a handful of urban students from low to moderate income families while school was out for the summer. Admitting he could not remember was not something Andrews could easily do. He would rather play the odds and tell a white lie.

"Well, we just got the good news that she will be our intern again this summer. She starts on Monday," Laura said.

"Wonderful," Andrews said as he relit his pipe that had been sitting in the ashtray since earlier in the day. (Wonderful, in this context, was a dismissive euphemism for Who-gives-a-shit.)

Andrews put a two-inch thick stack of papers into his brief case as work he would take home. The papers would return on Monday, having never been read or even withdrawn from the case.

"Laura, if there's nothing pressing in the stack I just put in my briefcase, I'm going to call it a week. And you should too." He was now using a pipe tool to tamp down the remaining tobacco in his pipe. He applied a flame again briefly to help ensure the tobacco burned evenly.

"Sergeant Major Rodriguez has a leave form that I put on the top of the stack. If you approve it, you won't have to carry it home," Bennett said.

As Andrews fished out the Army form that soldiers used to request time off, Laura Bennett added, "It's for a week in late August, but he's going to be out of town and he wanted to be sure you were okay with it before he locked in travel arrangements for his family."

Andrews reviewed the form quickly, noting the dates, checked *approved*, signed his name, and handed the form across his desk to his secretary.

"Yep. He mentioned it to me the other day," Andrews said. "Now, go on. It's close enough to quitting time. It's unlikely anyone will call, but ask one of the NCOs downstairs to cover the phones just in case."

"Thank you, sir, if I manage to finish early, I'll do that."

Laura knew that the handful of sergeants who worked in other offices in the headquarters building would do her any favor she asked, but she also knew they resented the dismissive way Andrews treated enlisted soldiers. Besides, she had no intention of leaving early. In fact, she was very careful to account for any time off because of her distrust of the colonel—a distrust that had never lessened—even after two years as his secretary.

Early Years

3

So, how did a person so few liked or trusted manage to rise to the rank of colonel and come to be selected to command an Army installation?

The bloated size of the Army during and in the waning days of the Vietnam War was part of the answer. Fleming Andrews was smart enough to sense when to be visible, when to take credit (whether earned or not) for successes, and when to fly under the radar so as not to be noticed if things went poorly.

It never took long for people to conclude Andrews had an enormously inflated self-image. Many were put off by this. Most confused his arrogance and lack of consideration as a manifestation of huge self-confidence; they were wrong. However, this misinterpretation was fine with Andrews.

He was a man with many personality flaws and little acumen in social settings. He countered his short-comings and insecurity around others, especially women, with arrogance, bravado, a conviction that every woman he found attractive wanted to get into his pants. When he was alone, pornography helped him boost a macho self-image.

Three months into Andrews' tour in Korea in the mid-1950s, mail from his first wife, Helen, stopped arriving. The only mail he received from that point on were letters and packages from his mother.

Helen was smart, active, and popular throughout high school. And though it wasn't the norm for young women in the 1940s, she was a college graduate. She had been awarded an academic scholarship to Marymount College in Tarrytown, New York, where she excelled.

Near the end of her sophomore year, her five-year relationship with a high school sweetheart began to unravel. Their phone conversations became strained. Finally, he admitted he was drinking a good bit and had experimented with drugs. She inferred from some of his comments that he was seeing other girls despite promises and assurances to the contrary.

When Helen went home for the summer after her sophomore year, she was surprised to learn her boyfriend would be leaving Fordham University and had been accepted at Berkley. He told her he wanted more freedom than his relationship with her would allow.

Helen returned to Marymount in September angry and confused, but resolved to be cautious in her relationships with boys. It wasn't hard for her friends to convince her to join them at a fall social event across the Hudson River at West Point. These were future leaders of the country; the men who had won World War II. It was there she met third-year Cadet Fleming Andrews.

Andrews had always done well academically and the regimented environment of the military academy suited him well. He soaked in the history and the indoctrination that told him he was among the country's elite. The sheltered (all male) environment also masked his social inadequacy. Despite this, he came across to people as a mature, responsible young man.

Their meeting could not have been better timed. Helen needed someone in whom she could have some degree of faith, someone with a serious approach to life in post-WWII America. For his part, Andrews reacted surprisingly well to the confident, albeit somewhat controlling nature of this smart young woman.

They married a month after their mutual graduation ceremonies. Andrews was commissioned a second lieutenant the day he graduated from West Point. Early Army schooling and his initial assignment kept the young couple on the east coast of the U.S. It was apparent early to Helen that she was not cut out for the white-gloved life of an Army officer's wife in the late 1940s. She had a college degree, idolized Eleanor Roosevelt, and had career aspirations of her own.

In the summer of 1952, with the Korean War ongoing, Andrews was transferred from the Infantry to the Military Police Corps and moved from Fort Benning, Georgia to Fort Riley, Kansas. Helen stayed at Fort Benning, preparing for the move, while Andrews was given temporary duty at the Army's school for military policemen at Fort Gordon, Georgia. She was pleased her husband would not be going to war, but was not happy about being in Kansas. After two years in Kansas, he was reassigned to Korea on what the Army called an unaccompanied tour of duty. It was 1954 and, although the situation remained tense, a ceasefire had been in effect nearly a year. Helen remained in Kansas because the Army told Andrews he would likely return to Fort Riley for an additional year after spending not more than twelve months in Korea.

Helen was miserable in Kansas. Fort Benning had been boring and tortuously rural for a city girl, but at least it was on the East Coast. She and old friends would periodically drive to a mid-point for mini reunions. She missed New Jersey. For years, she had missed the ability to go to New York City any time she wanted. She missed her friends and her family.

That Thanksgiving, Helen traveled to her hometown of North Arlington, New Jersey, to be with her parents. The day after Thanksgiving, she ran into an old high school friend who carried a flame for Helen that had never gone out. They had a cup of coffee together. He convinced her to go to the town's Christmas tree lighting ceremony with him on Saturday. She declined his advances over a drink after the event, but there was an attraction. They met for brunch after church on Sunday and had each other for dessert Sunday afternoon in his apartment.

She went back to New Jersey for Christmas. Their meetings during that visit were not by chance. By Valentine's Day, she had put her married life in government quarters at Fort Riley, Kansas, behind her and was living with her lover in northern New Jersey. Friends and neighbors all seemed to believe her lie that her no-good husband had written her from Korea to tell her that their marriage was over and he wanted her out of his life.

Her last letter to Andrews arrived in Korea in mid-March. She was over her guilt, convinced that her marriage to Andrews had been a mistake from the start. She ended her "Dear John" letter by saying she would treasure the good times they had together. She wasn't sure what that really meant. She was compelled to add a post script, "Honestly, Fleming, it isn't anything you did. It's me."

"You're goddamn right. It's all you, bitch," he said aloud when he finished reading her letter, even though he was alone in his room in a secure Army facility in Seoul.

He was humiliated. He was also furious. A cold-heartedness came over him. He folded the letter and secured it, ensuring it would not be damaged or lost. He knew it would be needed and very useful when he went to see the JAG lawyer there and when he returned to the States to divorce her formally.

Andrews was resolved never to marry again. He didn't know if he could ever trust a woman in a husband/wife relationship. In fact, he had little interest in long-term relationships with women. "Burn me once…," he would confide to friends who asked about his social life.

Over the intervening years, he had occasionally driven many miles from his duty station to be sure that he would not be recognized when he solicited a prostitute or tried to pick up a woman in a bar. Between those times, he satisfied himself with his small, but eclectic collection of porn and bold talk of past conquests when drinking in an Officers' Club.

It was not uncommon for the wife of a fellow officer to invite him over for dinner so that she and her husband could match him up with a female friend. Most often, the dinner encounter would be the extent of it. But, every now and then, Andrews would call the woman for a second date. Dinner and a movie, nothing more.

Rarely, if the woman was overly eager to become the wife of an Army officer, there would be sex, but it would be cold and unemotional on his part. Andrews made it a rule that, when this happened, it would be in the woman's residence or at a hotel. Typically, when the woman awoke in the morning, Andrews had been gone for hours. Another date was never in his plan.

4

After his time in Vietnam, Andrews was assigned to Fort Gordon, Georgia, as the installation's Provost Marshal. This was a big deal to Andrews. Fort Gordon was the home of the Military Police Corps. It was where he learned the fundamentals of being an Army policeman.

Most importantly for his career advancement, Fort Gordon was commanded by a two-star general who was himself a product of the Military Police Corps. Success working directly for this general, Andrews believed, would not only lock in his promotion to colonel on schedule, it might even get him selected early (below the zone) and could well be a stepping stone to wearing stars on his shoulders.

This rosy scenario was dealt a blow when Andrews met with the commanding general to receive his annual performance evaluation. It was a positive report, certainly good enough to keep him competitive for promotion. It wasn't the written evaluation that surprised Andrews, however.

"Thank you, sir, for the evaluation and for your supportive written comments," Andrews said and stood to leave the general's office.

"Fleming, one more thing," the general said. "Please sit back down."

"What is it, sir?"

"Fleming, this is a little awkward for me; so, I am going to consider it off the record…as though it never happened. Agreed?"

"Sure, sir."

"I've considered mentioning this to you before, but I held off. Look, I am going to be brutally honest with you, Fleming, because it's the only way I know how to be."

"I'm fine with that, sir." Andrews stiffened his back not knowing what the commanding general was about to say. Rapidly in his mind, he started recalling the few prostitutes he had encountered so many miles away over the last six months. Was he spotted buying porn in a magazine shop? He even tried to think if he had ever had one too many at the Officers' Club and said something stupid or rolled through a stop sign on the way home.

The commanding general was clearly uncomfortable; Andrews found that unsettling. His anxiety increased as he waited for the general to come to the point.

"Fleming, I know you talk a big show around your friends and we all exaggerate at times. Sometimes, it's to hide something else, but I don't think that's the case with you. No, I want you to know that I for one do not think you're a queer. I will admit…"

"What?" Andrews said without adding the "sir" or considering that he was interrupting his boss. The general simply held up his hand and continued.

"Fleming, I said that I'm *not* saying you're a queer; you know, a homo or anything like that. In fact, I would be very surprised to learn if that was the case; however,…well, Fleming, I've got to tell you, it just isn't right for a man your age, in this business, not to have a wife."

"Sir, where is this coming from?"

"Fleming, whether you're the world's biggest playboy or if your social life is in your head, this man's Army has expectations regarding the institution of marriage."

"I know, sir, but…"

"Fleming, it's the truth whether you like it or not. Look, I think you're a sure thing for promotion, but I have got to tell you, there will be people on the promotion board who'll wonder about a lieutenant colonel who doesn't have a wife. They won't have any way of knowing if every woman in the state of Georgia is in love with you, but they will be able to see in your personnel file that you are not married. And there will be doubts about why this is the case. Not everybody, mind you, but, once planted, doubts linger with promotion board members."

"Sir, I'm sure you know my wife left me when I was in Korea. And I can't believe anyone would…"

"Fleming, take a breath. You don't have to convince me. I'm talking to you as someone who has sat on his share of promotion boards. I know the comments that get tossed around. Hell, if I happen to be on the Board that considers you, I'll be in the room and I'll be able to stop it when that kind of talk starts up. But Fleming, it just doesn't look right for a man your age not to have a wife. I'm not telling you to get married tomorrow, for God's sake, but what I am telling you is to be open to finding a woman who you can see yourself spending the rest of your life and the rest of your career with. Just be open to the possibility and it just might happen."

Andrews didn't know how to react. No one had ever been so direct with him on the subject. He knew the general meant well and that he was almost certainly right about the candid, off-the-record conversations that would occur in the privacy of the promotion board meeting room.

"I got it, sir. I accept your guidance in the spirit it was given."

"Just give it some thought, Fleming. I wouldn't want it to be the discriminating factor that keeps you from pinning on those eagles when it's your time."

Andrews never forgot that meeting and often wondered if people were talking about him behind his back. They were. Or questioning his sexuality. They were doing that, as well. He was solidly heterosexual and, although he wasn't a muscular athlete, it came as a shock to him that his bachelorhood might be viewed by some—especially a promotion board—as a sign of something he considered deviant. It would be an understatement to say the general got his attention when he told him that his marital status might keep him from getting promoted to colonel and beyond.

As distasteful as it might have been, Andrews took the general's advice to heart and almost immediately became more willing to accept the blind date dinner invitations at the homes of married fellow officers. Two years before he became eligible for promotion to colonel, he met Nancy.

Nancy Filmore was born and raised in Augusta, Georgia, the town outside of Fort Gordon and the long time home of professional golf's Masters Tournament. Her father had a moderately sized law practice in the city, handling wills, divorces, and some personal injury cases. Mr. Filmore had been a captain in the Army's Judge Advocate General's (JAG) Corps assigned to Fort Gordon, Georgia. Though a native of Pittsburgh, he liked the lifestyle and pace of the South. The decision to practice law in Augusta after his discharge from the Army seemed like a natural. With his wife and their smart as a whip daughter, they settled down to a peaceful existence in a home just outside the city.

Nancy's excellent high school grades and her nearly perfect SAT scores earned her scholarship offers from many colleges. She chose Georgetown University in Washington, DC, because they made her the most attractive offer and because she hoped the proximity would help her achieve her long-term goal of getting a follow-on degree from Georgetown Law School.

Natural talent, hard work, and persistence made that dream appear to be a pending reality. Nancy graduated with honors and did well enough on the LSATs to be accepted into Georgetown Law.

Those plans were dramatically interrupted when her father was killed and her mother confined to a wheelchair as the result of a car accident on Route 1, just across the Virginia–North Carolina border, as they drove home from Nancy's Georgetown graduation ceremony.

Despite her mother's objections, Nancy withdrew from law school without attending a class and returned home to care for her mother. Nancy became a secretary in the law offices of one of her father's former competitors and soon attained her paralegal certification.

She did occasional volunteer work in Fort Gordon's Red Cross office which is where she met Mary Jo Mahoney, the wife of Lieutenant Colonel Kevin Mahoney, an instructor at the Army school on the base, teaching young, newly commissioned officers in the Military Police Corps. Six months before the Mahoneys introduced Nancy to Lieutenant Colonel Fleming Andrews, Nancy's mother died, never truly recovering from the physical and emotional trauma of the accident that killed her husband and changed their daughter's life nearly fifteen years before.

It was not love at first sight. What may have made their eventual marriage more likely might well have been the fact that Nancy was even less interested in the blind dinner date at the Mahoney's than Andrews was. They laughed about it when, several dates later, they admitted to each other that they both had been the frequent victims of well-meaning friends who incorrectly assumed their friendships translated well into matchmaking services.

There was something about Fleming that made Nancy think there was more to this man than she could ever learn at an arranged dinner at the house of a mutual friend. Andrews, too, came away from the dinner wanting to know more about Nancy.

"Fleming, why don't you join me for a cigar while the girls do their thing and prepare dessert?" Kevin Mahoney said.

"Kevin, you know I'm a pipe man, but I will make an exception and take you up on your fine offer," Andrews said.

Andrews accepted Kevin's selection from the humidor. They both sat in the living room to enjoy their cigars.

"So, what do you think, Fleming?"

"What do I think about what?"

"About Nancy, for God's sake. She's really nice, isn't she?"

"Come on, Kevin. Let's not have this conversation."

"Well, I mean she's attractive, smart, nice body. Would you go out with her again?" Mahoney said.

"Tell you what, Kevin. If I tell you that I plan to ask her out again, would you agree to change the subject?"

"Hey, that's great, Fleming. I don't usually go for this shit, but, when Mary Jo suggested that you and Nancy might like each other, I had to admit she was right."

Andrews sat silently, drawing deeply on his cigar, watching the exhaled smoke dissipate as it rose.

"Yeah, she was right, all right. That's just great," Mahoney said.

In the kitchen, the conversation was not much different. Nancy told Mary Jo Mahoney that she thought Andrews was interesting and that she wouldn't mind if he asked her out for a second date.

"Nancy, as tough as it is for me to say, you no longer have any ties to this town and I think could do a lot worse than Fleming Andrews," Mary Jo said.

"Mary Jo Mahoney! I told you I wouldn't mind going out with the guy one more time and now you have me married and moving away," Nancy said. "If you want to know the truth, I think he's putting on a bit of an act. Nobody is that self-assured. I'd like to see behind whatever screen he's putting up."

"Well, you never know," Mary Jo said. "You might like what you see."

"I can hear it now, 'let's get married because we can each do a lot worse if we wait.' Oh, brother," Nancy said.

Fortunately for both Nancy and Andrews, this topic did not make its way into the dessert conversation, but Mary Jo and Kevin exchanged knowing looks and less-than-subtle smiles throughout.

"Mary Jo, dessert was wonderful, but I'm afraid I have an early day tomorrow," Nancy said, as she stood to help clear the dessert dishes.

"I'm in the same boat," Andrews said. "Mary Jo, Kevin, thanks so much for dinner, but I have to hit the road as well."

Andrews stood and picked up his dish.

"Nancy, I'll see you to your car, if that's okay."

"That would be great, Fleming. Thanks."

Mary Jo had a broad smile on her face as she made eye contact with her husband. *We did it,* her smile said silently.

"Don't be ridiculous. There are only a few dishes. Kevin and I can take care of them," Mary Jo said. She took the plates from Nancy and waved at Andrews, indicating he should put his dish and coffee cup back on the table.

"You just run along, if you have to. We're happy you were able to come by and hope to do it again soon." Her husband made a slightly pained expression at this reference. Only Mary Jo seemed to notice.

They said their mutual goodbyes and expressed appreciation for the dinner. Andrews held the screen door for Nancy. They walked down the front porch steps and the driveway to their cars.

There was no physical contact. In fact, Andrews had his hands buried in the pockets of his pants as they walked. When they got to Nancy's car, they stopped. She turned to face him.

"Kiss her. Kiss her, damn it," Kevin Mahoney said as he watched through the blinds in the dark front bedroom on the second floor of their house.

"Oh, Kevin, be quiet," Mary Jo said. She had one arm around his waist and lightly slapped his chest with the other. "You can be such a child." Her eyes had not left the couple on the sidewalk.

"*I* can be a child? You're the one who dragged me up here to watch two adults say goodnight on a public street, wondering if they would hug, kiss, do a high five, or jump in the back seat and screw each other in front of our house."

Mary Jo looked at her husband with an intentionally over-exaggerated look of disbelief. "Kevin, I never suggested…"

"Uh oh," Kevin said.

"What?"

"Oh no."

"What? What happened?" She looked out the window. "They're gone?"

"Yep," Kevin said. "They're gone. It doesn't take but a second to shake hands."

"Shake hands? Did they only shake hands?" Mary Jo put her head on her husband's shoulder. "Damn," she said. "Mahoney, we've failed again, you freakin' Irishman."

"*We?* Did you say *we?*"

"Yes, I said *we*. Now come downstairs and help me with the dishes."

He pulled her even closer. They laughed and turned to go downstairs.

5

What the Mahoneys didn't know was that as Nancy and Andrews were walking to their cars, they had agreed to go out the next weekend. The handshake was Nancy's call. Andrews wanted a kiss, expected a hug, but settled for the handshake and the knowledge that they would be going out again in less than a week.

Friday was burgers and a movie and generally superficial conversation (hobbies, books read, his year in Vietnam, and other past assignments). Andrews mentioned that he also spent a year in Korea early in his career. Nancy assumed he had seen combat both in Korea and Vietnam and Andrews did nothing to change her mind. He intentionally said nothing about his marriage to Helen.

"Fleming, I thoroughly enjoyed the movie and who doesn't like a good hamburger and French fries? But it has been a long day and I think I had better head home."

"Big plans tomorrow?" he asked.

"Oh, sure. If you call house cleaning having big plans," she said.

"Would you consider meeting for a cup of coffee?"

"Um, sure. Aren't you tired of being around me, Fleming?"

"Not at all," he replied.

Her question may have been in jest, but, if asked, Andrews would not be able to explain the logic behind his asking to see her again the next day. He would have been embarrassed to admit that something he hadn't felt since he dated his first wife might be stirring in him again. He wasn't ready to call it love. He wasn't sure he could ever love again; he wasn't sure he could ever let himself love again. His mature side was curious, the socially immature side of his personality was confused. He wanted to know more about this woman. He wasn't a kid anymore. Besides, he could easily imagine Nancy as the wife of a colonel or even a general.

He couldn't deny the underlying motivation that continued to play somewhere in his brain. *The promotion board will wonder about an unmarried senior lieutenant colonel.* Fortunately, at least so far into the young relationship with Nancy, he did not have to force his interest in her. She was certainly smart; she was more than reasonably attractive, and she seemed to be honestly interested in him, or at least curious to learn more about him.

Andrews was not acquainted well enough with the city of Augusta to suggest a place to meet the next day. Oh, he knew it was the home of the Augusta National Golf Club and the annual Masters Golf Tournament. Other than the April gathering of the world's best golfers, Augusta was a fairly typical town of haves and have-nots.

Andrews, the military policeman, knew about the undesirable places because they appeared regularly on the daily police blotter linked to instances of soldier misconduct. Some of the venues would be troublesome enough to make the commanding general's list of business establishments declared off limits to soldiers assigned to Fort Gordon. Andrews oversaw the maintenance of this listing. None of those places was in the running for the next day's rendezvous with Nancy.

Augusta wasn't a major metropolis, but it had grown into an active city in America's still-segregated south. Andrews was aware of the African-American neighborhoods where whites would not venture, and of the white areas where Negroes were not welcome unless they were employed to perform some kind of domestic service.

"Where would you like to meet tomorrow, Nancy?" Andrews asked.

"Oh, I don't know. Do you have any place in mind?"

Rather than admit to his unfamiliarity with the city, Andrews said, "I figure most people in town know you and you aren't ready to be seen in public with a lowly soldier. So, I ..."

"Fleming, that's not the case at all. I suppose many people in town do know me pretty well. I've lived here all my life, except when I was in college, but I am certainly not embarrassed to be seen in public with you."

"Well, I was going to suggest we meet for a late breakfast at the clubhouse of the golf course on post. I've eaten there before and the food's pretty good."

"Fleming, are you sure you won't be embarrassed to be seen with a local girl around all those high-ranking soldiers?"

"Touché," he said. "Okay, where would you like to go? I'll drive."

"Tell you what, let's plan on the golf course clubhouse and if I come up with a better idea, I'll give you a call."

Andrews didn't know what to make of her comment, but he agreed.

6

Andrews' phone rang at 9:00 on Saturday morning.

"Fleming, I hope I haven't called too early," Nancy said.

"Not at all. Is everything okay?"

"Yes, yes, everything is fine. Fleming, I hope you don't misread what I am about to say…"

"…But something has come up and we'll have to reschedule. Right?" he finished her sentence.

"What? Oh, no. I was going to suggest you come here. I can put a pot of coffee on. I have the fixings for bacon and eggs or maybe an omelet. I made muffins last night as well."

"You made muffins? I thought you were tired last night."

He had never been this relaxed in conversation with a woman—or anyone for that matter.

"I was, but I couldn't sleep."

"So, you baked muffins?"

"Well…yes. A little silly, huh?"

"I would be happy to come to your house. Do you still want to meet at 10:30?"

"Sure, that still works, but feel free to come over any time before then. I'll be here."

"Great. I'll see you soon," he said.

Andrews arrived at Nancy's front door with a bouquet of flowers not more than 45 minutes after their phone conversation.

She met him at the door, drying her hands with a dish towel.

"Flowers. How sweet." She took them from him and kissed him on the lips. It wasn't the impassioned kiss of a lover. It was more the kiss with which a wife would greet her husband at the end of the work day. Still, it stunned him.

Nancy had surprised herself. She hadn't planned to kiss him. She gave no forethought to the reception she would give him when he arrived. She turned quickly with the flowers in her hands and walked down the hall toward the kitchen, hoping he would not notice how flushed she had become.

"Yeah. Who knew there was a florist in Augusta who opened at 9:00 on Saturdays? My lucky day," he said.

"No, mine. I got the flowers," she said. Please make yourself at home, Fleming, while I put these in water. Can I get you a cup of coffee?

"Sure, but I'm happy to pour if you point me to a coffee cup."

Her kitchen was small. After Nancy snipped the stems of the flowers and put them in a vase, she passed behind Andrews on her way to the dining room table. As she did, she placed a hand on the small of his back, in part to ensure he didn't back into her, but also because it seemed like a normal thing to do.

Again, her contact surprised him, and, at the same time, impressed him with what he read as a demonstration of her self-confidence.

"Can I pour a cup for you, Nancy?"

"No thanks. I already have one on the go. Let's sit in the living room for a few minutes before I start cooking breakfast. I guess it will be more brunch than breakfast," she said.

They sat and talked, relating more about their lives to that point. It was after 11:00 when Nancy looked at her watch and jumped to her feet.

"I am so sorry, Fleming. You must be starving. You'd probably fire the mess steward if he forgot to prepare a meal on time."

"No. That's why we still have firing squads," he replied.

"It will only take a minute to cook a couple of omelets. Ham and cheese okay with you?"

"That sounds good, but only if there are homemade muffins to go with them. Let me help." He was a few steps behind her, heading toward the kitchen.

She laughed and turned. Standing in the short hallway, they were very close to each other. He put his hands on her waist. "I understand you make the best muffins in Augusta."

She responded by putting her hands on his chest. "The best in Georgia, I'll have you know." Their second kiss lasted much longer than their first.

Nancy looked down and took a step back. "I had better start cooking."

"Nancy, I'm sorry."

"For what?"

"Well, for kissing you if you weren't ready. Sometimes my timing is…"

"There's nothing wrong with your timing, Fleming. In fact, I'd say it's pretty good." They kissed again.

After that morning, they made no effort to hide the fact that they were dating. Nancy was surprised to learn Andrews had been married before and was sorry to hear how the marriage ended. She wished her parents could have lived to see her in a serious relationship with a man, but knew how difficult it would have been for them to be comfortable with a divorcé.

7

"Who would have thought the first time you two were here for dinner that you would have hit it off so well?" Kevin Mahoney said as he passed the meat platter to Andrews.

"Why? Did we seem a little cold toward each other?" Andrews asked.

"No way," Mary Jo said. "I knew it would work out from the start, but Kevin wasn't so sure. Did he ever tell you that he wanted to watch the two of you walk to your cars when you left here that night?"

"Really?" Nancy looked surprised, but not nearly as surprised as Kevin, who wasn't expecting Mary Jo to mention it or to credit him for what had really been her idea.

"Yep, but I told him we had no business snooping on two adults—and friends at that," Mary Jo said. "Isn't that the way you remember it, Kevin?" Mary Jo's eyes sparkled as she looked to her husband.

"Absolutely!" he said after a pause. "That's exactly the way I remember it, dear, and I apologize for even suggesting such a thing."

"Funny," Nancy said. "I could have sworn Fleming and I saw two silhouettes watching us from a second floor window that night."

The other three looked at her with surprise on their faces that quickly brightened when she began to laugh.

"On a serious note, Nancy and I have been going out for just about a year. And I have you two to thank for that."

"*We* have the two of you to thank," Nancy said. "Fleming, why don't you tell them?"

"Are you sure?" he asked.

When Nancy nodded her approval, Andrews said, "Since you two introduced us, we thought you should be the first to know that Nancy and I are engaged."

"I knew it!" Mary Jo Mahoney said. "I just knew you two were perfect for each other."

"Holy shit. Fleming Andrews is going to tie the knot. I never thought it would happen."

"When the Army let me know I was going to be reassigned in the summer, I knew I didn't want to move without Nancy. Besides, there's a promotion board coming and a wise man once told me that unmarried lieutenant colonels don't get promoted."

After an awkward silence that followed Andrews' remark, the dinner continued with toasts and laughs over stories from the Mahoneys about their first years of marriage. Mary Jo could always find the humor in what others might consider the daily routine of life. In recognition of the role they played in bringing Nancy and Andrews together, Mary Jo and Kevin served as the matron of honor and best man at the civil ceremony six weeks later.

Lieutenant Colonel and Mrs. Fleming Andrews honeymooned for a week in Florida and returned to begin their new life together in the house she inherited from her mother.

Nancy was surprised to see her new husband's ability to be rude and demeaning to some of the wait staff and hotel employees while they were in Florida. Rather than say anything directly to him, she compensated by being extra nice to the individuals to whom Andrews was inconsiderate.

Back home, she was put off by the way he would talk about certain colleagues at the dinner table. And, as they prepared to leave Fort Gordon, Nancy saw more signs of his selfish nature. She was surprised at his lack of gratitude toward the people under his command. He routinely discounted the role they played in his success in this assignment. When she voiced this to her husband, he initially responded dismissively, but then he became abrupt, drawing a definite line between the subjects he was willing to discuss and those he considered none of her concern.

"Well, I'm sorry to upset you, Fleming. But sometimes I think you believe you did well in spite of the people around you and not because of them," she said.

"Hmm. Actually, that's about right," he said. "Nancy, life has taught me that you achieve on your own and for yourself. Other people are sometimes willing to help you, but only when it is to their advantage as well. It's a cruel reality, but it is reality. Most of the time, other people are no more than obstacles to be cleared and not aids to a higher level of achievement."

"Fleming, I'm not going to argue with you, but I don't believe that's true. I find it a somewhat jaded view of people and humanity." She really didn't want to confront her husband, but she had never seen him so cold and she could not let him think she agreed with his view of others. She was also hopeful that he would clarify and, at the same time, mitigate what he had said.

He doubled down. "Nancy. Dear Nancy. Yours has been a sheltered life. If you had seen as much as I have, you would have no trouble agreeing with me. To think otherwise is, at best, naive and, at worst, simply stupid."

She turned, taking great offense at being called stupid, but chose to let it go. She was sure her pursuit of the discussion would not change his mind and might make him more upset.

This exchange made the next week fairly tense. It was made worse because the Army Personnel Center representative told Andrews that his next assignment might be leading an Army recruiting battalion, overseeing the work of recruiters in the Northeast region of the United

States. While it would have been considered a command assignment, Andrews knew the challenges of recruiting in 1965 and he had no intention of taking that kind of a career risk with his eligibility for promotion to colonel fast approaching. The Northeast was the toughest region in the country for recruiting. In addition to that, he had no tolerance for the generation of youth his recruiting teams would be targeting.

When he mentioned the possibility of the assignment to Nancy, she was surprisingly upbeat and positive, trying to turn the page from their argument as well as wanting to be a supportive wife.

"Nancy, you're joking, right? A southern girl like you in the Northeast?"

"Oh, I don't know. It could be fun. Remember, my dad grew up in Pittsburgh. He loved a big city. It would also allow us to visit Manhattan every now and then."

"The last place I want to be," Andrews said.

"Oh, Fleming, but the city is such an exciting place. Broadway, the television shows, and shopping."

"You left out the crime and the dirty streets. I can live without that excitement, thank you very much. And if you want to do more shopping, I'll subscribe to a few more catalogs for you."

"Really, Fleming. I remember you saying that an officer worth his salt never turns down a command assignment; so, I naturally thought you would be excited at the possibility," she said.

"Recruiting duty is not a real command. In today's climate, it's a prescription for failure. A real career killer. I made it through a year in Vietnam; I'm not interested in risking my life in the cesspool of liberals, draft dodgers, and faggots. That's pretty much what I think of the Northeast. Damn hippies everywhere."

Nancy didn't respond.

"So, tell me the truth, Nancy, do you really want to go to the Northeast?" Andrews asked.

Nancy thought about poking more fun at him, but, in the course of the conversation so far, she saw his impatience coming to the surface.

"No, Fleming, I couldn't care less about New York, but, if that was where you wanted to go or if that's where the Army ended up sending you, I would be there with a smile on my face."

"Now that's the little girl I married," he said, while literally patting her on the top of her head. He lit his pipe and went into the other room, unaware and unconcerned with how demeaning he had just been.

By week's end, Andrews' assignment officer found another interested and qualified candidate for the recruiting job. Andrews was off the hook and headed to an assignment he considered far more acceptable. He was to be on the staff of the Army's Continental Army Command (referred to familiarly as CONARC) at Fort Monroe, Virginia. The job was purely administrative. CONARC oversaw the Army's development of doctrine, training, recruiting, and other personnel-related activities.

In the short time between their marriage and their move, Nancy took charge of winnowing down much of the furniture they each brought to the household. Andrews told Nancy he had no emotional ties to any of his furniture or furnishings with the exception of his books, tobacco humidor, pipes, and pipe rack. He had a special fondness for the pipe rack. It was made for him when he was in Korea. It had five levels and could hold 60 individual pipes, each standing on its bowl with the stem vertical, resting in a niche.

In the end, they moved much less than a houseful of furniture with the intent to buy additional new pieces after they arrived in Virginia and knew the size of the quarters they would be assigned. Here, Andrews was also willing to surrender control to Nancy. In this area, she was probably the more frugal of the two of them. He was sure she would not overspend.

The move went well, and from the start the new job seemed to agree with him. For her part, Nancy became active in the Officers' Wives' Club (an expectation of military wives in the 1960s and 1970s). She also continued her affiliation with the American Red Cross, serving as a volunteer in the organization's Fort Monroe office.

Andrews often commented about his dislike of Army staff work, but Nancy could tell, from his day-to-day attitude and the overall climate in the house, that it appealed to him more than he was willing to admit. His responsibilities were in the realm of policy and planning. As a result, he had limited interaction with rank and file soldiers—certainly much less than he had at Fort Gordon. He was fine with that. He wasn't as stressed as he had been when he was responsible for soldiers and their daily routines and issues which he saw as annoying.

As far as Andrews was concerned, it was a great time to be a staff officer at a large headquarters. Here, he was able to join with senior leaders lamenting the performance and the difficulties folks "in the field" were experiencing. Vietnam raged and the Army continued to have trouble recruiting quality volunteers. The enlisted ranks were comprised primarily of conscripted draftees. Indiscipline was a significant problem in many units, challenging even the most talented commanders. Drugs, booze, and racial tensions often brought military barracks to the point of police lockdown. Although he would never admit it publicly or even to his wife, Andrews was happy to be analyzing the statistics at headquarters, rather than being a part of them at a lower organizational level.

At social events on Fort Monroe, Nancy would overhear her husband comment on how much he missed doing "real soldiering." She was always disappointed at his unwillingness to be honest about his professional preferences, even among colleagues who, unlike Andrews, freely admitted they were happy not to have to deal with the current challenges of being in charge of soldiers in the ranks.

At times, routinely after Andrews had cut her short or had an outburst of temper, Nancy would reflect sadly, wondering if he was merely puffing out his chest to be a man among men or if this was a hypocrisy extending to the core of his personality. She fought the feelings, but there were lonely moments in her marriage when she missed Augusta and the predictability of the life she recently left behind. She never let herself reach the conclusion that it might have been a mistake to have married this very complex man and hated herself for even entertaining the thought.

She hoped for better days.

8

When the Department of the Army announced the names of those lieutenant colonels to be promoted to colonel, Fleming Andrews' name was on the promotion list.

Demonstrated potential for increased responsibility was the Army's standard justification for selecting someone for promotion. It isn't enough to show you have the potential to perform at the next higher grade to be promoted, the Army requires a minimum number of years of experience before someone is eligible to be considered for advancement.

Officers are typically categorized by Year Group which generally corresponds to the year in which they were initially commissioned as a second lieutenant. All that is prelude to say that each year the Army reaches a year into the younger cohort to select an extremely limited number of high performers for early promotion. The Army has always been stingy with this option, in part because every person selected early literally displaces an officer who might have been selected for promotion in due course.

Andrews had been openly disappointed the year before when he was not selected early, ahead of his contemporaries. He blamed it on a promotion system that gave the best breaks to the ass-kissers. He was happy to be on the promotion list, but felt no sense of gratitude to the Army or anyone in particular in the Army. In his mind, he deserved to be a colonel and his selection was not only earned, it was overdue. Andrews' aspirations didn't stop at colonel. He was convinced he would be promoted at least to one star and, frankly, the sooner the better.

Taking a cue from his wife and recalling her reaction to his remarks at his departure event at Fort Gordon, Andrews said all the right things a few months later when he was promoted to colonel. He said all the right things, even though they were insincere. Andrews' boss, a 2-star general, officiated at the ceremony. He and Nancy each pinned a shiny silver eagle on the shoulders of Andrews' uniform.

Soon after his promotion, he learned that he had subsequently been selected to command an Army installation.

"Nance, this could mean big things for me—for us. Taking command of a major Army installation could be the next step to a star," he said when he came home with the good news.

"Fleming, that's wonderful."

"Nancy, tell the truth. Don't you want to be a general's wife?"

"I'm content being your wife, Fleming."

A few weeks later, when he was on the phone with his assignment officer, he learned what the Army had planned for him.

"Where the hell is Cameron Station? Is it in the United States?" Andrews asked.

The phone call continued with Andrews' half of the conversation consisting of lines like:

"Really?"

"What do they do there?"

"Sounds like I might get a lot of unwanted help from all those resident generals, if you know what I mean."

At some point in the conversation, his assignment officer's patience ran out.

"You know, Fleming, there are a shit load of colonels who would be happy to command Cameron Station. You can decline the command and I'll find something else for you to do either in the States or overseas. Of course, you can always decide to retire, but that would mean giving up the eagles and leaving as a lieutenant colonel."

"All right, man, I get the message. You don't have to turn on the hard-ass routine with me," Andrews changed his tune. "Of course I accept the command. I just never heard of the place, but I'll be the best commander Cameron Station ever had."

The call ended moments thereafter and, after hanging up, Andrews couldn't resist the urge to say under his breath, "Asshole."

Not surprisingly, his assignment officer had the same comment on his end of the now-discontinued phone conversation.

In June 1968, Colonel Fleming and Nancy Andrews relocated to Alexandria, Virginia, for what was expected to be a three-year assignment.

Summer 1970

9

On an average day, Andrews wore fatigues: an olive drab shirt, and trousers which he bloused into black leather combat boots. There were reports in the trade press that the Army would soon authorize a cotton/polyester, wash-and-wear version of this work uniform. But, for now, the accepted practice in most non-tactical environments was for the coarse material of fatigues to be professionally laundered, pressed, and heavily starched when worn in garrison.

Today, however, Andrews arrived at work wearing elements of the Class A uniform: a long-sleeved, poplin shirt with the regulation black tie. He also wore a black windbreaker that bore his eagle rank insignia on the shoulders.

Army regulations allowed him to sit at his desk in shirt sleeves. To conduct official business, however, the expectation was that he would don his uniform coat with its shiny brass buttons and assorted awards and accoutrements. Actual medals were not worn on this uniform as a rule. Instead, Andrews had a few rows of military ribbons over his left breast pocket representing various levels of achievement and service. This was the Army's equivalent of a business suit, appropriate for meeting with an outside visitor, such as the representative of the city with whom he was scheduled to meet later in the day.

"Good morning, Laura," he said as he walked past Laura Bennett's desk and into his office. Something he hadn't expected nearly stopped him in his tracks, but he continued to his desk without a noticeable hesitation.

As he passed her, he caught the peripheral image of a young woman in a short black dress standing more toward the center of the large outer office, which also served as a reception area for individuals with appointments to meet with Andrews. Without emptying the contents of his briefcase, Andrews removed his jacket, picked up his coffee cup, and headed to the office coffee pot, past Laura's desk, at the far end of the reception area. He was confident Laura had already brewed a fresh pot. She had.

Had he waited a few minutes, he knew Laura would walk in to retrieve his cup and return it to him filled with coffee, as she did every day. Today, he was more than a little curious about the woman in the black dress.

"Oh, Colonel Andrews," Laura said as she saw him walk by.

He stopped, unfilled cup in hand.

"You remember Marie Garrett…our intern from last year? Today is her first day back with us for the summer."

"Why, of course." He reached out to shake her hand. "Welcome back. It's good to see you. I hope you had a good school year."

His words were perfect and welcoming, but Laura could not help but notice that the colonel was obviously looking up and down at the attractive young African American with the hemline well above her knees. The skinny high school sophomore had transformed over the past school year into a young woman. Her hips and breasts had developed noticeably and she had come a long way in her use of makeup.

"There's a fresh pot of coffee ready to go, sir." Laura sought to break the suddenly awkward silence and hoped to get the colonel to do something other than stare at Marie like the lecherous man he was.

Andrews was smart enough to take advantage of her cue. He again shook Marie's hand, welcomed her a second time, and moved to fill his coffee cup.

The day proved to be routine. Susan Braswell wore a blouse that was unbuttoned sufficiently for Andrews to appreciate a generous amount of cleavage during his meeting with the representative from the city of Alexandria, Ed Anderson. Throughout the day, he also consumed more coffee than usual, using it as his rationale to view and encounter Marie Garrett.

Such had become the personal life and professional career of Colonel Fleming Andrews, U.S. Army. The vast majority of his responsibilities were administrative and, though he admitted it to no one, not even his wife, the job was never much of a challenge and hardly interested him anymore. After two years, there was nothing new to learn. No major initiatives. Nothing that would catch the eyes of his superiors. Despite this, it had not yet become clear to Andrews that this job was not going to get him his coveted brigadier general's star. Not when the biggest crisis he had to face since he took command was the unexplained decline in the koi population in the small lake that was a landmark on Cameron Station.

Greatly impacted by his sense of missed opportunities and the system's lack of fairness, at 43-years old, he became unenthused about many things, to include his marriage. There was hardly any intimacy between him and his wife. His marriage to Nancy had taken on all the woodenness of the well-timed professional move recommended by a mentor years before. He was incapable of sustaining the chemistry they appeared to have had early in their relationship.

Not surprisingly, Andrews didn't see it that way. He still had an active eye for most skirts that passed through his field of vision. To him, he hadn't really lost interest; she became less interesting. It was her fault. While he never surfaced the issue with Nancy, he actually blamed her for his return to pornography and the growing, eclectic collection he had stashed in their basement, hidden the way a teenager would hide a stolen copy of *Playboy* magazine.

When he gave it any thought, he rationalized the porn as a much better alternative than having an affair or sneaking out to hire a hooker. He was sufficiently self-delusional to have no doubt there was a long list of women in and around Cameron Station who would welcome his advances, but he never thought any woman was worth the risk to his career.

It wasn't enough that he stared at Susan Braswell whenever they were in the same meeting. He was now ogling a 17-year old black girl entrusted to his organization for the summer. He couldn't help but notice this young woman had already fallen into the pattern of dressing in a way he considered provocative. He certainly enjoyed looking at her and expected she was well on her way to idolizing him.

On Thursday of Marie's first week in the office, Andrews asked Laura to close the door when it was just the two of them in his office.

"Laura, what do we know about Marie Garrett?"

"I don't know what you mean, Colonel."

"Her background, her academics. Is she a serious student? Does she come from a stable family? Is there any chance she will embarrass the installation by her behavior either on post or off post after duty hours or on the weekend? That kind of thing."

"Well, sir," Laura said. "I know she had to apply for a summer position through the Civilian Personnel Office here on post. I have an information sheet on the program she's a part of. It indicates that all the participants must not be discipline problems in school and that they are getting passing grades. A friend of mine in the Personnel Office told me that all the kids are considered at risk because of their economic situations. The program is designed to engage them in useful activity during the summer. They make a little money and stay out of trouble."

"We *hope* they stay out of trouble, right?"

"Yes, sir, sure, but as far as Marie is concerned, she worked out well last summer; so, I had no hesitation accepting her again this year. Is there something specific that concerns you?"

"Well, now that you mention it," Andrews began. "It strikes me that she dresses a bit like a tramp and I'm not sure that's appropriate for the headquarters."

"Oh, Colonel, I don't agree. She wore a very nice outfit today. Girl's skirts and dresses may be shorter than they were when I was a girl, but it's just the style."

"Well, I'll take your word for it, but we can't forget this is a military headquarters."

"Yes, Colonel. I'll keep an eye on her and I'll talk to her if I think she's dressed inappropriately."

"That sounds good, Laura. I will not hesitate to let you know if I have other concerns. We'll go from there."

"Yes, sir. Anything else?"

"No. Thanks, Laura. I appreciate your insights. I want you to know I intend to do my part to ensure she has a positive experience this summer…one that will serve her well for the future."

"Well, that sounds great. Thank you, sir."

Laura was confused. *Was this the same person who was just about undressing Marie with his eyes earlier in the week? Now he has concerns with the way she dressed, but he is going to do his part to ensure she has a positive experience?* She always thought there was an underlying element to everything he said, and was now surprised by the conversation she had just had with him. Two years and counting and she still could not figure out Colonel Andrews.

Fundamentally, Andrews couldn't understand why women dressed the way they did and were then offended when a man took a healthy interest in them. He knew he couldn't express this sentiment aloud—certainly not as the installation commander—without career and legal consequences. But there was no law against his thinking this way and he knew he was right. He saved his diatribes for conversations with his wife: his rants about, as he often put it, "females dressing like common whores and bitching when they are treated that way."

Nancy never enjoyed it when he was feeling especially self-righteous. They might discuss the issue. They might even debate it strongly, but Nancy avoided arguing with him. It was as though she feared the consequences of winning an argument. She didn't know what they would be, but she didn't want to take the chance.

Despite his comments, or maybe because of them, Andrews took an interest in Marie Garrett that Laura Bennett found a bit over the top. While last summer he could have easily walked past Marie without noting her gender or even her existence, this year he was including her as an observer at meetings, spending time with her before and after meetings (ostensibly to talk about what had happened) and inviting her to join him on his routine inspection rides around the installation. He described it as professional development for her and delivering on his promise to make her summer enriching.

"Marie, this is Mr. Henry. Mr. Henry this is Marie Garrett. She will be with us this summer and I thought it might be instructive for her to come along on some of our rides around post."

"Hello, Miss Garrett," Henry Washington said. He touched the brim of his cap as he nodded his head, a slight smile on his face.

"Pleased to meet you, Mr...," Marie hesitated a bit, "Mr. Henry."

Andrews instructed Marie to sit behind the driver's seat

as he moved to the right rear door of the Chevy Blazer, the position prescribed for the senior occupant of any military auto.

"Mr. Henry, let's just drive on some of the main streets so Marie can become more familiar with our little city."

"Sure, Colonel. No problem." Washington's response was casual and more familiar than Andrews would have preferred, but he did not comment.

"Marie, you may remember some of this from last summer, but it'll be a good refresher of what we have here. And if you see anything you think is not right, you just let me know." He smiled at her. "I will order it to be fixed."

Marie returned the smile and thanked him. She had a pen and a small note pad in her hand, resting on her lap.

They drove along, with Henry Washington deciding the route through the base with only a few suggestions from Andrews. The main part of the installation was little more than a collection of two- to four-story administrative buildings, sets of military housing units, and a handful of retail operations sponsored by the military. Beyond these, single-story warehouses ranging in age from 10–40 years dominated the installation.

Washington brought the vehicle to a gradual stop as they approached the lake near the southeast boundary of the installation.

"So, Marie, that's the brief tourist's spin around Cameron Station," Andrews said. "Let's take a few more minutes for a quick stop at the rail yard. Would you take us there, Mr. Henry?"

"Of course, Colonel."

Now, this will be a quick stop," Andrews said to both of them. "We've been out of the office a while. Marie, Mr. Henry knows very well that I visit the rail yard often because it is an important part of the post. Commercial trains pass through routinely. Maybe we'll get to see one today. And the area is always ready to receive trains carrying military supplies or equipment. I like to be sure that nothing will go wrong there."

"Sounds really interesting, Colonel. I love trains. We have tracks not far from my house. I can always hear them," she said.

"You can't imagine how important this place is to me, Marie. I really do love it. In fact, Mr. Henry often drives me here when he knows I'm under a lot of pressure from the job."

"Is there a lot of pressure in your job, Colonel Andrews?" She asked.

"You better believe it."

"I just mean that, as the person in charge, you can pretty much tell other people what to do, right?"

"Well, I do tell other people what to do, but I have to decide what it is they are supposed to do and then find ways to ensure they follow orders properly and to my high standards. You will also find out, as you go out into the world, that everyone has a boss. Everyone has someone they have to answer to…someone they are responsible to. And they taught me years ago at West Point that people do what the boss checks; so, it's important to check and double-check."

"Okay," she said. "I didn't realize you went to West Point. Was it hard?"

"Oh, you know it. It's the best college in the country. People talk about Harvard, Yale, and Stanford, but I'm telling you, West Point is the best," he replied.

Henry Washington reacted to Andrews' inflated description of his responsibilities and his declaration about West Point by looking into the rearview mirror and rolling his eyes. He couldn't believe Andrews' sanctimonious tone.

Washington had heard much of this before with other guests, but today Andrews was outdoing himself.

"You know, Marie, they are starting to let girls attend West Point. Maybe you ought to consider it, if your grades are high enough and you're a leader in school."

"I'll think about it."

It was unclear which of them was being more insincere in this exchange. Marie had never given any thought to the Army and Andrews was one of many West Point alums who opposed the inclusion of women in the corps of cadets. He thought it ridiculous that a black girl from the inner city might gain admittance to the school, let alone graduate and be commissioned a second lieutenant in the Army.

They were spared having to continue the conversation as the Blazer came to a stop outside the gate of the rail yard, not far from the dumpster.

"We're here. Let's step out of the vehicle, but I'm afraid there isn't time to walk through the yard today."

They approached the gate on foot, but did not go in. Andrews held onto the chain link fence with one hand as he spoke.

"I have to tell you, Marie, being here gives me a sense of calm. Here, I seem to be able to clear my head so I can go back to the office able to focus on the really difficult parts of the job. Does that make any sense to you, Marie?"

"I guess."

"Marie, someday, you'll have a place like this to come to. A place where you can find release from the pressures of the day and the challenges that life sends your way."

"Yes, sir. My mother always tells me that's what church is for."

"Okay. I get that. This is a kind of a church for me, I guess. I will tell you one thing that makes me very angry.

Look through the fence at some of those cars. Do you see that? Vandals have painted graffiti on some of them. It's criminal behavior to do that—defacing someone else's property."

"Yes, sir," Marie said. "But that car over there is kind of pretty."

"Pretty? Which one?"

"The one with the rainbow painted on the side."

"The person who did that clearly has some talent, but he needs to apply it somewhere where it isn't against the law. You wouldn't happen to know the person, would you?"

"Me? Oh, no, sir," she said.

"Well, that's good. Marie, we'll come back when I can spend more time here, but I wanted you to at least see it. Now, my dear, I think it's time we head back to headquarters before they consider me AWOL."

She wasn't sure she knew what AWOL meant, but she returned his smile just the same. For a few moments they stood there with Andrews looking into her eyes, saying nothing.

"Well, okay," he broke the brief silence and turned toward the waiting vehicle. "Let's get back to the office."

10

As the month of July progressed, Andrews became infatuated with this young woman—this girl. He made up reasons to go on multiple inspection rides during some weeks. He found it exciting to share the back seat of the Chevy Blazer with Marie. He was sure she felt the same way. How could she not?

Andrews actually blushed slightly when Marie mentioned seeing him as the Grand Marshal of the Fourth of July parade and how great he looked in his Army blue uniform with all his medals.

When Marie placed a folder or a piece of paper in his in-basket, he could not resist the temptation to look up from his desk to watch her as she walked back to her work area. Even after work, at home with his wife, Marie would come to mind. He would remember what she wore that day, how she walked, how she crossed her legs, how she looked at him admiringly.

Andrews would mention Marie to his wife, but only in the context that she was a bright, young student with enormous potential, who probably idolized him. Unaware of the rest of the equation, his wife encouraged Andrews to mentor Marie in the short time she would be there. Nancy even mentioned inviting Marie and her parents for dinner.

"Not your best idea, Nance. She's technically a subordinate and, frankly, I don't even know if she has a… if her father actually lives with the family. You know how those people can be."

"Oh, Fleming, really? I grew up in the South, but I swear, you are more prejudiced than most people I have known. How can you say that about the girl? I'm sure she has a solid family life. I understand she is a subordinate. I'm not stupid. We've hosted your subordinates in this house before, Fleming."

"That's different."

"If you say so. Well, maybe we can have her over for dinner during the school year, when she no longer works for you."

"We'll see," he said. Andrews was never a fan of being chastised by his wife and he had a low threshold of acceptance before he would react with unmistakable anger in his voice. Nancy was acutely aware and was generally careful not to push him to his limit, but she had decided early in their marriage that it would be wrong to be a total pushover with him. She refused to condone his generally low opinion of women or his bias against Blacks. They weren't married very long before Nancy learned to walk a fine line between the man with whom she fell in love and the person she feared he could become.

Andrews knew his feelings about Marie were inappropriate, but he told himself his feelings were rooted in her obsession with him. He was confident he could control himself before crossing any lines. He also knew she would soon return to school. Out of sight, out of mind. Until then, the pleasure it gave him was very self-affirming. If only she wouldn't look at him with those adoring eyes.

He was no psychologist, but he figured all this was completely understandable and totally not his fault. If anything, she should be more rational—more mature. *For God's sake, just look at her; she's a woman.*

Andrews half expected Marie to view him as a father figure, but he was surprised and gratified to have concluded she considered him some kind of hero. He was convinced she was also drawn to him physically. It only made sense to him.

11

When another driving tour took them to the rail yard, a voice in Henry Washington's head told him to break with his routine practice of staying in the Blazer and join them for the walk-through. He opted instead to ignore his intuition. He waited in the car outside the gate.

While walking through the yard and out of sight of the vehicle, Andrews placed his hand on the small of Marie's back to guide her around a trash can. The move was instinctive, but the feeling of excitement that overcame him was not something he anticipated. These feelings were stronger than he expected. He became aroused.

As he pointed to one of the boxcars not far off, he turned to face her. He put his hands on her shoulders, looking into her face, though she had turned her glance downward. "Marie, you have turned into quite a lovely young woman. I think I know what you may have in mind, but, while I'm flattered, I have to tell you that it just isn't possible. Oh, it would be great, but we…"

Marie, staring directly into his eyes, interrupted saying, "Colonel Andrews, is there something you need to inspect, sir?"

He squeezed the upper part of her arms slightly; then dropped his hands to his sides.

"We should go."

"Yes, sir."

They walked to the car in silence and did not speak during the ride back. Andrews busied himself, making notes and lighting and relighting his pipe until they arrived at the headquarters building.

"Marie, if I spooked you back there, I apologize," Andrews said as they walked from the Blazer. "I apologize. I was trying to pay you a compliment and ensure you know I consider myself to be a professional mentor to you." He was improvising and rightly concerned that his insincerity was coming through.

He wasn't sure if his voice gave away the concern he had at the realization that Marie was in a position to cause him a lot of trouble if she decided to tell anyone about their exchange in the rail yard. He wondered if she was sophisticated enough to realize this. Would she turn to him now and tell him how full of shit he was? That would make it crystal clear.

Maybe she was coy enough to play him: tell him she had no idea what he was talking about, while banking this damning piece of information for some future use. Maybe, just maybe, he fantasized, she might be bold enough to make a sexual advance. After all, she had been subtle with her teasing. Maybe she was ready to be more direct. Handling that could be a challenge.

"I understand, Colonel. Thank you," she added. It didn't feel right to show even that level of gratitude regarding the awkward moment, but she didn't know what else to say.

The next day, they barely made eye contact with each other. Just before lunch, Marie carried a few folders into Andrews' office and placed them in his in-basket. She picked up the papers in the out-basket and turned to leave.

"Oh, Marie."

"Yes, sir?"

"Are you sure you're okay? After yesterday, I mean."

"Yes, sir. I told you that I understood."

"I know you did, but I couldn't help but think about the wrong impression you must have gotten. I'm sorry if I made you uncomfortable or if I misread your intentions."

"I'm fine, Colonel."

"Good. Good. Thanks."

She turned again to leave.

"Marie, one last thing. Did any of the people you talked to about this misunderstand or get the wrong impression?"

"Colonel, as far as I am concerned, nothing happened yesterday; so, there was nothing to mention to anyone."

"You told no one?"

"No, sir."

"Thank you, Marie. That's very mature of you. I hope you know that any concerns you ever have can always be brought to my attention, right? I'm here for you."

"Yes, sir." She turned to leave and, as she did, Andrews watched her movement.

Despite their seemingly calm conversation, Andrews remained on edge by what happened that day in the rail yard. While he knew he could be held responsible, he had told himself it was Marie who was to blame. She was beautiful and she certainly knew it. *They all know it.* She flirted with him constantly. She sensed his weakness and took advantage of it. She had been doing it all summer.

Normal. That's how he would explain his reaction to her, if anyone really wanted to know. Andrews also knew that, if he was ever asked about this, it would be by someone whose mind was already made up against him.

A few days later, Andrews walked up to Laura Bennett's desk: Marie sat near Laura at a desk along the wall.

"You know, ladies, I think I'm going to go on this inspection ride solo today. Marie, I feel as though I've kept you from learning more about what Laura does and how things operate inside the headquarters—especially when you're with the boss who's riding around looking for shortcomings in the nooks and crannies of Cameron

Station." After a quick chuckle at his own remark, he added, "What do you think, Laura, can you keep Marie gainfully employed for the next hour or so?"

"Of course, sir. No problem." Laura wondered if the relief in her voice might have been obvious. The less one-on-one time Andrews had with Marie the better as far as Laura was concerned.

Later in the week, he went on another ride with only Henry Washington. Laura didn't know what caused this change, but she was pleased by it. Maybe the colonel realized his behavior toward Marie was nothing short of juvenile. She doubted that was the case, but, whatever caused the changed behavior, Laura was all for it.

On Friday, August 14, Andrews resisted his desire to invite Marie on another inspection ride. This was the third consecutive ride without Marie. One week later, Andrews prepared to join Henry Washington in the parking lot for another of his regular driving inspections of the installation.

"Marie, how about joining me for one last ride around the installation before you bid us farewell?"

Even Laura smiled at the suggestion, since it would be Marie's last opportunity. The next week would be filled with administrative requirements related to her out-processing and, of course, the customary farewell lunch with some of the headquarters staff, primarily the secretaries in the building.

"Hello, Mr. Henry," Andrews said as they approached the Blazer. "Young Marie here has only one more week before she leaves us. Let's mark the occasion by going to the rail yard one last time. There is no telling when you will be able to visit there again; maybe next summer."

"Gonna miss you, young lady," Washington said.

"Mr. Henry, she is actually going to take off the last week of the month before she goes back to school. Can you imagine a full week off, Mr. Henry?"

Even in a setting that had become very familiar, Andrews struggled to say something humorous. He assumed Henry Washington would play along with his comment, but, as if to drive home the point, Washington responded, "I think she deserves a small summer break, Colonel. She's a fine young woman."

"Indeed she is, Mr. Henry. You are correct. She is fine. Indeed she is." Henry Washington caught the implication and gave Andrews a hard, disapproving look in the rearview mirror, but Andrews did not notice because, as he made the comment, he turned to Marie, who was again sharing the backseat with him. With no forethought, Andrews' words were accompanied by a gentle pat on Marie's right thigh which was only half covered by her flowered skirt.

Though most of his left hand landed on material, his index finger and thumb touched the smooth, bare skin of Marie's leg. He sensed it instantly, of course; Marie did as well. He reacted by pulling his hand away and by turning to look out his window.

Marie reacted by also turning to look briefly out the window on her side of the car. When she again looked to her right, she discovered Andrews eyeing either her legs or her breasts.

He must have sensed her attention because he shifted his gaze so quickly that she could not determine on which part of her body he had been focused. When their eyes met, Marie gave an embarrassed smile and looked down with what could only be described as a confused look on her face. For his part, Andrews shook his head slightly and turned to look out his window.

For the entire ride from the headquarters to the rail yard, Andrews could not help but think of the feel of Marie's thigh and the look she had given him when they looked at each other. *What message was she sending? How could a young girl be so suggestive?* Henry Washington had said it himself. *She is a fine young woman; a fine woman. Very fine.*

"Look over there, Colonel. There's the boxcar with the rainbow painted on it," Marie said as she stepped over one of the tracks, walking through the yard next to Andrews. "I think I'm going to remember this rail yard the most."

"Oh, I understand, Marie. By now you know how much I enjoy coming here." He lit the pipe he had packed with tobacco before they left the office. "The way the tracks run parallel and then crisscross at the switch points. And then there's the handful of box cars, mostly empty, but some with vital supplies for the Army. Crazy, isn't it? But it is very special to me."

"There's another one with a rainbow. It must be something the artist likes to paint," she said.

"I wouldn't call them artists, Marie. More like vandals is what I think."

"I understand, Colonel, but here's one with butterflies painted on it. They're really pretty."

"Okay, Marie, you win. They are well done."

They walked through the yard, occasionally stopping so that Andrews could point out a feature that he may have noted on previous visits or something they hadn't seen before.

"Look, Marie, there's a sparrow's nest up there in a nook near the top of that boxcar." He pointed to the upper part of the end of a boxcar, bending his knees and twisting a bit to see between the cars. Marie moved next to him, also bending her knees, torquing her body slightly to see the nest.

"I don't see it," she said.

"It's right there." He pointed with the stem of his pipe

in his left hand, as he lightly placed his right hand on her back, sensing the point at which her bra hooked together. "Do you see it?"

"Oh, there it is. Neat."

They both straightened and began walking toward the exit gate and the vehicle. Andrews eyed her up and down as she turned to walk to the driver's side rear door. When Andrews climbed into his seat, Marie was already seat-belted in, straightening her skirt.

"Well, that was great. Thanks, Mr. Henry. Let's head back to HQ."

By 4:45, Andrews had packed his briefcase, rinsed his coffee cup, and emptied his pipe of its tobacco ash. He was ready to call it a day and a week. Laura was already gone for the day. She left the office at noon, taking a few hours of personal time, to get a head start on a weekend in Rehoboth, Delaware, with her husband.

At 5:00, Marie stood in the doorway of Andrews' office to say goodnight. She had a thin sweater over her arm and a small purse suspended from her shoulder.

"Have a great weekend, Marie."

"Thank you, sir. You, too."

"One more week and you will be free of us."

"I'm going to miss everyone, Colonel."

He couldn't help but watch her turn and walk away. Andrews thumbed through a few more pages on his desk, deciding to add one more sheet to his briefcase, returning the remainder of the stack to the desktop. As he reached for his hat, he looked out the window and saw Marie walking across the parking lot. Each day, she walked several blocks on the base to the Cameron Station front gate at Duke Street, where she caught a city bus for home.

Andrews watched the movement of her hips and how

the breeze flared her skirt. He turned from the window, tossed his hat on his briefcase, and walked down the hall to the restroom. As he washed his hands, an enormous clap of thunder startled him and rattled the windows.

12

"What the hell was that?" he said aloud to no one. He was alone in the restroom.

He walked to his office, noticing the sky had darkened in the brief time he was in the men's room. There was another very loud boom and the rain began in a torrent. Andrews picked up his hat and briefcase wondering if he should wait out the storm or run to his car. The initial raindrops seemed to bounce off the summer asphalt of the parking lot, producing brief puffs of steam as they hit.

"Marie!" Andrews said, with a sense of urgency. He dashed from the building to his car which was parked close to the rear entrance in the space reserved for the Post Commander.

He found her walking quickly a block and a half from the headquarters building, her shoulders hunched as if that position would somehow keep her from getting wet.

"Marie, let me give you a ride," he said through a half-opened passenger side window.

Marie did not recognize Andrews' car. It was not the first time a male had suggested she join him in his vehicle. She pretended not to have heard him, but the driver—whoever he was—knew her name. The car did not pull away. Instead, it moved along at her pace. He tapped the horn.

"Marie, it's me, Colonel Andrews. Come in out of the rain," he said a bit louder and more emphatically.

With that, she moved to the car as he came to a stop along the curb.

"It's okay, Colonel. There's a shelter at the bus stop. I'll be fine."

"Nonsense. You'll catch your death of a cold. Hop in."

She did.

"Thank you, Colonel. It's pouring," she said. The sound of the rain hitting the car caused them both to raise their voices.

"Let me at least take you to the bus stop," he said. "You're soaking wet." He could see how the lightweight material of her blouse was now practically sheer from the soaking rain. "I tell you what: I have one stop to make, then I'll take you home."

"Oh, no sir. I couldn't ask you to do that."

"Oh, Marie, it's no trouble at all and I would feel awful if I let you get on a bus as soaked as you are."

He pulled from the curb and made a couple of turns before he spoke again.

"Marie, there's a blanket on the back seat. Feel free to wrap it around your shoulders if you're cold."

The soaked Marie was indeed chilly. Andrews had the air conditioner in the car running on defrost to keep the windshield from fogging.

"Thank you," she said, as she turned to reach back between the front seats.

Andrews turned slightly to look at her. In his quick glance, he clearly saw the outline of her right breast through her wet blouse and bra. He forced himself to return his attention to the road.

"Better?" He asked as she wrapped the blanket around her shoulders.

"Much," she said. "Thank you."

They drove a little while in silence. She again offered

to get out at the bus stop, but, by then, they were moving away from the gate, deeper into the base.

"This looks like the way to the rail yard," Marie said, after they rode for about ten minutes.

"Marie, it isn't fair that summer is coming to an end. You are getting to know this place as well as I do," he said. "There's something I forgot to do at the yard and then we can be on our way."

Andrews pulled up to the gate of the rail yard.

"Marie, can you reach my briefcase behind my seat?"

"I think so," she said. As she turned to retrieve his briefcase, she let the blanket fall off her shoulders. She was not nearly as wet as she had been, but she was by no means dry. Her reach for the briefcase gave Andrews another opportunity to note her shape. Marie pulled the briefcase to the front seat, careful not to hit him or the rearview mirror.

"Here it is, sir."

"If you don't mind, Marie, just pop it open and hand me the key ring. It should be right on top."

"Yep. Here it is." She handed him the keys.

"Great. Thanks. If you would close it up and put it back behind my seat, that would be great. I'll unlock the gate and be back in a flash."

She watched him through the windshield as he pushed open the gate. He gave it a bit of a shove, returned quickly to the car and drove through the opening, well before the gate made its gradual, gravity-induced return trip to the closed position.

Andrews continued forward with both hands firmly on the steering wheel. He exhaled audibly as he heard Henry Washington's words from their first visit to the rail yard: *It don't lock, o'course, but damn near looks like it.*

He rolled to a stop, only after he had turned slightly

left, resulting in the maintenance shack blocking a clear view of the car from the entrance. The rain had lightened considerably to a mere drizzle.

"Marie, it's only drizzling now, but there's no need for you to be out in the rain again. I'll just be a minute. Unless you're super curious, of course."

"If it's okay with you, Colonel Andrews, I'll stay in the car."

"No problem, my dear. I'll be right back. I'll leave the A/C on low, but feel free to adjust it if you are too cold or too warm."

"Okay. Thanks."

Andrews puffed his pipe and moved quickly from the car to the far side of the nearest boxcar. From her vantage point on the opposite side of the boxcar, Marie could see only his black combat boots and the bottom of his bloused green fatigue trousers.

He stepped on the first rung of the two-step access bars below the opening of the boxcar door and disappeared within.

Marie had no idea how long she sat in the passenger's seat before she began nodding off. The drizzle that followed the torrential downpour now gave way to bright sunshine. Marie initially squinted because of the glare. Gradually, she closed her eyes and drifted off, but it wasn't sleep. Not really. She never truly lost awareness that she was in Colonel Andrews' car or that he had been in the boxcar for what seemed like forever.

She was soon aware of something else. What was it? A presence. It was as though she was not alone in the car, but she was sure no one else was there. Andrews had not returned. If he had, she would have noticed. Even if she had fallen asleep, the sound of the car door opening and closing again would have awakened her.

There had been no sound. She was alone. No. Someone was there with her. She could keep her eyes closed no longer. Her mind told her that she was alone, but other senses told her that she was very much with someone or something. She knew her heart rate had increased. She could feel it. Despite the car's air conditioning, wrapped in the blanket, perspiration now dampened her upper body.

She had to know. She opened her eyes.

Standing just outside the passenger door was Colonel Andrews. She knew it was Andrews, though she couldn't see his face. From her seat, she could see his mid-section and his hands. His left hand was propped on his belt buckle; she could see a glimmer of sunshine reflected off the stone of his West Point class ring.

She knew he had been standing there staring at her as she dozed. She didn't know for how long, but she knew. Her hemline had slid up to expose more of her thigh than she would have liked. *Has he been staring at my legs? The man is a creep.*

Alarm replaced her brief disorientation. She tried not to notice, but the coarse material of his Army fatigues did little to hide the fact that he was aroused. She didn't know what to do. Before she could make a move, he had opened the car door and extended a hand to her. The aroma of his burning pipe tobacco filled her nose.

"Come on, Marie. You've got to see this."

"Oh, no sir. I really should be getting home."

"Come on. It will just take a minute."

His hold on her forearm was firm, but not harsh. It was more the hold of someone trying to keep another from falling than a grasp meant to cause pain. He noticed with appreciation her unsuccessful attempt to keep her knees together and simultaneously swing both legs as he helped her out of the car. He led her around to the open door of the boxcar.

"Marie, look. It's your favorite…the boxcar with the rainbow on the side," Andrews said.

The contrast between daylight and the darkness within made it impossible for Marie to distinguish any shapes within the boxcar.

"Let me step up first, Marie. Then I can help you."

"Colonel Andrews, I really should be getting home, sir."

"Marie, I promise. It'll only be a minute. Here, take my hand and step on the bar there."

She did as he instructed. Maintaining one's modesty while climbing into a boxcar is simply not possible when one is wearing a short skirt. Marie knew the colonel had taken advantage of whatever opportunity her entrance provided him.

Her eyes adjusted to the darkness. She could now see a stack of flattened cardboard boxes against a rear wall. It was at least three feet high and was covered with what appeared to be a padded blanket, the kind used by professional movers.

"What do you think?" Andrews asked.

"Excuse me. Sir? I don't understand."

"This." He waved his arm toward the stack like the prize girl on some cheesy television game show. "I even put a big old rock at the end…under the blanket…as a kind of pillow."

"Colonel Andrews, I don't understand and it is getting very late. I think I should leave, sir. My family is expecting me. Please take me to the bus stop."

She turned to leave the boxcar, but Andrews put his hands on her shoulders and faced her.

"Oh, Marie, don't pretend you don't understand. I did

this for you. I know you're headed back to school soon and I know how much I mean to you. I want you to know you mean a lot to me, too"

"Mean to you? I…"

"Don't play dumb with me, Marie. I've seen the way you look at me. Those subtle smiles. The suggestive way you dress. Do you think I haven't noticed? Of course I've noticed. And now we are going to give each other what we want and you will go back to school a much more experienced woman."

"Colonel Andrews, I don't know what you're talking about."

He pulled her to him. She tried to push away, but failed. He kissed her. The more she tried to resist, the more force he exerted to maintain control. With his left hand pressed firmly in the center of her lower back, he allowed his right hand to explore.

"My God, what a fine ass you've got."

Her shock at being touched there caused her to open her mouth, only slightly, but it was enough for Andrews to take advantage. He kissed her deeply.

She shifted to break the kiss. Andrews easily wrapped his left hand around her left wrist and slid his right arm around her waist. He led her to the stack of flattened cardboard.

"You're hurting me," she said, as she used her free hand to try to loosen his grip on her left wrist. His hold was secure.

"Too late to turn back now. Come over here with me. It'll be the best you ever had."

"No! I don't want to." Marie raised her voice for the first time. She was frightened and could no longer contain her fear. It showed.

Andrews pushed her down on the blanket covering the bed of cardboard.

"Just lie here on the bed I made for us."

Marie started to squirm just as soon as her back hit the blanket, but Andrews never lost contact with her. Before she could get any leverage, he was on top of her.

He tried to kiss her again, but she managed to keep her lips from his. He kissed her neck repeatedly and groped her roughly. Her resistance continued.

Finally, he pushed up from her by placing both hands on her shoulders, pinning her to the blanket.

"Don't fuck with me, Marie. You and I both know that you want this. You've worn down my resistance and there's no turning around now. I'm taking all the risk. You know it and I expect you to be grateful. You've wanted this all summer. Don't be a bitch."

In his mind, his logic was solid, but his voice was clearly that of a delusional man who was becoming angry and losing patience with Marie's refusal to accept what was going to happen.

When he stopped talking, he moved to lower himself onto her again. Instinctively, she lifted some of her torso in the brief interlude between his lessening the pressure on her shoulders and the full weight of his body pressing on hers.

Andrews' reaction to her movement was quick and decisive. He caught her with both hands and aggressively pushed her back down. As soon as he did, he cupped her face in his hands and kissed her deeply, again. She was nearly nauseated by the taste of his tobacco-laden breath. She was still.

"That's a good girl. No resistance. Now we can both enjoy the moment."

Andrews didn't know if he had been asleep for hours

or minutes, but he opened his eyes with a start. He quickly realized where he was. The memory rushed back to him as he pushed up from Marie's upper body. In what must have been nanoseconds, a thousand thoughts ran through his mind. *Boxcar. Marie Garrett. Lightly scented perfume. Wait! She's here. I'm with her. We made love. We had sex. She stopped moving. She isn't breathing.*

"Shit!"

13

Andrews had broken into a cold sweat as he began to fully realize the depth of his dilemma. No one had to tell him. He had completely lost his self-control and had surrendered to his basest instinct. The discipline that enabled him to survive and thrive as a member of the military was broken by this stupid woman—this slut.

He got to his feet, but nearly fell when he took a step because his unzipped fatigue pants had comically fallen to just below his knees. He dressed himself in a rush, breathing heavily.

"Shit. Shit. Shit! Shit!" His curses grew in intensity. He punched the wall of the boxcar, creating an echo he instantly regretted. "Damn it! What have I done?" He began to pace back and forth as though he were on duty, unconsciously guarding Marie's body.

"Okay, take a breath. Get control of yourself." The panicked, nearly whispered monologue continued. *You can't change what happened*, he told himself. *Get back in control.* "Back in command, Fleming."

He took a few steps back to the makeshift bed. He stood over Marie's lifeless body.

"Do you see what you made me do? You bitch. You no good black bitch!" Andrews wiped the sweat from his face, placed his hands on his hips, and looked down on Marie. He exhaled audibly and moved to the door of the train.

He looked left and right before cautiously stepping to the ground. He walked to the end of the boxcar; he eyed his car, the engine still idling.

Andrews drove the car around to the open door of the

boxcar. His actions were hardly those of a sophisticated criminal, but his instincts were of a reasonably intelligent man in survival mode. With the car parked, he opened the trunk and returned to the boxcar.

After wrapping Marie's body in the mover's blanket that had served as the sheet for their bed, he shifted her to the edge of the boxcar. He stepped back down to the ground and carried her sheathed body to the trunk of his car. He again returned to the boxcar to ensure no personal items were left behind; he saw none. Andrews tossed the rock pillow to the ground near the rear of his car and scattered several of the flattened boxes within the interior of the boxcar.

After adding the rock to the trunk, he backed up his car, made a U-turn, and then applied the brakes. He sat behind the steering wheel of the idling car, mentally recounting the steps he had just taken to remove evidence from the boxcar.

Something clearly came to mind as he threw the shift into Park, got out of the car, and went back into the boxcar. He repositioned the two pieces of cardboard that had been just beneath the blanket so that he could reach them from the ground. He examined them in the sunlight and, just as he feared, some of Marie's blood had seeped through the blanket and stained the top piece of cardboard, but only the top piece. The second piece was dry. Nonetheless, he removed both pieces.

He had to bend the cardboard slightly to get it to fit in the trunk along with Marie's body. Andrews pushed open the gate and drove out of the yard, stopping very close to the dumpster as the gate to the yard slowly slid closed.

Andrews turned off the engine and got out of the car. He slid open the dumpster's side door, unlocked the car trunk, and lifted her body. He couldn't stop his hands from trembling as he strained to raise her feet sufficiently to position them on the lip of the dumpster's opening. Andrews re-gripped her body to provide a more secure hold. In the process, he could distinguish that his left hand, the one closest to the dumpster, was at her pelvic area. No mistaking it, his right hand was on one of Marie's breasts.

As he elevated her head, he felt her body begin to slide into the dumpster. He tightened his grip to prevent that from happening because he didn't want the body to slip out of the blanket. When he repositioned his feet to support a tighter hold on Marie's torso, the end of the blanket separated slightly. It was enough for Andrews to find himself staring into the open eyes of Marie's corpse. Her mouth was open. A slight stream of blood flowed from her nostrils and left ear. Her hair looked damp from the blood of a head wound.

Using his shoulder to help support the body, Andrews managed to free a hand to cover Marie's face, but he lacked the courage to try to close her eyes. With a twisting motion, he gave the body a shove, and managed to propel it close to the center of the dumpster.

The odor inside the nearly empty dumpster was already mildly unpleasant; Andrews knew it would worsen over the weekend. Would anyone notice the body? The smell that would come before Monday? Not likely. Just another case of track kill that the yard crew dumped in the trash rather than calling Animal Control. *Even a small rodent can stink bad for a few days.* His words to Henry Washington came back to him. Andrews then dropped the rock in as well, careful not to hit her body as he did. Finally, he lowered the two pieces of cardboard into the dumpster. They settled on Marie's body. That done, he began to slide the dumpster door closed.

What was that? As he slid the dumpster door, the metal-on-metal contact must have made a sound almost like…*no, that's not possible; it's ridiculous. It couldn't have been a human moan.*

Whatever it was, it was loud enough to scuttle the three crows perched on top of the rail yard fence. They flew off, cawing loudly in response to whatever it was…whoever it was.

No. Marie was dead. Definitely. He was hearing things. Andrews re-opened the door and listened. Nothing. He slid the door closed again, but the sound did not replicate; so, he opened it once more—very quickly this time.

Still nothing. With the dumpster door shut, he locked the fence, smudging the fingerprints he left behind, but intentionally not wiping the lock clean. Slowly, he drove off, hoping that he had not been observed. He had not.

In fact, the first time he saw another human being—another living human being—was after he had put more than a mile between himself and the rail yard and, more importantly, the dumpster just outside the gate of the rail yard. If he remembered the routine, it would be very early Monday morning before the dumpster would be emptied. A lot could happen between now and then. Andrews hoped for a lot of good luck. It would be a very tense weekend.

A thousand thoughts ran through his mind—many delusional. *Did I really murder someone? Will I be caught? How could she have tempted me all summer and then acted so pure and innocent when a man offered her what she had been asking for? She didn't suffer. I spared her any suffering. Her death was painless and sudden.* That's what he told himself. He discounted her terror in the moments before her death. *It was pretty much all her fault, anyway.*

When he got in the car after disposing of Marie's body, Andrews was sweating heavily. The ride from the rail yard at the relatively slow speeds mandated on Cameron Station, allowed the car's air conditioning to cool him significantly.

Back on the main part of the installation, rather than drive directly home, Andrews wanted to stop somewhere to ensure he didn't look like a man who had just done what, in fact, he had just done. His office was not a good option because, even at this hour on a Friday evening, there would be too many people working late for him to come and go unnoticed. By now, the staff duty officer would be at his desk on the first floor with a view of the parking lot.

The man with a key to nearly every door on the base felt restricted as to where he could go without being recognized, even after regular duty hours. He decided to go to the Exchange. It would be busy with people who had shopping on their minds. If he moved inconspicuously, he might not even be noticed since all he really wanted to do was use the restroom which was located not far from the building's main entrance. He could get there without even setting foot in the main part of the store. Instead, he would walk through the small snack bar portion of the complex, directly to the restroom.

He avoided the close-in parking that was available; especially the spaces with the signage "Reserved for General Officers and Colonels."

Andrews walked purposefully through the snack bar and into the men's room. In one of the stalls, he patted the dust from his pants, straightened his uniform shirt, and used toilet paper to clean the small bit of rail yard mud from his boots.

A few minutes later, while he wasn't ready for inspection, he looked presentable enough, especially for a soldier in a work uniform at the end of a very long Friday in August.

He rinsed his face with cold water, straightened his hair, and turned to leave the restroom. At the doorway, he encountered a young soldier walking in, who clearly had an urgent need to pee. His eyes widened noticeably when he saw the colonel's eagle on Andrews' uniform collar.

"Evening, sir. Excuse me," he said on his way in.

His urgency made Andrews smile slightly.

"How ya doing, young man? Have a great weekend."

"Roger that, sir. You too," came the voice already standing at the urinal.

Andrews actually impressed himself with his composure during the unexpected encounter. His heart was racing, but the soldier didn't notice. Andrews was cool and calm on the outside and that's what mattered most at this point. A sense of discipline seemed to be returning to his life—normalcy. He was a colonel again; the installation commander. He felt emboldened enough to stop at the flower shop within the Exchange building to buy cut flowers to take home to his wife.

As he walked through the parking lot, he told himself he was back in control. "You didn't have to get me flowers, sir," one of two sergeants joked. They both saluted Andrews as they walked toward the Exchange.

"Sorry, fellas, the flowers are for the Mrs." He carried the flowers in his left hand; so, he was able to return a sharp salute.

"Damn, sir. Now I'm disappointed." The sergeants played along with Andrews as their respective steps in opposite directions took them further apart. More evidence that things were getting back to normal.

He was indeed back in control. In a perverse way, he was actually already beginning to suppress the memory of the murder he had committed only about an hour earlier. *Is my mind playing tricks on me? Maybe I played some role as an agent of a higher authority meting out justice to a woman who deserved death.* He'd have to be more of a sincere churchgoer to believe that. Strange thoughts entered his mind. *Could it be that I imagined all this? Maybe I didn't kill Marie, after all.*

Maybe she got home okay. Maybe my imagination got the better of me. There's no way I'm going back to the rail yard to confirm anything. No returning to the scene of the crime for me—even if there proved not to be a crime. I'll just work to get this out of my mind over the weekend and, who knows, maybe

Marie will show up Monday morning to begin her final week at the headquarters.

Could that be it? Was he lying to himself?

What the hell is going on? he wondered.

This bit of daydreaming as he walked through the parking lot brought Andrews closer to his car. He noted where it was and nearly simultaneously began reaching into his pocket for his car key.

Wait. Something was wrong. His mind must really be playing tricks with him now. He must be more stressed than he thought. He could swear he just saw someone in the passenger seat of his car.

No way. Could it possibly be Marie? Probably a shadow.

Andrews didn't realize that he had stopped walking and was now standing motionless in a driving lane of the parking lot, staring at the outline of what was clearly a young woman in the passenger seat of the car. *That's a girl. In my car. I think she's a Negro.*

He was also unaware that a car was idling right behind him, waiting for him to start walking again. Finally, a slight tap on the car horn brought Andrews back to reality. The teenage girl in the car was African American, but she was not Marie. She exited the car and joined her mother, walking toward the Exchange.

Andrews never noticed the girl's mother. He assumed the car—same make, model, and color—was his. He waved an apology to the driver of the car he had been blocking and started walking toward his own car. There were more cars in the lot now than when he arrived less than a half hour ago.

Andrews sat still in the driver's seat. He had already inserted the key into the ignition, but had not started the car. He switched the flowers to his right hand and placed them on the passenger seat.

Again with the goddamn mind games.

He could swear the seat was still warm from Marie's presence. *It's August, damn it, of course the seat is warm.*

He moved his hand to the seat's back. Damned if it didn't feel damp from its contact with Marie's rain-soaked clothes.

Andrews looked down at the steering wheel trying to clear his mind before he started his drive home. He told himself, *the seat is dry and Marie Garrett is not the reason it's warm to the touch.* He moved his right hand from the passenger seat to the ignition key and, as he did, he sensed something peripherally.

A face!

The chill that ran up his back was immediate. The hair on his arms and the back of his neck stood up. Goosebumps appeared on his arms in an instinctive reaction.

"What the…"

"Hello, Colonel Andrews." The face smiled a friendly smile. "Sorry if I startled you." The general manager of the Post Exchange waved as she looked into the car through the passenger window.

Andrews stepped out of the car and made eye contact with Mrs. C.J. Wax.

"I'm sorry, C.J., I was thinking of something and didn't realize you were standing there."

"No problem, Colonel. I just wanted to say hello and wish you a good weekend," she said.

"Thanks. The store looks good, C.J. How are sales?" Andrews felt obliged to feign interest.

"They were a little slow last month, what with summer vacations and all. But they have really picked up thanks to all the back-to-school shopping."

"For sure. School is about to start, isn't it? Well, C.J., I've got to go, but it was good seeing you. Have a great weekend."

"You too, Colonel. Say hi to Mrs. Andrews for me."

Andrews got back in his car, started the engine, turned on the A/C. He reached for his pipe sitting idly in the car's ashtray. It wasn't there.

With his hand still stretched out toward the ashtray, he felt another chill go up his spine.

"Oh, shit."

Where's the pipe? Andrews kept up to a half dozen pipes in his office. His Friday routine was to leave the office with a pipe to rotate it with one of the others in his pipe rack at home. He couldn't recall the last time he had gone home without one of his pipes.

Maybe he didn't leave without one. Maybe he dropped it in the boxcar. He tried to think of everything that happened. He could not remember having the pipe in the boxcar, but it was such a part of him, he couldn't imagine walking out of the headquarters without it.

Could Marie have taken the pipe as a kind of memento? Maybe she did. "It would be just like her, the way she idolizes me," he said aloud. *The pipe would have been cool enough for her to have slipped it into her purse.*

Her purse.

"Oh, fuck!" He smacked the steering wheel at the thought. *How many surprises can I take? Where is Marie's purse?*

Did she have it with her when she got out of the car? Women always take their purses with them. But I woke her and helped her out of the car. I don't remember a purse.

He leaned over to check the floor on the passenger side. No purse. Wait. A little bit of chain was visible under the seat. Andrews pulled on it and Marie's purse slid along the floorboard into view. It was much smaller than he expected. No more than five inches across and maybe two inches wide at its base, tapering to well less than an inch at the top where a zipper secured the contents. With that, he also noticed her white sweater that had fallen next to the seat. The sweater would present more of a challenge to conceal.

He looked up, taking stock of the activity in the parking lot. He decided to back out of his spot and move to a remote end of the lot, where no cars were currently parked. Once there, he put Marie's purse and her sweater in his briefcase. He made sure it was locked before he put it behind the passenger seat and began the drive home. He would deal with the evidence later.

14

"Nancy, I'm home," Andrews said as he walked into the Army-owned house in which he and his wife lived on Cameron Station. He and Nancy had no need for a four bedroom house, but this set of government quarters, as they were called in the military, were designated for the installation commander regardless of the size of his family.

"Nance?" No answer. Andrews placed the flowers on the kitchen counter and went upstairs to change into civilian clothes. Just as he went into the second floor bathroom, Nancy Andrews walked in from the backyard where she had been pulling weeds.

"Fleming? Is that you?" she said as she slid her feet out of her gardening shoes and removed the gloves she wore when working in the yard.

"Fleming?" Her voice was only slightly raised above normal conversational level and certainly not loud enough to be heard on the second floor. But Nancy Andrews thought of herself as a lady—a colonel's wife—and ladies do not yell.

She stopped when she reached the kitchen and smiled, picking up the bouquet of flowers, taking in their fragrance.

"Oh, how sweet," she said as she withdrew a tall glass vase from the top shelf of a kitchen cabinet. She went to the bottom of the steps, but abandoned any thought of going upstairs when she heard the sound of the shower.

"Hmm," she said. Her husband didn't routinely shower as soon as he got home from work.

Back in the kitchen, she arranged the flowers in the vase and moved it to the center of the table in their dining room.

By the time she started turning the pages of a magazine in the den where she and her husband probably spent eighty percent of their waking hours at home, Andrews was coming down the stairs, having showered and changed out of his uniform.

The flowers earned him a brief, but genuine hug in addition to the perfunctory kiss when he joined her in the den. He packed tobacco into a pipe he had removed from his pipe stand, lit it, and sat in his customary chair, tamping down the tobacco with his pipe tool. He relit the pipe and noticed the gin and tonic she had placed on a coaster on the table between their chairs.

"Thanks for the drink, Nance," he said as he half raised it feigning a toast before he took a sip.

"So, how was your day?" Nancy asked.

"You know," he said. "Same old shit."

"Oh, really, Fleming? How did I know you were going to say that?"

"Because I say it every day. Miss Nancy, mine is a job with a great deal of pressure from all directions. I deal with sensitive and highly classified information." He puffed on his pipe, striking a pose he hoped would appear insightful, but it only matched the self-serving sanctimony of his rhetoric.

Nancy absolutely hated when he spoke down to her. She heard this speech many times. Each time implied she was to assume the role of an inexperienced little girl.

"I have no interest in reliving the day's events at home in the evening and definitely not on a Friday evening," he concluded.

Nancy thought about coming back at him to point out that he was again overreacting to a simple question, but she knew it might ruin the entire weekend. So, she said nothing more about it; opting, as she usually did in similar encounters with her husband, for silence over confrontation.

He picked up the newspaper on the coffee table and began scanning the front page.

"C.J. Wax was asking for you," he said without looking at Nancy. "I ran into her at the PX when I stopped to buy the flowers." Andrews felt compelled to break the silence that came as a result of their most recent exchange.

"Oh, that's nice. I don't think that woman ever takes a day off. She's very dedicated."

"She runs that store very efficiently and she knows what it means to be in charge," he said, never turning from the newspaper.

"That was quite a downpour we had this afternoon, wasn't it? she said.

He thought quickly. "I got caught in it and then the humidity kicked it. I had to get out of my fatigues and take a quick shower as soon as I got home. I called for you, but you must have been in the yard."

"Yes. I thought I heard you, but, by the time I got in the house, you were already upstairs. Oh, my! It's getting late. I'd best put dinner on the table."

Andrews reached for a second helping of nearly everything on the table in a successful effort to demonstrate to his wife that nothing had happened during the day to cause him to lose his appetite. He was also legitimately hungry. He knew he could share it with no one, but he found it morbidly humorous that killing someone and dumping her body seemed to really work up a man's appetite.

After dinner, they returned to the den and sat in front of the television in their respective chairs. Nancy started at her knitting, while Andrews puffed his pipe and worked in pencil on the newspaper's crossword puzzle.

"Fleming, I'd like to tell you a little about my day."

"Oh? What's that?" he said without looking up from the crossword puzzle or removing the pipe from his mouth.

"I represented our Red Cross office at a meeting at the national Red Cross building in DC."

"Really? Why you?"

"Well, Fleming, I *am* the most experienced Red Cross volunteer in the office. I've been involved with the organization longer than I've known you."

"Good meeting?" he asked.

"Very. After the meeting, one of the VPs pulled me aside to tell me about a vacancy they have in the DC office. He wants me to apply for the position," she said.

"Oh, Nancy, you can't be serious. It wouldn't be right for a colonel's wife to work as a secretary, even if it is the Red Cross."

"Fleming," there was a muted anger in her voice. "It happens to be a management position and I think I'm interested."

"Come on, Nancy. You have to see through this. Why would they hire you for a management position? Clearly, they're hoping hiring you would gain them some influence with me."

Andrews had not taken his eyes off the crossword puzzle. As a result, he missed the near rage in her eyes as she stared directly at him. Nancy put her knitting in the basket and walked into the bathroom off the hall, where she remained for several minutes.

15

When she returned to the den, her husband was asleep in his chair. As a rule, Nancy would not disturb him until it was time to go upstairs to bed. Tonight, in light of his demeaning treatment of her on two occasions in a matter of minutes, Nancy enjoyed waking him, even if it was only to ask if he wanted coffee and dessert.

Andrews declined both. Nancy had no interest in reinitiating conversation with him; so, they sat with the audio of the actors in a television sitcom serving as the only conversation in the room. It was a little after 9:00 when the phone's shrill ring broke the silence between them.

He would periodically get a phone call at home after duty hours about some issue on the installation, but it was not the norm. As soon as the phone rang this time, he knew the call was about Marie. *Why hadn't I anticipate this? How could I have deluded myself into thinking it would be quiet this weekend? How could I have failed to plan for this?* He felt cold sweat on his forehead and an increase in his heart rate. *Could they have found her body?*

"I'll get it," Nancy said.

"No! I'll get it," he said.

She had already stood from her chair when she turned to look at him with a confused look brought on by the abruptness of his response.

"What?"

"I said I would…. Never mind. It's okay; you go ahead."

She moved again toward the phone in the kitchen, shaking her head slightly at his reaction to the ringing phone.

"You really must have had a rough day."

She answered the phone with a casual tone that quickly faded.

"Fleming," she said. "It's Jack Ewing. Something has happened. He needs to talk to you." She was visibly concerned by the tone of the caller's voice.

Lieutenant Colonel Jack Ewing was the installation Provost Marshal, Cameron Station's sheriff. He told Andrews that the Alexandria police contacted him through the staff duty officer because Marie Garrett's mother had reported that Marie did not arrive home after work.

Everything had been going so smoothly and Andrews seemed so in control, but he never thought about the inevitable phone call that would be coming once Marie's family became concerned and called the police. *How could I have been so stupid? Why didn't I think this through?*

Andrews knew his wife was watching him to try to read his reaction to whatever he was being told. He also sensed that his face had lost its color. His mind shifted into overdrive again.

"Jesus, Jack," he said. "That's awful."

Did I overplay it? Hard to tell.

"What does it have to do with us? Oh, I see. Yes, she was at work today," he continued. "No, I'm pretty sure she left at the normal time. Nothing unusual. I have to assume she was heading home, but I have no way of knowing for sure, of course."

"Who, Fleming? Did something happen to Laura?" Nancy asked.

He ignored her inquiry, except to shake his head. While continuing with the phone conversation, he was trying to collect his thoughts. He knew he would be telling the same story more than once tonight and in the days ahead.

"Yes, sure, Jack. Your office? I'll be there in less than 15 minutes."

He hung up the phone and turned to face Nancy.

"Oh, Fleming, what's wrong?"

"It's Marie Garrett. Our summer intern. She didn't make it home today after work and her mother called the city police who reached out to Jack through the duty officer."

"Oh, God, Fleming. I hope she's okay."

"What?" He seemed distracted. "Oh, of course. I hope so, too. I'm sure she will be. I have to go to Jack's office to meet with the city police."

"Why you, Fleming?"

The directness of her question caught him off guard. Had he given her some reason to think he was involved?

"Nancy…" *Can she hear the nervousness in my voice? Probably not.* "…I'm the post commander and one of the last people to see her in the headquarters today. They will probably want to get a statement from me. As the commander, I'm involved on the outside chance it turns out that something happened to her while she was still on the installation."

"You don't think someone on post did something, do you?"

"Nancy, how do I know? I guess anything could have happened to the poor kid. It's extremely unlikely anything happened on post, though, but anything is possible, I suppose."

"Do you want me to come with you?" she asked.

"No. No need." He wanted to ask her what good she could possibly do, but thought better of the sarcasm in this instance. "I'm not sure how long I'll be there; probably not all that long. Frankly, there isn't much I'm going to tell them…nothing that would be useful. I'm sure of that. I've conducted similar interviews in my career when there's a chance a crime was committed. It usually works out fine, but the cops have to do their job. And sometimes that means assuming the worst."

Andrews thought about wearing his uniform to the Provost Marshal's office, but opted to change from his blue jeans to khaki pants and a short-sleeved shirt with a button-down collar. The drive from the commander's quarters to the Provost Marshal's office took Andrews no more than ten minutes. He was met at the front door by Jack Ewing, also in civilian clothes, who walked with him through the small lobby and into the conference room where he was introduced to Detective Bob Decker of the Alexandria Police.

Someone had set up a coffee pot at the far end of the conference room and, as the conversation among the three men developed, Andrews poured himself a cup and took a seat at the head of the table, trying to appear as relaxed as possible.

"Colonel, before I say anything else, I want you to know how much I appreciate the support we are already getting from your folks, especially Jack Ewing here," Decker said.

"I'm glad to hear that, but I'm not surprised, Detective."

"We haven't been here a half hour and Jack told me to set up here in the conference room and to consider it my on-post base of operations for as long as we need. Although I doubt we'll be here more than a day or two."

"I figured it was a lot better than asking them to operate out of the back seat of their cars or the rear of a van," Ewing said. "It also ensures we communicate with each other."

"Makes perfect sense. Detective, we're on the same team. You're welcomed for as long as you can stomach Army coffee," Andrews said.

"Appreciate that, Colonel. I understand you are a military policeman in addition to being the post commander. That's great."

"Well, my law enforcement days are pretty much behind me at this point in my career. I was a desk jockey at Fort Monroe in my assignment just before I assumed command. I guess I still know enough about police work to be a pain in Jack Ewing's ass," Andrews said in a rarely voiced expression of modesty—false modesty at that. "Jack's the professional who is on his way to colonel's eagles if I have any say in it."

When Andrews walked into the building, his anxiety level was fairly high. He was most concerned that his demeanor would be a wordless, but unmistakable admission of guilt. He was surprisingly relaxed now. In his element. He realized that, rather than being questioned as a suspect, he was being updated and consulted as the installation's commander—among the most respected positions on base in the mind of the city's citizens. And there was the added benefit of being a fellow cop.

After refilling his coffee cup, Andrews returned to the end of the long conference room table where Decker and Lieutenant Colonel Ewing were seated.

"Well, I suppose you'll want a statement from me covering my actions this afternoon and this evening," Andrews said.

"Nah. Not right now, Colonel. We'll get to it, of course. At this point, though, I consider the fact that you were one of the last people to see Marie Garrett today to be fortunate. It gives me a definite and reliable starting point to figure out what the hell happened."

Andrews remained on guard, but he was pleased with the tone the conversation had taken.

"Any chance you can recall when Marie left the office?"

"Not exactly, but she has been a very reliable kid. The other day, my secretary mentioned that Marie has never been late for work in the morning and that she wishes we could keep her permanently. So, I'm guessing she walked out precisely at 5:00 or a little after, but never early. You know, she stuck her head in the door of my office to say goodnight. I told her to have a good weekend, but didn't check my watch."

"Did you stay at work long after that?" Decker asked.

"I stayed for a while. Don't know how long exactly. I finished up a few things, packed my briefcase for the weekend, and then went home."

"Hmm. Any chance you remember what time you got home? What was on TV when you walked in the door? Anything like that can help me with a timeline."

"No, I don't. And to add to the uncertainty, I didn't go right home."

"Oh?"

"No. I went to the PX. Picked up some flowers for my wife. I talked a bit with the store manager. Sorry, not very helpful."

"No, Colonel, it all helps," Decker said. "How about the rain?"

"What about it?"

"Well, it rained like a son of a bitch for about 15 or 20 minutes this afternoon. Remember? Was Marie still in the office when it started raining?"

"No. She definitely left before then. In fact, the second floor was pretty deserted when it rained. I was in the latrine when I heard a very loud clap of thunder. I remember that because I thought there is no better place to have the shit scared out of you than in the latrine. I actually laughed out loud at my own joke even though I was alone in the bathroom."

"I think everyone in the city heard that boom," Ewing laughed. Decker agreed.

"It wasn't long after that the skies opened up," Decker said.

"No it wasn't," Ewing added. "And it was only minutes after 5:00."

"I know. I got soaked," Andrews said.

"So, you headed home when it was still raining?" Decker asked.

"What? No, I was at my desk. Let me clarify. I was at my desk working for some time after 5:00. Just my luck, I went to my car to get my pipe tobacco pouch about thirty seconds before the skies opened," Andrews explained.

"So, you went from the restroom—the latrine—to your car before returning to your desk," Decker said.

"That's right. When I heard the thunder, I thought I'd better get my pipe tobacco before it started to rain. Clearly, my timing could have been better."

"That's funny."

"What is?"

"I don't usually carry my car keys to the bathroom when I have to pee," Decker said.

"You might, if you knew you had to go to your car."

"I suppose," Decker said after a slight pause. Think about it, Colonel. Within the timeline you just laid out, do you think there's a chance Marie got caught in the rain or was there enough time for her to have made it to the bus stop?"

Andrews was on edge now, concerned that he was digging himself a hole. He tried to think far enough ahead to avoid being caught in a trap hiding in a seemingly benign question. He took a slow drink from his coffee cup.

"So, she takes a bus home?"

"That's her routine. She walks to Duke Street and catches a bus headed east," Decker answered.

Andrews took another slow drink of coffee.

"Jeez, Detective. I couldn't say, but I suppose it's possible."

"Are you working on a theory, Bob?" Ewing asked Decker.

"Not really. She could be off on a lark somewhere as we sit here talking, for all I know. Her mother says she's not that kind of a kid. We don't know enough about her at this point in the investigation. If there was foul play, was it a pure assault or might it have been an abduction?"

"Not on my post," Andrews interjected. "Sorry," he added. "I'm a bit protective of our image."

"No. I get it completely," Decker said. "I'm admittedly into a hypothetical here. If she was abducted, I'm thinking it was probably a result of one of two things. She's a pretty girl, right? Someone might have been stalking her for a while and decided to grab her today. It could also have been something unplanned. An abduction, for sure, but a crime of opportunity."

"What are you thinking?" Andrews asked.

"Well, her mother said Marie wore a short flowered skirt with a white blouse today."

"I don't recall," Andrews lied.

"Her mother said she didn't have an umbrella with her," Decker continued. "If she got caught in that storm, her clothes were probably sticking to her like a see-through outfit. Some guy driving by might have lured her out of the rain and into his car because he liked what he saw."

"Again, I want to think that would not happen on Cameron Station," Andrews said.

"I know," Decker said. "And neither scenario is pretty. Of course, her mother says Marie would never get into a stranger's vehicle, but she's a kid and if she was getting soaked, who knows?"

"I have no idea. Hell, I'd like to think I would have offered her a ride home in the bad weather, but for all I knew, her mother drove her home every day," Andrews said. "Never even knew she took a bus."

"I know it's too early to say and I know these are hypotheticals," Ewing said, "but I really don't like the sound of where this is going."

"Well, like I said, an abduction is only one possibility," Decker said. "You know, she could have just as easily decided to go off with some friends. Maybe they started drinking and she'll have to sleep it off. She could come home in the morning or later tonight with her tail between her legs, embarrassed, and in trouble with her mother."

"Can I ask a pretty blunt question, Detective?"

"Sure, Colonel, go ahead."

"And I don't want you to think I'm making light of the situation or that I don't appreciate the potential gravity here."

"Fire away," Decker said.

"Well, isn't it a bit premature for the Alexandria Police Department to be investing this much effort and manpower for the case of a kid who has been missing—what—five or six hours?"

Decker smiled. "Do you have my phone bugged, Colonel?"

"I don't understand what you mean."

"I asked my superiors the same question."

"And did you get an answer?"

"Just between us, it wasn't very satisfactory. I was told that it had been decided to open an investigation now and that the decision was not open for discussion."

"Huh," Andrews said. "Seems to me somebody somewhere has a few preconceived notions about this situation and is assuming the worst. Of course, there is an election in November. No one would insert politics into a police investigation. Would they?" If anything, Andrews stressed his sarcasm, rather than try to hide it.

"Look, Colonel, I can assure you I'm not drawing any premature conclusions, but I want to capture as much information while the facts are fresh. I've got uniforms checking with her neighbors, friends, and classmates. They'll check out any of the places she likes to go."

"You keep mentioning her mother, Detective, only her mother. Are her parents divorced? Is her father out of the picture?" Andrews asked.

"No, not divorced, but he is kind of out of the picture most of the time. He's a long-distance truck driver. Drives a big rig across the country. Mrs. Garrett says he was scheduled to leave Arizona today, headed for a delivery in San Diego. When I left her, she was expecting him to call when he stopped for the night. He's probably called her by now."

"I see," Andrews said, as though he was processing Decker's response. "Can't say I'm surprised there is no strong male influence in her family. That could explain any questionable behavior."

Decker continued. "That's not completely true. She also has extended family in the area. She's close to an uncle who works here on base. He's the one who told Marie's mother about the summer job program on Cameron Station. I haven't talked to him yet, but her mom said he's already blaming himself for whatever might have happened to Marie."

"That doesn't make any sense," Andrews said.

"Yeah, but the guy's probably not thinking straight. I'll bet he's working on pure adrenalin and emotion," Ewing added.

"Do you know the uncle?" Andrews asked.

"No. I don't think so. If I know the guy, I'm not aware that he's Marie's uncle. I'm just speculating on how I would react if I was in his place," Ewing responded.

"I'll talk to him in the morning, if we don't find Marie tonight," Decker said. "And I'm guessing it's going to be a long night."

"Look, you obviously know what you're doing, Detective. Other than brewing more coffee, what else can we do to help?" Andrews asked.

"Can't think of a thing right now. We may be here through the weekend, though."

"Stay as long as it takes. Jack will have to report the activity through Provost Marshal channels and I will ensure my superiors are aware. They'll want periodic updates; so, please keep us in the loop for anything that relates to Cameron Station and we will share whatever we have. I will also call the general officers who work on post, as a courtesy."

"Jack already mentioned the requirement to report up the chain. I understand, of course," Decker responded. "And I've assured him we would stay in close contact."

"Great. If you don't need me for anything else, I'm going to hit the latrine and head to the house, but I'm available 24/7."

"I know that. Thanks, Colonel," Decker said.

As they shook hands, Andrews added, "Find this girl safe and sound, Detective, and get her home."

"That's my plan."

"Jack, can I have a minute before I leave?" Andrews said this as he walked out of the conference room and headed down the hall to the men's room. He knew Ewing had walked into the hall. Andrews waved over his shoulder and said, "I'll be right with you, Jack. Let me pee first."

"Yes, sir."

Standing at the urinal, Andrews exhaled audibly and looked up at the ceiling. He didn't know if he was smiling, but he thought of a line he once heard an after-dinner speaker attribute to the comedian George Burns: *The key to success is sincerity. If you can fake that, you've got it made.*

He was convinced his faked sincerity appeared to be genuine in his conversation with Decker and Ewing. As he washed his hands, he came to the essential realization that, once you have murdered someone, lying about everything else is relatively easy. He sensed what could only be described as a power that made him feel as though he controlled what did—and didn't—happen. He would steer police attention away from his installation and to the streets of Alexandria: somewhere between the front gate of Cameron Station and Marie Garrett's front door.

Jack Ewing had moved down the hall so that he and Andrews would have more privacy when Andrews stepped out of the men's room.

"Jack, please call Dan Grady. Tell him what's going on and ask him or Susan Braswell to meet in my office tomorrow morning. Let's say 10:00. You should be there, too, of course. I'm sure the press will be calling by then."

"I got it, sir."

"By the way, it was brilliant of you to have the city guys use your conference room. Keep an eye on them. Think about giving them an NCO you can trust to stay with them as much as possible."

"Okay, sir."

"I don't want these bastards freelancing on my installation. I have to think the only reason why they are so engaged without waiting the standard 24 hours before they investigate a missing person is because the mayor and the police chief are eager to cast suspicion on the Army. These politicians hate having us in the middle of the city on prime real estate and I believe they enjoy pitting the Army against the community."

"Can do, sir. But, I thought you and the mayor had a pretty good relationship…what with being the Grand Marshal at the Fourth of July parade and all."

"You know the old saying, Jack. Keep your friends close and your enemies closer. I deal with the mayor as much as possible, but always with a level of suspicion and distrust. Asking me to be the Grand Marshal was just a way to soften me up," Andrews said as he applied a flame to relight his pipe. "Keep an eye on them."

"Yes, sir."

Driving home, Andrews caught himself thanking God for permitting things to go without complications. In Andrew's mind, God understood the exigent circumstances that led to Marie's death and, with a wisdom that is uniquely divine, how Marie actually bore responsibility for what took place in the rail yard.

16

It wasn't until the next morning that Andrews got a
reminder that at least some of God's creatures might not
share his opinion that he and the Lord enjoyed a special
complementary relationship. When he stepped outside to
collect the Saturday newspaper, he noticed that his car had
been generously coated with bird droppings.

"Holy shit," he said aloud and, as soon as he did, he
laughed slightly.

"Holy shit, indeed." Andrews had not noticed General
Charles Abell walking his dog on the sidewalk in front of
Andrews' house.

"Hey, good morning, General. I didn't see you there."

"Morning, Fleming. It appears to me you pissed off
the animal kingdom something fierce. I've never seen a car
covered with that much bird shit."

Andrews feigned amusement with the situation and
acted as though he didn't mind being embarrassed in front
of a superior officer.

"I was at the Provost Marshal's office most of the night.
I must have parked under a tree filled with birds who had to
go real bad and very often. It certainly didn't happen here:
there isn't a tree for nearly a hundred feet in any direction."

Lieutenant General Abell was the senior officer on
Cameron Station—a highly decorated Army helicopter pilot
who now led an element housed on the installation that
did extensive work with Army intelligence assets, the CIA,
the State Department, and occasionally, the FBI. In fact,
its very existence was barely acknowledged by the Army.
As a result, Andrews knew virtually nothing about Abell's

organization and Abell had never shown any inclination to broaden Andrews' understanding. To put it in Andrews' terms, this is one set of locks to which the man with the largest key ring on post had no access.

"Say, Fleming, I heard about the missing girl. Tough story. You must have your hands full. If there's anything I can do to help, just ask," Abell said.

Andrews walked to the end of the driveway, wondering how Abell became aware, but resolved not to concede that the 3-star might be a step or two ahead of him.

"Yes, sir. I was going to call you, General Schwab, and General Macri later this morning to bring you up to speed." Schwab and Macri were the two other GOs leading tenant organizations on Cameron Station. "It's not clear if she is missing against her will or if anything actually transpired on post," Andrews continued. "We're working closely with the Alexandria police."

"Fleming, I'm confident you're doing all the right things. You can call Rick Schwab and Nick Macri, but I don't need any updates. If you think of a way in which I can be helpful or if you think any of my people are involved, give me a shout. Otherwise, I plan to stay the hell out of your way," Abell said.

"Thanks, General. I appreciate that." Andrews truly appreciated the vote of confidence, especially since he knew, were the roles reversed, he would be far more intrusive into whatever the post commander was doing. It never occurred to Andrews that this might be one of the leadership differences separating Lieutenant General Abell, an accomplished professional, from Colonel Fleming Andrews, a colonel who would never wear a general's star, let alone three stars.

As soon as he went back inside, Andrews phoned both Major General Rick Schwab and Brigadier General Nick Macri. He felt a sudden sense of urgency because he didn't want General Abell beating him to it. Again, were the roles reversed, that's precisely what Andrews would have done. As further evidence that Andrews wasn't half the leader General Abell was, it never occurred to Abell to make such phone calls.

Andrews also spoke to the on-call duty officer for the Army Materiel Command, which had oversight responsibility for Cameron Station because of its logistics mission. He gave the duty officer the basics and asked to speak with the commanding general as soon as possible.

When he hung up the phone after the call to General Macri, Andrews said yes to Nancy's offer of scrambled eggs and bacon for breakfast. It was the smart thing to do since she had already put the eggs and bacon in their respective pans. That aside, he actually was hungry this morning. He poured a cup of coffee and dropped two pieces of wheat bread into the toaster, double-checking to ensure the setting was on "Light."

He ate heartily and engaged Nancy in conversation. He was somewhat surprised at how easy it was to mentally and emotionally compartmentalize yesterday's events. Fewer than twenty-four hours ago, he had raped and taken the life of a young girl whose body lay like a piece of common trash or, more precisely, track kill in the dumpster at the rail yard.

On another day, the sight of the bird shit on his car would have been enough to set him off for the day, but not today for some reason. Despite this, or maybe because of it, Andrews mustered the courage to face whatever news coverage about Marie Garrett was in the paper.

He looked above and below the fold on A1. No mention of a dead girl in *The Washington Post*. Well, there wouldn't be, would there? At this point, Marie was still missing. Another bit of knowledge that he shared with God. Only they knew that Marie was dead. From Andrews' hands to God's with no middle man. Powerful.

"Fleming." Nancy's voice was piercing, as she broke his spell. "Fleming, are you all right?"

"Yes, of course. Why do you ask?"

"I said your name four times before you heard me."

"Oh, sorry. I was looking in the paper for news about the Garrett girl, but there's nothing here."

"That's because it's here in the Metro section." She turned the paper so that her husband could see it. Front page of the section, below the fold.

ALEXANDRIA GIRL MISSING

Police: Clues Scarce

So, that's how Abell already knew about it. "Have you read the article, Nance? What does it say?"

"I haven't finished it, but it says basically what you told me when you got home last night and the bits I overheard you tell General Schwab and General Macri. It says the police don't have enough information yet to formulate a theory on what happened and that Cameron Station authorities are cooperating fully."

"I called a meeting for ten o'clock with Jack Ewing and Dan Grady from Public Affairs. The press will be asking about this. Always looking for news to make the Army look bad—especially on a slow news day."

"You mentioned that last night. I just feel so badly for her poor family," Nancy said.

"Of course," he said. "The truth is that we don't know much about her family, do we? We don't know if she stayed out late most Friday nights or if she has been in any kind of trouble before this. The police are trying to figure that out."

"I know," she said. "But from the things you've said about her, she sounds like such a nice girl."

"I'm sure, but people are often not what they seem,

Nancy. Cops said her father isn't around much. Drives a damn tractor trailer across the country. Ridiculous. Children need a father, if you ask me." As he said this, he got up from the table—a clear sign that the conversation was over and he was not interested in Nancy's opinion on the subject. He put his plate in the sink and headed upstairs to shower, shave, and get dressed for the meeting.

17

Ewing saw Andrews pull into the parking space marked for the installation commander.

"Jesus, boss, what the hell happened to your car?" He was standing at the base of the short cement staircase leading into the rear entrance of the headquarters.

"Last night I parked under a tree at your building and the car was attacked. I didn't notice it until this morning."

"I can have someone pull out a garden hose and wash down the car, if you'd like."

"No. That's all right. I'll take it through a car wash on my way home. Let's get inside. Is Dan Grady here?"

"I'm pretty sure. I think that's his car over there. I just got here myself."

Dan Grady was a career government civilian employee. He had worked briefly for a small, Alexandria-based weekly newspaper after college before being hired by the Cameron Station Public Affairs office. He became the Public Affairs Officer (PAO) five years ago, after a ten year rise through positions within the same organization. Grady had a good working relationship with the community leaders, the reporters from the military trade papers, and the military reporter for *The Washington Post*.

He had never handled a situation with the dynamic potential of Marie Garrett's disappearance. He had no doubt whatever happened did not occur on Cameron Station.

Andrews and Ewing walked into the headquarters. Dan Grady met them just inside the front door. He had been standing there talking with the duty officer, who, after greeting Andrews, advised him that he had just brewed a fresh pot of coffee for the meeting.

Andrews shifted his briefcase to his left hand to shake hands with Grady. As he did, he had the cold realization that the briefcase still contained Marie's sweater and purse.

"Why don't you fellas get a cup of coffee and we'll meet in the conference room," Andrews said. "I'll grab a pipe and my coffee cup in my office and meet you there."

"I put notepads and ink pens on the conference room table for you gentlemen," the duty officer said, apparently hoping to gain some favor with the installation commander.

"Hey, that's great. Thanks for doing that," Andrews said without changing course for the stairs to the second floor and his office. "Brown-nosing A-hole," he added under his breath when he was sure he would not be heard.

In the privacy of his office, Andrews paused, looked up to the ceiling, and exhaled audibly.

"Shit," he whispered. He couldn't believe he had lost sight of what was in his briefcase. He was a bit shaken by the prospect that he very nearly walked into the conference room and popped it open. He took a few seconds to compose himself, during which time he selected one of the five pipes that stood in the rack made to hold six.

With the pipe in hand, he looked around the office for the sixth pipe—the one he had reached for in his car and the one either Marie took or he left somewhere in the rail yard. The ashtray on his desk was empty. Had he left his pipe sitting in the ashtray, he knew from past experience, the contract cleaning team would have left it and the ashes alone.

The ashtrays on the coffee and end tables were also clean. *What if her body was found and his pipe was in her pocket?*

He felt a cold sweat allover his body. He slowly packed

tobacco into the pipe he had selected. Her skirt had no pockets. *I would have noticed. Maybe it is in her purse. I'll check later—when it's safe. No, I have to know.*

He placed the pipe he had just filled with tobacco in the clean ashtray, quietly swung his office door closed and stood his briefcase on his desk. He dialed the three-digit combination, laid the briefcase on its side, and carefully opened it, with the lid facing the closed door.

Was it the clicking of the latches echoing in the office? Or was it something else? He concluded his mind was playing tricks on him—not the first time in the last twenty-four hours.

No. It was very real: more of a tap–tap than the click of the briefcase latches.

He looked around. *What the hell is that noise?* He turned toward the window behind him as though to protect himself in the event someone was spying on him through the second floor window.

Tap–tap.

There, outside on the windowsill, was a crow. Was it staring at Andrews? Andrews was convinced it was.

The crow again tapped twice on the window.

"Oh, fuck you," Andrews said softly, but defiantly.

The crow straightened and cawed loudly at Andrews before taking wing and coming to rest on the branch of a tree across the parking lot, joining several other black birds.

Andrews slowly shook his head and turned his attention to his briefcase. He lifted the lid and looked down on Marie's sweater and purse. He again looked left and right, as though to ensure no one had entered while he was distracted.

The sweater and the purse made it real. Any illusion that yesterday's events were imagined and that Marie would be found safe was gone. She was dead. He had killed her.

He pressed down on Marie's sweater with an open palm. No hint of the missing pipe there. Marie's purse was so small and soft that, even if Marie *had* squeezed his pipe into her purse, the pipe would have created a clearly visible outline in the fabric. He opened it anyway. Two keys on a small ring, lipstick, tissues, and $12—two fives and two singles. No souvenir pipe taken from her idol.

He zippered the purse and slid it into an inconspicuous compartment of his briefcase. The compartment had a zipper of its own. He lowered the briefcase lid, snapped the latches closed, and set the lock dial to all zeros. He double checked that the latches were secured and placed the briefcase in the well of his desk. He picked up his lighter and pipe tool from the desktop, retrieved today's pipe from the ashtray, grabbed his coffee cup, and exited his office.

Andrews walked into the conference room after pouring his coffee and took a seat at the end of the table, flanked by Ewing and Grady.

"Where are we Dan?" Andrews asked as he went through his pipe-lighting ritual: light, tamp, relight.

Grady told Andrews that he had received inquiries from *The Washington Post*, the three networks, local television affiliates, and the *Army Times*. Together, they settled on a statement expressing the military community's concern for the Garrett family, confidence that Marie would be found safe and unharmed, and a commitment to cooperate with the Alexandria Police.

"Generally, missing persons cases are resolved within a week," Ewing said. "Two to three days with a positive outcome. Increasingly less likely as each day goes by."

"What's your gut, Jack?" Andrews asked.

"Well, I don't know the girl, but, if she was hanging out with the wrong crowd, this could be drug or sex related."

"Jesus!" Andrews said, "I never took her to be that bad a kid."

At that, Grady spoke up.

"Colonel, we have to be very careful not to suggest anything negative about her character."

"No. No," Andrews replied. "That's why I want you to be our voice, Dan. She did dress a little provocatively, in my opinion, but those are today's styles. And, as I said, she seems like a very good kid to me." He said what he thought was expected. "Laura thinks highly of her."

As he said this, Andrews tamped his tobacco with his pipe tool, relit the pipe, and took a deep drag.

"Let me summarize and give you my bottom line," Andrews said. "I want to be seen as being responsive to all inquiries, but I don't want you feeding the flames, Dan."

"No, sir. I'll stick to the patter line we've agreed to," Grady said.

"You're the only person I want talking to the press. When this is all over with…and little Miss Garrett is back home with her mommy and maybe even her daddy…it might be appropriate for me to make a statement. But, until then, you're the man. Got it?"

"For sure. I can handle it."

"Be sure all the public affairs weenies up through the chain understand that they are to resist the temptation to open their damn yaps except to refer inquiries to you. If any one of them starts speculating with the press, I will ensure his nuts are cut off."

"Right, sir."

"Jack is our liaison with the police. He has already been in communication with the military police commands, including Army CID. Right, Jack?"

"Yes, sir. They are happy to stay out of this one…at

least in the eyes of the press. CID may want to get more involved, but they won't grandstand with the public."

"You two are the lead dogs. Cooperate with each other, but stay in your own individual lane. I'll handle any confusion or overlap, but don't make me play referee."

"Understood." They both replied and smiled at each other because of their common response.

"I'm expecting a call from the CG at Materiel Command sometime this morning. I'll let you know if he trumps my guidance, but this is the way I want to handle things. I've already talked to the three GOs on post and they are content to keep hands off. Any disagreement?"

Both Ewing and Grady shook their heads. Andrews leaned forward over the tabletop as though he was about to share a secret with them.

"Dan, I've already told Jack, but you ought to know that I don't trust the boys from Alexandria. I'm sure they want to solve the case and make a good arrest, if a crime has been committed. But I am also convinced, in the absence of finding Marie Garrett unharmed or of arresting someone who looks clearly guilty, those bastards will do all they can to cast doubt on the U.S. Army, Cameron Station, and its commander—yours truly. Now, Jack Ewing here thinks I'm a paranoid old shit, but..."

"Come on, sir," Ewing interrupted, sensing Andrews was less than serious. "I didn't say you're paranoid. I was just surprised at your view of the Alexandria PD. The more I think about it, though, I see your point and I think we should keep our guard up."

"You're goddamn right we should," Andrews said. "Dan, whenever you see an opportunity to turn the tables, I want you to direct attention to the city police and the likelihood that the answers to the press's questions are to be found outside the boundaries of Cameron Station."

"I understand, Colonel."

"Come in," Andrews reacted to the soft knock at the door of the conference room.

The duty officer stuck his head in the door. "Sir, there's a call for you from…"

"The commanding general of Materiel Command?" Andrews finished his sentence.

"Yes, sir."

"Can you transfer it to this phone?" Andrews pointed to the corner of the room where the conference room phone sat on a small table.

"Yes, sir."

"Please do."

Andrews stood and walked slowly toward the phone, anticipating its ring. Ewing and Grady stood to leave the room to give Andrews privacy.

"No, sit down, guys. Stay here. This won't take long and we'll all know what the boss has to say about our plan."

Andrews picked up the phone even before the first ring ended. He recapped the approach he planned to take, omitting the part about not trusting the bastards from the Alexandria PD. The call lasted less than five minutes.

The four-star commander of Army Materiel Command endorsed the course Andrews proposed. He asked to be kept informed as necessary and made it clear he expected Andrews to minimize damage to the Army and Cameron Station.

Andrews hung up and returned to his seat at the table.

"Well, the CG said to proceed with our plan and to make sure none of the stink gets on his uniform, if you know what I mean." Andrews exhaled audibly through his nose and looked at the two men sitting at the table with him. He relit his pipe.

"What's left? What should we be doing that we haven't done?" Andrews asked both men.

"I think we're in good shape, sir. I expect we'll be hearing from the Feds before too long, but I'll keep you posted," Ewing said.

"Why the Feds?"

"The FBI and Army CID will nose around until the investigation eliminates the post as the location of any criminal activity. If she was kidnapped from inside the gate, the Feds may claim jurisdiction. At the very least, they'll work with the city police."

"And won't that be fun for us all?" Andrews said. "Dan, do you have what you need?"

"Yeah, I'm good for now. I'm going to go to my office and return some phone calls," Grady said.

"I'll be at my quarters all weekend. If I'm not there, I'll be in my office."

"One last thing, boss. Despite what Decker told you, you should expect to be questioned at length since you are probably one of the last people to see her on Friday," Ewing said. "Not for nothing, but you may want to talk to the JAG."

"Shit, Jack. I expect to be interviewed for just that reason, but I don't think I'm suspected of anything, do you? I actually thought Decker was being straight with me when he clearly implied that I was not only not a suspect, but that I could help fill in his timeline. I broke my own rule about not trusting these bastards."

"My guess is that they've got nothing right now. They'll talk to everybody to try to reconstruct yesterday afternoon. Until they do, everyone is, by definition, a suspect to some degree. Nothing to worry about."

"Right. Of course," Andrews said. He relit his pipe and

continued, "Dan, while you're making calls to the press, give Laura Bennett a call. The police may want to talk to her."

"They may have already talked to her," Ewing said. "They asked me for the contact information on everyone who worked in the headquarters and who might have had contact with Marie."

"Already? They really are moving fast on this one," Grady said.

"This stuff goes cold fast. Like I said, the longer it takes the less likely it is to turn out good."

"Oh, God, I hope not," Grady said.

"Let's hope you're wrong, Jack. Keep me posted." Andrews stood. The meeting was over.

When he approached his car, he was reminded of the assault it took the night before. He unlocked the door, got behind the wheel, and started the engine. As he shifted his focus to look in the rearview mirror before backing out of the space, his eyes were drawn to the front and to the windshield. It looked as though it had snowed while he was inside.

"Oh, for God's sake."

Andrews' windshield was coated with a healthy deposit of recently produced bird droppings.

"Damn birds."

The wipers first smeared and then, with a few sprays of the washing fluid, eventually cleared most of the windshield. Andrews backed out of his parking space and drove in the direction of the installation's back gate because of its proximity to the off-base car wash.

About a quarter mile down the road, had he gone straight instead of making the final right turn that led directly to the exit, Andrews would have soon come to the often unnoticed side street that led to the rail yard. He gripped the steering wheel tightly as he fought a nearly unconscious urge to go there.

"No thank you," he said, as though the briefcase on the passenger seat was a person. "There will be no returning to the 'scene of the crime' for me—not just yet."

18

He felt the eyes of the community on him as he advanced slowly in the line to enter the car wash. He sensed that everyone recognized him as the person most closely involved in the case of the missing girl.

Stop looking at me, assholes, the voice in his head said. *She's dead. I know it and God knows it. Just the two of us; so, stay out of it.*

His senses were betraying him, of course. His was just another anonymous car waiting for a low quality, automated car wash. If asked, a couple of the attendants would have remembered the car covered in bird shit. But no one ever asked.

Just before he drove forward enough for his left front wheel to engage the automated track that pulled the car through the wash, an attendant approached the car, signaling for Andrews to lower his window.

"Drive forward and put it in Neutral when I give you the signal." *How often must he say this on a busy weekend?* As he gave Andrews instructions, he handed him a damp cloth the size of a standard washcloth.

The cloth was ostensibly provided as a service, allowing the driver to dust off the dashboard and parts of the interior during the wash cycles. The true purpose was to cause the customer to stop long enough to return the cloth to one of the attendants, hand him a tip, or drop something in the large plastic tip jar, crudely labeled "TIPS" in hand-printed marker.

Andrews used the car wash several times before; so, he was familiar with the process. Because he did not want to stand out in any way today, he made sure to drop a dollar bill in the jar when he returned the washcloth to the attendant. Too large a tip and they would remember him. No tip would also make him memorable. His mission today was not to stand out.

Andrews hated the concept of tipping someone who did a mediocre job of drying his car after an automated wash. *Everybody wants a little extra for doing the bare minimum.* Even before he joined the ranks of rapists and murderers, Andrews believed the car wash attendants would make a point to screw with his car next time if he did not tip.

Andrews glanced over at the cars using the coin-operated vacuums.

Holy shit! I'd better vacuum this thing. God knows what evidence she left behind.

With the wash completed, he parked next to a vacuum that offered easy access to a 50-gallon drum being used as a large trash can.

If the opportunity presented itself, Andrews would execute a newly-hatched plan. Before he got out of his car, he unlocked his briefcase and withdrew Marie's sweater. He dropped it to the floor at his feet. He would do what he could to transfer whatever dirt was on the floor of the car and the bottom of his shoes to Marie's sweater.

While the briefcase was open, he slipped his hand deeper into the case to the hidden, zippered compartment. He tapped the area to reassure himself that Marie's purse was still there. It was, of course, but he needed the reassurance. He hoped to come up with a plan to get rid of her purse, but, for now, he was comfortable dealing with only the sweater.

The sweater was no longer a bright white. It looked nothing like the garment Marie had carried over her arm yesterday afternoon. Yet, he wanted to make it look even more like an old rag. As he got out of the car, Andrews tossed the dirtied sweater over to the floor of the passenger side of the car. He deposited the quarters necessary to start the vacuum for what was advertised as a 5-minute vacuum. He was sure it would be something shorter than that, but he didn't really care. He had plenty of spare change in the center console of the car.

He noticed that the trash barrel was a little less than half full and, based on a quick look, appeared to have several dirty rags and wadded sheets of paper towel. He also saw bags, wrappers, and paper cups from fast food restaurants. As he leaned in to vacuum the floor on the passenger side, he used his free hand to make the sweater into the tightest possible ball while he rubbed it across his floor to dirty it more.

He stepped toward the vacuum as though he was uncoiling the hose and, as he did, he added the sweater to the garbage with a flick of his wrist intended to cause some of the contents to stir and possibly cover enough of the sweater to make it less distinguishable from the other pieces of trash.

He turned toward his car and nearly bumped into a large woman with a half-empty cup of soda and a bag of empty food wrappers from McDonald's. Andrews and the woman did the awkward mirrored shifting back and forth twice, only to block each other's path each time.

"I am so sorry, ma'am. Here, let me throw all that away for you," Andrews said.

"Why, thank you. I appreciate that," she said. She surrendered the bag and the cup. Andrews made sure to empty the bag as he dropped it into the trashcan, obliterating the outline of the sweater. Letting the half-empty soda spill onto the material was a bonus.

He spent every bit of time offered by the vacuum focused on the front passenger seat and its floor. He looked extra hard for any hairs caught in the upholstery.

When the time ran out, he inserted more coins for

a second vacuum cycle, turning his attention to the car's trunk. The vacuum captured what might have been small pieces of the cardboard that had been in the trunk with Marie's body. There may have been fibers from the blanket or a hair or two from Marie. Andrews wasn't sure, but he was taking no chances. All the while, he sniffed the air in the trunk, wondering if there was a detectable smell of death. There wasn't.

He pressed even harder with the end of the vacuum hose when he thought he picked up the fragrance of Marie's perfume. If anything, the trunk of his car had no smell other than that of the spare tire. There was no odor, no fragrance.

Andrews felt a sense of accomplishment. He was convinced he had successfully gotten rid of the sweater and that it would never be found, let alone associated with Marie. The bird droppings on his car might have been a blessing in disguise. He took this as more evidence that someone was watching over him and, almost certainly, that he bore no blame for what happened to the young woman who tempted him all summer.

I don't think I would have remembered to vacuum my car—passenger seat and trunk—if I wasn't at the car wash. And washing my car wasn't even on my to-do list before I discovered the bird shit.

"Ha," he said aloud. "Almost like manna from heaven. Well, thank you, Jesus!"

Despite the definite sense of relief he now felt, the drive home was difficult. Andrews struggled, trying to come up with a way to dispose of Marie's purse and its contents. He ran through possibilities in his mind, but none satisfied him. Every scenario he could imagine came with the risk of being seen by someone who just might link his action to the search for the missing girl.

He turned into his driveway resolved that the best

course of action, for the time being, was to keep the purse in his locked briefcase and to ensure he and his briefcase were always together.

Back at home, he gave Nancy a brief, sketchy update on the morning's meeting, after which he lied, "You know, babe, the truth is that I am so troubled by how this all might turn out that I really don't want to talk about it anymore today. Is that too selfish a request for me to make?"

Nancy sensed his increased level of stress which she attributed to Marie's disappearance and his role as the commanding officer of Cameron Station. She agreed not to bring up the subject again, but only after he promised to keep her apprised of any developments—a promise he was pretty sure he wouldn't keep.

Andrews wasn't particularly productive the rest of the day. He tried to read the paper, but couldn't stay focused on it. He sat in front of the television watching several innings of the nationally broadcast baseball game, but it never captured his interest.

Eventually, he wandered into their den ostensibly to get some work done. In fact, he sat at his desk, staring at his unopened briefcase, trying to come up with a plan to deal with Marie's purse, until Nancy called him for dinner.

The next morning, they were in the front pew of their regular on-post Sunday church service. Ever conscious that someone attending any Cameron Station gathering might be looking at the installation commander, Andrews did his best to make it appear he was participating fully, to include bowing his head deeply when the congregation prayed for Marie Garrett's safe return to her family.

Nancy Andrews could not have been more sincere or genuine. Her husband, on the other hand, was becoming increasingly concerned that the voice he was hearing and the thoughts he was having might eventually drive him mad if he did not maintain control over his emotions. At one point in the service, he let his eyes move across the congregation.

All prayers are answered, the voice said silently to the faithful. *Sometimes the answer is NO, fools.*

Had he cracked a smile? He hoped not. He clearly heard the voice. He was sure—pretty sure—no one else had.

Stay in control, Fleming. The voice isn't real. If you ignore it, it will go away.

What are you going to do, Fleming, kill me, too?

The voice sounded pretty real to Andrews.

Shut up!

As the conversation in his mind came to an abrupt end, Andrews was not aware that he had tightened his grip on his wife's hand. She reacted to the pain by pulling her hand away slightly in a motion that was apparent to no one else in the church.

"Fleming, are you okay?" she said softly, as she lightly rubbed her hand.

"Yes, sorry," he whispered in response, "I'm just concerned about her."

Nancy took note of her husband's apparent increased concern for Marie Garrett. It pleased her to see him express empathy. She credited it to the prayerful environment. Yet, the pain in her hand lingered as did her doubts about his sincerity.

When the service ended, Andrews and his wife exited the chapel through the main doors at the rear, where the celebrant stood to greet the congregation.

This week, Andrews' cursory handshake at the chapel door was prolonged when Father John Hughes (who was also a U.S. Army major in the Chaplain's Corps) held Andrews' hand with both of his.

"Colonel, I can only imagine how much of a burden the uncertainty surrounding Marie Garrett must be on you—both professionally and personally. I want you to know that you and the entire staff are in my prayers. God's will be done, but I'm praying hard for a positive outcome."

"Why, thank you, Chaplain. You have no idea how much that means to me."

Andrews loved that line. He had been using it for years. The person on the receiving end takes it to mean his words carry great weight when, in fact, he has no idea how little his words really mean to Andrews.

Most of the congregation left the chapel and followed the walkway around the side of the building into a general purpose room for "Fellowship," a euphemism for coffee and doughnuts.

Early in his tenure, Andrews' realized that his attendance at the post-service Fellowship permitted the rest of the congregation to corner him with a pet peeve, a complaint, or a suggestion on how the base could be better managed, more efficient, and improved overall.

After his first Fellowship, Andrews began referring to it as Benevolent Bitching. Fleming and Nancy Andrews made it to three consecutive Fellowships. The third was their last. Instead, they adopted the routine of going to brunch at the Officers' Club, which provided a pleasant environment in which Andrews was treated like royalty.

"Fleming, do you think it would be bad form if we went to brunch at the Club this morning?" Nancy asked as they left church and walked to their car.

"Nance, we go to brunch every Sunday after church. Everybody's concerned about the missing girl, but I have an obligation to reassure people that there is a steady reliable hand on the controls. Let's go to brunch."

He wasn't sure how much he believed his own rationale,

but, not surprisingly, Nancy complied without openly questioning his judgment.

Andrews started the car and pulled on the lever to wash the windshield. There in his line of sight, more than one bird had deposited a small deposit of bird shit on his windshield.

"Son of a bitch," he said under his breath.

"What's that, honey?"

"Nothing. I think the birds around here are gunning for me."

He spoke twice with Jack Ewing throughout the day and told Nancy that there was nothing new to report. On base, the Army's criminal investigators, teamed with the Alexandria police, continued their search. Andrews had no idea how extensive Alexandria's city-wide effort was. What he knew in that regard came from local news reports. Lieutenant Decker was less than forthcoming on that part of the investigation.

By sunset, Marie's body was fewer than twelve hours away from joining piles of garbage in a Prince William County landfill more than 30 miles south of Cameron Station. The police needed a lucky break.

19

Andrews was pleasantly surprised that he had been able to compartmentalize Friday's events to this point. Late Sunday afternoon, however, his level of anxiety began to increase. Until then, he had not focused on what the discovery of Marie's body would mean: the certain loss of his freedom and the end of the lifestyle he had known since his late teens. But it was the realization that his hopes of being an Army general would be lost that scared him for the first time since the scene in the boxcar when he became aware Marie lay dead beneath him.

On Sunday, he found himself staring at the phone each time he walked past it, expecting a call with the news. Even worse, there might be a knock at the door. He supposed both Decker and Jack Ewing would be there to take him away.

Decker would be ecstatic. He landed the big fish. Jack wouldn't be able to look Andrews in the eye.

Andrews considered himself a mentor to Jack Ewing and presumed it would crush him to see his boss fall from grace in this way. Nancy would raise her voice to near panic, begging Andrews to reassure her that it was all a mistake as he was escorted away.

As afternoon turned to evening, any noise Nancy made in the kitchen or upstairs startled him. Sunday night traffic on Cameron Station was never heavy and there was virtually no traffic on the street where Andrews and the three resident general officers resided. Yet, the headlights from a passing car were enough to cause him to shift uncomfortably in his chair.

Neither the television nor his concentrated effort to think of something else could keep him from returning to the image of his own arrest—possibly moments away. There would be no advanced warning of a big arrest from Jack Ewing—not when the person being arrested was the installation commander himself.

Andrews couldn't remember the protocol he previously knew so well. Would he be taken into custody by military or civilian authorities? His mind was rushing and he couldn't recall basic procedures of military law enforcement. Would he face civilian trial or a court martial? Did Virginia use the electric chair or the gas chamber?

His eyes were closed when he imagined himself standing blindfolded, hands tied behind his back, in front of a military firing squad.

Ready, aim, fire! When the shots rang out in his head, he shifted abruptly in his living room chair, bringing himself out of his unwelcomed reverie.

"Fleming, are you okay?" Nancy asked.

"What? Oh, yeah. I'm fine. Must have dozed off."

"Oh, you dozed off, all right. You were mumbling something, but I couldn't make out what you were saying."

"What was it?"

"You're not listening, Fleming. I said I couldn't understand your mumbling. I'm not even sure they were words."

"I'm sorry, Nance. I don't feel well. I think I may be coming down with something. I have a nasty headache."

"Fleming, I'm beginning to worry about you." Nancy knew his symptoms were because of the tension he felt regarding the Marie Garrett situation. Until Marie was found safe or until there was clearly no link between Cameron Station and whatever happened to her, she knew the strain on her husband would grow. Andrews had also mentioned to her that he learned the board constituted to select this year's crop of future generals had finished its work and an announcement could be made in a month or two. Even if Marie Garrett was found safe and sound, the self-imposed stress of the pending announcement would be enough to impact him.

Andrews went to bed at his usual time, right after the weather report on the eleven o'clock news. But he barely slept.

The brief periods of sleep were interrupted by his restlessness. He used the bathroom several times and even slipped downstairs for a shot of bourbon, but it was little help. When he managed to nod off, he had visions of Marie. In most of the dreams, she appeared scared and in pain as she looked out from the open dumpster door.

In one dream, she hobbled away from the rail yard toward a main road, her flowered skirt badly soiled and her blouse torn. In another, she approached a military police car. Dried blood was visible from her nostrils, mouth, and ears. She handed something through the window of the car. It was Andrews' missing pipe, with a hint of smoke coming from the still-smoldering tobacco in its bowl. Lieutenant Decker was in the passenger seat of the military police car. He was smiling as he attached the EVIDENCE tag to the pipe's stem.

Repeatedly, sleep would find him, but only long enough for one of the dreams to play in his subconscious. The dream would wake him and the cycle would start again.

As the sun began to lighten the Monday morning sky, Andrews awoke with a start. Moments before, as he again dozed off, he felt the sensation of falling. He wasn't sure if it was another dream about the undead Marie, but it woke him for the day. Doctors refer to this as a hypnic jerk that commonly occurs as someone transitions between being awake and asleep. It can be caused by anxiety, caffeine, or a dream. Andrews had his share of each since Friday.

He was sweaty. He plodded off to the bathroom, tossed his pajamas and underwear into the hamper, and stood under the running shower for several minutes before beginning to wash. He had no way of knowing that, as he showered, a truck was lifting the rail yard dumpster into the air. As the steel forks in the front of the garbage truck returned the dumpster to its place outside the rail yard fence, the mechanism in the rear compressed Marie's body with the trash.

The driver and his helper hadn't noticed the dozen crows sitting on the rail yard fence when their truck approached. It was only natural that the birds would take flight as the forks engaged the dumpster with a metal-on-metal slap.

"Did you get wind of the stink coming out of that son of a bitch?" The helper asked as he climbed back into the cab on the passenger side.

"Sure did. Must have been one helluva big piece of track kill them bastards threw in the dumpster," the driver responded.

"You ain't shittin'. They aren't supposed to do that, right?"

"No," the driver said. "But nobody complains 'cause there ain't no houses nearby. I don't give a shit. It all stinks bad in the end."

"I suppose. Hey, look over at the sidewalk."

"What?"

"We must be being followed by some birds. I can see their shadows out there ahead of us."

"Good eyes, my friend. I think you're right."

"Did you see the ballgame yesterday?"

As their conversation shifted quickly to baseball, both driver and helper lost track of the birds overhead. From the rail yard to the land fill, whenever the truck was in motion, an unnoticed phalanx of six or eight or sometimes ten crows flew high above.

With each stop the trash truck made, Marie's body would be further compacted until the fully packed truck dumped its load near the top of a growing mountain in the landfill. By the end of the day, the smell of her rotting flesh would be one with the stench of the weekend trash from various parts of Northern Virginia.

20

Andrews wasn't sure if he had ever spent as much time standing under a running shower head as he did Monday morning. While toweling off, he caught an unmistakable aroma that told him something was out of the ordinary.

On most mornings, Andrews got fully dressed for work before going downstairs. But, on most mornings, he was not greeted by the smell of bacon cooking. Wearing only a robe and slippers, he went downstairs to find Nancy, also in a robe and slippers, standing at the stove.

"What's the occasion?" he asked.

"You had such a restless night; I thought I would try to give your day a better start."

"So, I ruined your night's sleep, too?"

"That's not it at all, Fleming. I just hate seeing you so tense and on edge. I know it's the Marie Garrett mystery. I can't help with that. Making you a decent breakfast is the least I can do."

Nancy had turned and placed her palms flat on Andrews' chest. He responded instinctively by putting his arms around her, resting his hands on her robe at the small of her back.

She kissed him gently on the lips and, as she did, slid a hand down and inside his robe.

"Maybe I can help that headache of yours, as well."

Neither remembered the last time they were intimate, but Andrews could not control the physical evidence that indicated he clearly welcomed her overture. Nancy was pleased at his reaction. She kissed him again with more passion, now with both hands suggesting they should go back upstairs.

"The bacon's burning," he said without warning, as he stepped away from her, retying his robe.

When she brought the plate with eggs, toast, and bacon to the table, Andrews didn't look up from the newspaper she had retrieved from the driveway and placed on the table while he was in the shower.

By the time she put a small portion of eggs and a strip of bacon on her plate and walked into the dining room, Andrews was nearly finished with his breakfast. She didn't touch her food. He never noticed. She sat watching him with a look of pained sadness in her eyes—something else he failed to see.

He stood, picked up his plate and coffee cup and took a step toward the kitchen before stopping.

"Did you get the paper in your nightgown and robe?"

She never moved her hand from her chin or her elbow from the tabletop.

"No. I'm not wearing a nightgown and I didn't want to get my robe dirty; so, I took it off and went outside buck naked."

At first, he didn't react to her response. He moved to the kitchen, put his plate and cup on the counter, and started up the stairs.

"Sometimes, you're pitiful," he said from the third step up.

"By the way, the birds left you a surprise again this morning." She didn't know if he heard her. He had, but she didn't hear him call her a bitch under his breath.

When he came downstairs dressed and ready to go to work, he noticed Nancy hadn't moved from the table. Her chin still rested in her hand. He sensed that even the perfunctory have-a-good-day kiss would be awkward. He decided not to press it.

"I'm going to work," he said, as he put on his hat and picked up his briefcase.

She couldn't respond.

"By the way, thanks for breakfast," he said. "It was good." The door closed behind him.

Still not moving from the table, she shut her eyes tightly and began to cry. She was humiliated at how dismissive he was of her touch. His words echoed in her head: *It was good.*

Was it? She thought. *If it ever was, it certainly wasn't good now.*

21

Andrews wanted the Alexandria police contingent to see him taking an active interest in the case. He planned to delay his departure for the office on Monday so that a stop at the Provost Marshal's conference room en route would guarantee the Alexandria crew would be there.

At another time, he might have welcomed extra time in the bedroom with Nancy, but the current tension between them would have made it a fool's errand this morning. Besides, despite the morning's harsh ending, his lengthy shower and the surprise breakfast did the trick. He was confident the timing was right for him to head out.

He parked near the Provost Marshal's office, but before going to see Jack Ewing, Andrews turned into the conference room. Two Alexandria detectives and one uniformed policeman were busy making notes and sorting through sheets of paper. One of the detectives was speaking on the phone, but not loud enough for Andrews to overhear.

Sometime since Andrews' last visit to the conference room, they had brought in a portable chalkboard on which they created a timeline with points marking the few known activities in the life of Marie Garrett on Friday, August 21.

Andrews stood just inside the open door of the conference room. The detective who was on the phone noticed him and, as he hung up the phone, also noted Andrews' interest in the chalkboard.

"Morning, Colonel. How can I help you?" he asked.

"Just checking in. In the Army, we would call that a training aid," Andrews said, motioning to the chalkboard.

"Well, it isn't very sophisticated, Colonel, but it's a big help getting the job done. Is there something specific I can do for you?"

"I was hoping to run into Lieutenant Decker, but I don't suppose he's here yet."

"Are you kidding, Colonel?" the cop asked. "He's been here and gone twice already this morning. I'm not for sure where he is. Wait, come to think of it, he said something about heading to your office."

"My office?"

"Yeah, that's right," the uniformed cop chimed in. "Lieutenant Decker left out of here for your office a while ago."

"I guess I better go meet him there. I'll probably see you folks later."

As Andrews re-entered the hall, he met Jack Ewing who was walking out of his office hat in hand.

"Hey, sir, good morning. I'm just about to take a spin around post…unless you need me for something," Ewing said.

"Jack, how come you didn't tell me Decker went to the headquarters this morning?"

"Decker went to headquarters? I didn't know. I haven't seen him today."

Andrews stepped closer to Ewing and lowered his voice so as not to be overheard.

"Look, Jack, you know I want us to cooperate with Decker and his team, but cooperation is a two-way street. He owes us some common courtesy. I don't want him thinking he owns the fucking place."

"Roger that. We'll keep an eye on him. To tell you the truth, sir, I pretty much have given him enough space to operate freely without us. I offered him an NCO, but he said no."

"I guess I'm not surprised," Andrews said.

"I get the sense his team won't be on post much longer and I'm pretty sure they've concluded that whatever happened to the kid happened off post."

"Well, if he doesn't need our help, then, he doesn't need your conference room. Let him drink his own damn coffee in his own damn precinct. And did *they* tell you specifically that whatever happened occurred off post, or is that something you are assuming?"

"Not in so many words, but I am pretty sure that's where they're headed. Every now and then I catch some of their side chatter. We'll know something if they begin packing up soon. Do you want me to put a tail on Decker? That won't be easy to do on post. He'd pick it up for sure."

"Nah, screw him. I think you're right; they'll be gone soon. Maybe I can help them along."

Andrews was aware that, over the weekend, Alexandria police rode around the base with personnel from the Army's Criminal Investigation Division, but he did not know the depth of the effort.

Together, the CID and the city police drove up and down nearly every street on Cameron Station. They stopped frequently to inspect many areas on foot. They knocked on door after door to interview residents. No one saw anything that would lead them to conclude Cameron Station was the location where anything happened to Marie Garrett.

In the industrial areas and around the office buildings, they spoke to anyone working weekend duty, snooped around vacant parking lots, and shined a flashlight into dumpsters—some with a considerable amount of trash, others nearly empty. They focused on areas that might have been out of sight or lightly populated on a Friday afternoon. They never stopped at the rail yard.

The Army Criminal Investigation Division was notorious for its aloofness, independence, and arrogance. Many CID agents saw no need to work closely with local commanders. When investigating internal Army criminal activity, everyone is a suspect initially, including the local command structure. As a result, there was an inevitable tension between those assigned to the base and the investigative invaders. Had the CID agents asked for assistance from Jack Ewing and his MPs, there would have been no chance the rail yard would have gone uninspected and Marie Garrett's body almost certainly would have been discovered.

In the neighborhoods outside the base, detectives and uniformed police conducted similar inspections and interviews without any positive results.

The local news ran a brief story about Marie's disappearance, put her photo on the screen, and asked for the public's help to find her. They received fifty or so phone calls. Each was checked and dismissed as a dead end or prank call.

When Andrews arrived at the headquarters building, he came face-to-face with Detective Lieutenant Bob Decker who was on his way out of the building.

"Detective, I thought I would have seen you in the Provost Marshal's office, not here," Andrews said.

"Morning, Colonel. I started my day there, but I wanted to visit with a few of Marie's co-workers as soon as they got in this morning."

"Didn't you call them at home over the weekend? Isn't that why you asked for their contact info?"

"Oh, sure," Decker said. "We talked to everyone on the list. We even tracked down several people at their leave addresses. It pays to follow up after folks have some time to think about the initial conversation."

"Really? Interesting. And was this a worthwhile follow-up?"

"It always is." Decker had reached the bottom of the stairs leading from the headquarters and stepped toward his car. "Well, talk to you later, Colonel."

"Right. Talk later," Andrews said, as he turned to enter the building and climb the stairs to his second-floor office.

"Good morning, Laura. How was your weekend?"

It was only as Laura looked up and began to respond that Andrews noticed she had been crying.

"Not good. I couldn't sleep all weekend: worrying about that poor girl and her family," Laura said. "I imagine this situation kept you busy this weekend, Colonel."

"Indeed. And I share your concern. Unfortunately, I don't have the luxury of putting the world on hold. I have an installation to run and responsibilities that don't simply go away because of one troubled young woman."

As he spoke, trying to make himself appear far more important than the facts warranted, Andrews realized how harsh he sounded. And, even though he believed his response was accurate, he knew he shouldn't have been so dismissive of Laura's angst. In his mind, he knew he was carrying a much greater burden than anyone else was aware; one he could not share. He continued to be surprised how easily he was able to put what he had done out of his mind for most of the weekend: how instinctively he was able to even blame Marie for her own death. Back in uniform, back in the office on a work day, the impact her disappearance had on others was sobering—even to him. Again, he was surprised. He wondered if it would help Laura and others if they knew Marie was dead.

"Oh, Colonel, how can you be so cold? She's just a girl. A very vulnerable girl. I shudder to think what might have happened to her. I feel so responsible."

Laura Bennett had never spoken so directly to any of the installation commanders for whom she had worked. Under normal circumstances, she would immediately apologize; maybe even offer to resign for her insubordination. No one would call these normal circumstances. Marie's disappearance brought Laura's disdain for Andrews to the surface. She was confused and uncomfortable. She had never felt this way about a supervisor.

Andrews turned to face her squarely. "Laura, stop that. There is no reason why you should feel any responsibility. You didn't do anything to cause her disappearance. None of us did."

What Laura wanted to say would have gotten her fired. She decided not to contribute further to what was clearly a pointless conversation. Andrews went to his desk without an additional word exchanged between them.

She had her doubts about Colonel Andrews. Andrews had often sensed the tension between them. Now he wondered what she might have said about him to Decker. In fact, she had told the detective that she never liked the way Andrews looked at Marie.

"Detective, my sister always tells me that I'm a prude; so, I may not be the best judge," Laura said to Decker when he interviewed her earlier that morning.

"Do you think he is capable of hurting her?" Decker asked.

"No. I don't think so. I'm just not sure. It was off-putting...when he looked at her the way he did. Last summer, I didn't think he knew she was alive, but this summer, it seemed he was always looking for reasons for her to be with him. I thought his behavior was inappropriate. At least that's the way it seemed to me. I should have said something. I feel so responsible."

"You're not responsible, Miss Bennett," Decker said, trying to console her. "Is that what you meant when you told the detective on the phone on Saturday that this summer was different?"

"Yes, exactly, Detective. But I am so confused. I really don't care for Colonel Andrews. I'll admit it. I'm trying to keep that from coloring my comments and clouding my opinions. As much of an egotist and selfish person that I think he is, I can't imagine him being so awful that he would do something terrible to Marie."

"People surprise us sometimes, Miss Bennett," Decker said. "People often disappoint us."

"Detective Decker, do you think she'll be found okay? Maybe she is disoriented and lost somewhere. Maybe she fell and hit her head." Laura put a tissue to her eyes as she concluded, "She might be lying on the ground somewhere, badly injured."

"Could have been an accident, I suppose," Decker said. "Could you ever imagine Colonel Andrews taking some liberties with Marie that might have gotten out of control?"

"Oh, God." Laura's eyes filled with tears as she blew her nose lightly. "I never would have considered that a possibility, but, now that you have mentioned it, I'm just not sure."

As professional as she was trying to be, Laura Bennett's disdain for Andrews was obvious to Decker. Laura was not alone in her lack of respect for the installation commander. Decker talked at varying lengths with officers, enlisted personnel, and civilian employees in the headquarters building. Some were less restrained than others, but not one person considered Fleming Andrews to be a good leader. Most concluded that Andrews would not have done anything to Marie—not because it would have been wrong, but because he would not want to jeopardize his chance at promotion.

Most commented that Andrews could not connect with anyone. More than one female employee said she was uncomfortable when Andrews was in the room, always sensing that he was staring at her.

"I probably shouldn't say this because it might be insubordinate or something," Sergeant Nick Carson began. Sergeant Carson was an administrative NCO working directly for the sergeant major. He was the first person Decker encountered at the headquarters that morning.

"This conversation will be kept confidential. If I need you to go on the record with a formal statement, I'll let you know," Decker said.

"Well, the colonel, he…"

"Colonel Andrews?" Decker qualified.

"Right. Colonel Andrews always talks down to me. I don't take it personally because he pretty much treats anybody below him in rank like a second-class citizen. He may not treat you like shit, you understand; he just sends the message that he's better than you are. I think all the women in the headquarters think he's a little creepy."

"Creepy…that's an interesting word to use. How about Marie Garrett? Does he treat her the same way?"

"Well, I'm not around them much. I talk to Marie every now and then. She never complained about the colonel to me. I mean like every now and then, you know, she'd tell me that the colonel took her to a meeting or on an inspection ride somewhere on post. That's about it. We're friendly and all that, but I wouldn't say that we are friends. Know what I mean? She hasn't been here that long."

"Sure. Did she ever say anything about her time alone with Colonel Andrews or anything about being uncomfortable around him?"

"Jeez, no." Sergeant Carson said. "So, you think the colonel did something to Marie?"

"I didn't say that. No."

"Detective, I just don't see that. I mean I don't think a lot of Colonel Andrews and all, but I can't see him doing anything to Marie. I guess you never know."

"Hey, Sergeant Carson, I don't want you spreading rumors. I never said anything about the colonel being suspected of anything. To tell you the truth, I'm asking other people in the building the same questions about you and others that I just asked you about Colonel Andrews. It's all part of the process."

"No. I get it. It's just that some of the guys joke about what it must have been like to serve in 'Nam with the colonel and whether or not we could see him walking through the jungle or in a rice paddy, popping off caps at Charlie."

"You don't think he has the courage?"

"Shit, Detective, there's no telling what a man will do when that shit is for real. I…we just don't see Colonel Andrews as a combat soldier is all. I think he pretty much had desk jobs over there."

"So, he's a REMF, right?"

"Hey, Detective, you said that; not me."

They laughed, stood, and shook hands.

"Don't go spreading any goddamn rumors, Sergeant. Okay?"

"No, sir. You got my word," Sergeant Carson said.

Decker decided to return to the Provost Marshal's conference room to review notes with his team. He knew that he had led Laura Bennett a bit too much and that she would be a very weak witness in any courtroom scenario. And Sergeant Carson had pretty much summed it up. Everyone below the rank of colonel did what Andrews said because of the eagles on his uniform. He appeared to inspire no one and was simply not someone people would follow if the organizational structure didn't require it.

When he got to the Provost Marshal's building, Decker stopped first in Jack Ewing's outer office, only to learn that Ewing was in his military sedan "making the rounds." He asked the secretary to let him know when Ewing returned and then walked down the hall to the conference room.

"What's shakin', fellas?" Decker said to no one in particular.

After the door had closed, the detective who conversed with Andrews said, "Your buddy, the colonel, was asking for you."

"Yeah, I know. I was walking out of his headquarters when he pulled up. He was not happy that I was there without his supervision."

"I think he thinks you consider him a suspect," the other detective said.

"Well that would be very perceptive on his part," Decker responded. "Because I do."

"Really?" The detective said. "I can't figure if he's a really bad guy or just a weasel."

"Oh, he's a scumbag, for sure. His wife may be the only person who knows him who has any affection for the guy."

"You didn't find a lot of fans at the headquarters? Maybe we should track down his mother; see how she feels about him."

"No one I would call a fan," Decker said. "And it seems the people who work closest to him like him least."

"Isn't that pretty much the message you got from Sergeant Major Rodriguez when you spoke to him on the phone over the weekend?"

"Yep, but the sergeant major did all he could to maintain a level of professionalism. It was tough to break through the sergeant major/colonel relationship and get him to talk about the Ed Rodriguez/Fleming Andrews relationship—especially over the phone.

"At the headquarters, I could see the discomfort in the eyes of the people I spoke with. They don't like him. And not because he's some military hard ass. They just don't trust him. Everyone doubted…at least to me…that he would have done anything to Marie. Not because he's a good guy or she's just a kid, but because it would put his career at risk and maybe keep him from getting his star."

"He sounds like a real sweetheart."

"You know," Decker said. "I can easily construct a scenario where he grabs her on her way out the door. His secretary was gone for the day. The sergeant major has gone home and everyone else pretty much leaves him alone."

"So, he pulls her into his office at the end of the day?" the detective asked, getting Decker back to his theory.

"No, I don't think so," he continued. "The duty officer stays in the headquarters building all night starting at 4:30. Maybe he offers her a ride or something. It did rain on Friday afternoon. And he takes her to a warehouse once he has her in his car. Somewhere remote on base."

"Just to kill her? What's his motive?" The first detective asked. "Do you think she was coming on to him in any way?"

"Doesn't matter. She's a kid; he's the adult. Anything that does or doesn't happen is on him," Decker responded.

The second detective picked up Decker's original thought process. "I see what you're saying Lieutenant. He takes her to a warehouse to get kinky with her. Maybe he figures she wants what he wants. But, being a kid, she gets spooked. Either she resists or he draws her in before she realizes what's going on."

"And in the process, he kills her," the first detective finishes the thought.

"That's about where I am with that scenario," Decker said. "If anything happened to her on Cameron Station, I can believe Colonel Do-You-Know-Who-I-Am is responsible. But there's also a 50/50 chance that whatever happened took place outside the gates in our fair city."

"I suppose that's possible," the detective said. "I'm not jumping to conclusions here, but the bus driver recognized Marie from the photo we showed him. He said she took his bus home everyday this summer and that he does not remember her on the bus on Friday. In fact, he waited at the stop an extra minute in case the rain had slowed her down. And neither driver of the buses before or after that one remembers seeing her."

"Come on in," Lieutenant Decker said in response to a knock on the door.

"That's not necessary, Detective," Colonel Ewing's secretary said. "I just wanted to let you know that Lieutenant Colonel Ewing is back in his office and he said you are welcome to stop by at your convenience."

"Hey, thanks. I'll be right there."

After the door closed, the uniformed cop said, "Are you being summoned, Lieutenant?"

"No. I asked to see him. I'm going to ask a favor and give him some good news."

"What's that?" the detective said.

"Start packing up your shit, fellas. We're going home: back to the precinct. We don't need to be squatters anymore."

"Amen to that," he said. "Their coffee is actually worse than ours."

22

"Colonel Ewing, you have been a great host. Very generous with your conference room and that unforgettable Army coffee. But I think it's time to bring my team back to the precinct and for you to get your operation back to normal," Decker said.

"Did you call my coffee unforgettable or unforgivable?"

"It's probably a little of both, if I have to be honest."

"You've only been here a couple of days. You know you're welcome to stay as long as you need to," Ewing said. "Have you come to any conclusions, Bob?"

"Only theories so far, Jack. Nothing I'm willing to hang my hat on. I would like to ask a favor, though. I'd like to bring cadaver dogs through some of your warehouses in the more remote sections of the installation. I've got nothing solid, but if somebody abducted and killed this girl on Cameron Station, I'm thinking it would have to have been done somewhere no one was likely to be on a Friday night. Something more remote."

"Well, Bob, there's a couple of things you ought to know. I just learned that the FBI is going to engage. They've asked for a briefing. It's not clear if they plan to take over the investigation or become an informed observer. I've been told they'll be here sometime after lunch today."

"I'll bet Colonel Andrews isn't very happy about that."

"Oh, he'll be pissed big time, but he doesn't know about it yet. I just called his office. He owes me a call back. I'll let him know what you want to do, as well. He won't like it, but we have to do everything to find that girl—alive or, and I hate to even say it—dead."

"Yeah, I thought my idea about the cadaver dogs would be the piece of info that ruined his day, but I think our friends at the FBI will keep me from topping his shit list."

"Trust me, Bob, there's plenty of room at or near the top of his shit list. When do you want to bring the dogs through and where do you want them to go?"

"Naturally, I'd like to do it as soon as possible. I made a few phone calls and I can get our dogs and the canine teams from both Arlington and Fairfax counties here this afternoon, but I guess I can wait until tomorrow morning if necessary."

"Let me talk to the colonel, but I think you should stick to the plan today. If you wait until morning, the FBI might want some say in the decision. If we move forward, you'll be started before they're finished with their briefing. By the way, I assume you'll be part of that session. I'll let you know when and where."

"That's great, Jack. Wouldn't surprise me if my chief will want to be in that meeting, too. I'll try to talk him out of it. The more brass, the less progress. I'm going to make it a point to find out if we have been contacted by the Feds, as well. To be honest, I thought they would have engaged over the weekend. They won't sit on the sidelines very long—especially if they think there's a chance to look good on television," Decker said. "I'll let you know what I find out."

"Thanks, Bob. Now, you still have to tell me where you want the dogs to go."

"Well, I was hoping you could help me with that."

There was a soft knock at the office door.

"Excuse me, Colonel Ewing, Colonel Andrews is on line one for you."

"I'll get out of your way, Jack," Decker said.

"Thanks, Bob. I'll come down to the conference room

151

when I get off this call and we can go over the post map in detail."

Decker and Ewing's secretary left the office together. She closed the door as Ewing picked up the receiver of his desk phone.

"Jack Ewing, sir. Sorry to keep you waiting."

"Hey, Jack, I'm returning your call. I was in the shitter when you called."

"No problem, sir. It happens to all of us."

"Right. What's on your mind, Jack?"

"Well, boss, I got a piece of good news and a couple of things that aren't going to make you very happy."

"Has she been found?" Andrews asked.

"What? Oh, unfortunately not. The good news is that the Alexandria police are getting ready to move off the installation and go back to their precinct."

"Good-fucking-riddance. You've made my day. What's the bad news?"

Ewing told Andrews first about the FBI deciding to engage. His reaction was unexpectedly restrained.

"You know, I don't like it, but I can't say I'm surprised. You said this might happen. We've got three general officers on the installation. The FBI will give the Army some overhead cover. As far as I'm concerned, they'll be more trouble to the Alexandria PD than they will be to us. There's also the 1-star list due out soon. If I'm on it, it will look good for me to be seen as supportive of the investigation: helping to turn over every stone to find this girl and get the bad guys."

"Couldn't agree with you more, sir," Ewing replied. Although he didn't follow Andrews' rationale about the FBI giving the Army overhead cover, disagreeing with him or asking for clarification didn't seem worth the effort, especially since Andrews' reaction had been so calm. Neither Andrews nor Ewing knew it was the Alexandria police chief who had asked the FBI to engage so early in the investigation. At this point, Decker was also unaware this was his own department's initiative.

Decker's interest in bringing in cadaver dogs got a different reaction.

23

"Tell me why I shouldn't tell him to go fuck himself," Andrews said through the phone line.

"Colonel, there's no way you can reasonably refuse without casting doubt, if not suspicion, on the installation…" Ewing paused, but found the courage to add, "…and possibly yourself. I checked with the JAG and, technically, you can make Decker jump through hoops to get authorization, but there's no doubt the Pentagon would tell us to cooperate."

"I can always count on the JAG to stab us in the back," Andrews said.

"Decker promises to keep it as low key as possible and asked that we have an MP with each dog handler."

"Great. So, now Decker looks like Mr. Reasonable. I still say he's trying to pin this on someone on Cameron Station and, if he can't do that, make the installation look bad in the eyes of the press and the public."

"I've got to say, sir, while it's only been a few days, Decker and the Alexandria PD have been pretty judicious in their dealings with the press. They've been playing it straight. There's been no grandstanding that I can see."

"Whose side are you on, Jack?"

Ewing didn't know if Andrews intended the question to be rhetorical, but he chose not to answer it. He was, in fact, a bit taken back by the question—rhetorical or not—and insulted that Andrews would make the statement.

"I assume he thinks the girl is dead. What makes him think her body ever was—or still is—on post?"

"I suspect he's just playing the odds, boss. When she went forty-eight hours missing, the likelihood is that something bad happened. No evidence. No ransom. No communication, etc., etc. Decker just has to assume the worst. Since Friday night, we've amped up security at the gates, stopping cars on the way out, opening trunks. So, he thinks it's worth a shot to let the dogs sniff around."

"And you agree?"

"And I agree. Yes, sir."

"Well, make sure he starts with my car and my quarters." As Andrews said this, he realized that, however briefly, Marie's body was in his car. He had no idea how sensitive the dogs' senses were or how long the smell of a body would linger in the trunk of a car.

"I'll tell him that, sir, but he wants to take the dogs to the remote parts of the post."

"Remote parts? Seriously? We're the size of a postage stamp in the middle of Alexandria, Virginia, for Christ's sake. What remote parts is he talking about?" Andrews asked.

"There's a decent chunk of warehouses on post that don't get a lot of foot traffic. He's thinking there might have been places where Marie could have been assaulted and possibly injured or killed without any witnesses."

"Could have, might have, and possibly. This guy sure ain't Sherlock Holmes, Jack. Fine. Fine. Tell him okay with me. Make sure our higher headquarters agrees and coordinate with our tenant organizations. Several of those warehouses belong to them and not even I have the keys to those locks." For once, Andrews was happy to be able to make that statement.

Before moving on to his next topic, Ewing promised to take care of all the necessary coordination with the other agencies on Cameron Station. He also asked Andrews to reach out to Generals Abell, Schwab, and Macri to advise them and get their support. Finally, Ewing worked out the details for the upcoming meeting with the FBI team.

"You know, Jack, I'm not happy about bringing those dogs on the installation, but I love the fact that they'll be here and nearly gone before the damn FBI boys have a clue. That's rich."

"Well, sir, I suggest we make a statement as part of the briefing to them. Very matter of fact. Let's see if they notice," Ewing said.

"Oh, they'll notice. Count on it. We might even get some questions from the press."

"I suppose," Ewing said.

"By the way, Jack."

"Yes, sir?"

"If one of those dogs shits on our grass, be sure they pick it up or have the MPs give Decker the damn ticket."

"Wilco, boss. I'll keep you posted."

"Jack, on a serious note, why don't we plan to have a working lunch here in my office. I'll have Laura set it up. It'll be good for her. She's been all weepy this morning. You, Public Affairs, and the JAG. As much as I don't want a lawyer's advice, we probably need to include one. We'll go over a game plan for the FBI meeting."

"See you at noon sir."

24

The phone call done, Ewing went directly from his office to the conference room. Andrews' reaction to the pending FBI involvement was not what he expected, even if he had warned him this might happen. In fact, there were several parts of Andrews' recent behavior that Ewing found unusual. This was the first time in as long as he could remember that Andrews had not overreacted to a piece of information—even something seemingly trivial.

"Oh, here you are, Jack. Right on time," Decker said. "I just asked the guys to spread out the base street map on the conference table."

"Great," Ewing said. As he walked toward the map, he checked his watch.

"In a hurry, Jack?" Decker asked.

"I just have a shitload to do all of a sudden."

"Well, this shouldn't take long."

"Bob, our meeting with the FBI team is at 3:00 in the command conference room in the headquarters. I have a lunch meeting with Andrews and some of the staff."

"I'm available if you need me," Decker said.

"Thanks, Bob, but this is going to be just internal staff. Say, is your chief coming to the three o'clock?

"No. Believe it or not, he told me he thinks I can handle it. He said he would just get in the way."

"Wow. That's pretty enlightened."

"Nah. If the Feds get pissed, he wants them pissed at me. And, by the way, the Feds want to meet with him at

5:00 today at our headquarters."

"Same team?" Ewing asked.

"I assume so."

"Lucky him."

"No kidding. The whole case could be theirs by the end of the day and that would be fine with me," Decker said.

Standing, leaning over the conference table with the Alexandria police team, Ewing helped identify twenty-six buildings in parts of the installation that appeared to be remote enough for someone to move about unobserved on an early Friday evening, when most people were focused on starting their weekends.

"Jack, I've got three dog teams that'll arrive at 2:00. I expect they will be nearly done between 3:00 and 3:30. All bets are off if they came across something of interest, of course," Decker said.

"Right and you understand that Colonel Andrews and I don't own many of the buildings we've selected. Actually, we've got the outside, but what's inside belongs to one of our tenant commands," Ewing said.

"Yep, you mentioned that earlier. Do I need to do anything?" Decker asked.

"No. Andrews is calling the three general officers and I'll close the loop with my points of contact after we're through here. We actually conduct periodic security and fire checks of those buildings; so, we've worked this before. I'm sure they'll have someone meet us at each of their buildings with keys and codes for any alarms."

"Great, but ask them not to unlock any doors until the dog team is on site with them," Decker said.

"Can do easy." Ewing looked around the room. "Looks like you're just about packed. You haven't been here long and I wish the circumstances were better, but it was good having you folks here. I only wish we had already found her alive and well."

There were handshakes all around.

"Well, my to-do list just keeps getting longer and most has to be done before noon; so, if you will excuse me, I'll get going," Ewing said. "Bob, if you don't hear from me, it means all systems are a go. How about if my deputy, Major Miller, meets your guys and the dog teams in the parking lot of the post movie theater? It's a large lot and no one should be using it until tonight around 6:00 or 7:00."

"Sounds good. Detective Birch, here, will be my lead, since you and I will be meeting with Mr. Hoover's finest at 3:00."

25

Despite all the things Ewing had to do, he was able to get to them and arrive at the headquarters building a full fifteen minutes before noon. A couple of things in the parking lot surprised him.

Andrews' car was parked in its usual space—the one reserved for the installation commander. It was closest to the door, but Ewing noticed that the car's trunk was open. As he parked and exited his car, Ewing saw Andrews leaning in an open rear door. He couldn't help but notice Andrews' car had once again been pelted with a generous supply of bird droppings.

"Sir, what have you done to piss off the bird population of Alexandria? Isn't this the second time in three days that they've attacked your car?"

When he heard Ewing's voice, Andrews stood up.

"It's the third time, but who's counting?"

"Is something wrong with your car, sir? Other than the obvious bird guano design modification?"

"That's the thing, Jack. I'm trying to figure out if there's something about my car that is attracting the bastards." Andrews was willing to engage in this banter because it enabled him to hide the fact that he was trying to air out any remaining scent of Marie that might be picked up by a cadaver dog, if one happened to get close enough to his car.

"Do you think there's something in the trunk?" Ewing asked. "That sounds pretty unlikely to me."

"Who knows? I just thought I'd give it the once over and maybe a little fresh air would be helpful."

"Well, my guess is that you have been incredibly unlucky and that you've been parking in the wrong place at the wrong time. But, hell, you could be right. Maybe there's something under the car on the frame or the drive train. Have you hit anything on the road? Old road kill could stay with the car for a long time," Ewing said.

"Don't think so, but that's not a bad thought. I'll run it through the car wash later today."

"Hey, sir, didn't you go to the car wash when they attacked your car the last time? I would've thought that would have done the trick if there was an odor."

Andrews thought quickly. "Me too, but I didn't get the most expensive wash that hits the undercarriage or the tires. I'll give it the deluxe treatment this afternoon."

As he said this, Andrews closed and locked the car doors and shut the trunk.

"Well, let's head upstairs. I see the boy lawyer walking toward the building and I think that's Grady parking his car."

The lunch meeting itself was unremarkable, with the exception that Andrews had Laura Bennett collect $4.85 from the other attendees to cover the cost of the sandwiches and soft drinks.

During the meeting, Andrews stayed focused on content, thanks in part to the fact that Dan Grady's deputy, Susan Braswell, was not in attendance. While the others were taking their seats at the conference table in Andrews' office and organizing their notes, Grady began.

"Colonel, I have to say that it's been relatively easy to hold the press at bay since there really isn't anything that I'm aware of to tell them."

"Well, the presence of the FBI and cadaver dogs may make them more curious and less happy," Andrews said.

"Oh, they're not happy, sir, but they seem to be focused on the Alexandria PD as the reason why they don't have a lot of information."

"Good, Dan, keep it that way. I'm happy when they're NOT happy." Andrews added his signature laugh at any of his own remarks he considered funny or clever. "And I'm especially happy when they take out their anger on somebody else. Know what I mean?"

Each of these men had been around long enough to respond to Andrews' prompting with a sycophantic chuckle, a "yes sir," or "you got that right."

"McGrath, do you have anything to add before Jack and I get to the substance?" Andrews asked of the young JAG captain.

"Only to restate what you've heard probably more than you want to hear," McGrath said.

"Let me guess: cooperate. Be a good boy. Kiss any ass available. Right?"

"Well, not exactly, sir. My legal guidance stops with cooperate. I don't see any reason why there should be any disagreement. In fact, I think cooperation with the FBI will be easy and even less awkward than working with the local Alexandria police," McGrath added.

"Captain McGrath, you are the eternal optimist and I hope you're right. I plan to cooperate fully—though our definition of *cooperate* may prove to be different. Let's see how it goes, shall we?"

"Of course, sir," McGrath responded, with a hard stare at the man who was clearly trying to belittle him. For his part, McGrath planned to stay in the Army only long enough to serve the time he owed as a result of the Army program that paid his law school tuition.

"Jack, you're up," Andrews said, turning from the attorney.

"Thank you, sir." Ewing had prepared a packet of six draft slides for each of them. He placed one packet in front of Andrews and slid the other two along the tabletop to Grady and McGrath. "I'll talk us through these slides and note any changes to be made. At 3:00, I plan to use transparencies and an overhead projector. I don't think we should have any paper copies of the slides. If anything gets leaked to the press, it will have to be from individual notes and not from something we handed to the FBI at this meeting. If that's okay with you, Colonel, I'll even collect these packets at the end of this meeting."

Andrews nodded his approval.

Ewing and Andrews changed the wording here and there and reduced the number of slides from six to four. Grady and McGrath didn't comment on the content of the slides. Grady especially liked the plan not to produce any paper slides, thereby reducing the likelihood of leaks to the press. For his part, Captain McGrath encouraged Andrews to be as cooperative and non-confrontational as possible. He also thought the absence of a paper trail was a smart tactic.

There was only a little small talk when they turned their attention to lunch. Dan Grady asked occasional questions ranging from the investigation to the makeup of the FBI team they would encounter. The consensus around the table was that there was a decreasing reason to be hopeful for a positive outcome in the case of Marie Garrett. Grady asked Ewing if the Alexandria Police had any leads or suspects or theories.

Ewing was truthful when he said he didn't know of any in either category. He was especially careful not to imply that he had any personal opinion because, in fact, he believed Lieutenant Decker suspected Colonel Andrews of being less than totally forthcoming and perhaps of something more serious. At first, Ewing thought Decker and Andrews just hadn't hit it off. Now, however, whether from innuendo or osmosis, Ewing thought Decker's dislike for Andrews stemmed from something more.

With this in mind, Ewing nearly jumped out of his chair when Andrews said, "That fucker is convinced she is dead and he wants to pin the murder on me."

"Jesus, Colonel. I'm sure that isn't the case," Grady said.

"Wow, sir. What makes you say that?" Ewing asked.

"When I met him on Friday, I got the sense he was on a mission to tar Cameron Station and the U.S. Army with the blame. When I talked to him on Saturday, I got the sense that he wants more. His shitty attitude this morning convinced me that he wants me to be the villain."

"He's gonna need some hard evidence to do that, sir," Ewing said. "Right now, I don't think he has any."

"He doesn't have shit, Jack. That's why his whole attitude has gone negative. He's frustrated, the asshole."

Andrews' comments were followed by a minute or so of stunned silence.

26

There was a chocolate chip cookie included with each lunch. Andrews never suggested anyone pour a cup of coffee to go with the dessert. He was the first to finish and wanted to send the message that it was time for the others to leave. After depositing his sandwich wrappings and empty soda can in the trash, he stood at his desk thumbing through a few papers.

"Sir, I've got a lot to get to before the three o'clock meeting and I'm sure Dan and Captain McGrath do, as well. So, if you don't have anything else for us, I recommend we break until then," Ewing said.

Andrews was pleased Ewing got the message from his body language. Grady, ever the reporter, would have been happy to stay for as long as anyone would answer his inexhaustible supply of questions. Captain McGrath was somewhere between Grady and Ewing. McGrath couldn't wait to leave the office, but, in the absence of any additional substance in the conversation, had effectively zoned out, figuring he would sit at the table until he was snapped from his trance by a relevant question or by Andrews' dismissal.

"No, Jack, you're right. I know we all have a lot to do. It's not like you had a choice, but thanks for making time for this meeting, gentlemen. See you at 3:00," Andrews said.

27

Andrews followed the three staff officers as they filed into his outer office, much like a herding dog ensures its sheep move into their pen without pause or delay. Grady actually paused at an end table by the sofa in Andrews' office to look at the mementos Andrews had on display. Before Grady could pick up a brass statuette of a soldier standing with a rifle, Andrews placed his hand on Grady's back and gently, but firmly, redirected him to the door.

They exited the outer office and entered the hall. Andrews stopped at Laura Bennett's desk, outside his office door.

"Laura, I'm going to run a quick errand, but I'll be back well before my three o'clock. Also, how about scheduling a command ride for tomorrow? I want to see how much damage the Alexandria police did while plodding around my installation this weekend."

"Certainly, sir," Laura said. "By the way, you'll have a new driver tomorrow."

"Oh, really? Is Mr. Henry on leave?"

"Mr. Henry? No, you mean Mr. Washington. The motor pool said that Henry Washington is taking some of his accrued leave, at least through the end of the month, and he may not return," she said.

"Did a rich relative die?" Andrews asked.

"No, sir." Laura's eyes filled with tears. "Marie Garrett is his niece. Apparently, Mr. Washington told his sister about the summer job opportunity two years ago and now he is blaming himself for her disappearance. He told his supervisor that he might not return to Cameron Station.

He's afraid it would be too painful."

"Nonsense," Andrews said under his breath, but loud enough for Laura to hear the tone and know he said something dismissive.

"Sir?" she said.

"Nothing. Nothing. I don't think Mr. Henry…Mr. Washington should blame himself. I can understand him wanting to take some time off, but giving up his career is a bit over the top, it seems to me," Andrews said. "Sometimes in life, you have to step into your big boy pants and play the cards life deals you. Of course, it does take a certain strength of character to do that. Anyway, a driver is a driver. It hardly matters."

Andrews stood by her desk, lit his pipe, gently tamped down the tobacco, and relit the bowl's contents. On the outside sill of the window behind Laura's desk, a crow stood, looking inside. Laura had no idea it was there. It caught Andrews' eye, and though he never paused from his pipe ritual, Andrews extended the middle finger of his left hand which was holding the bowl of the pipe. For a few seconds they stared at each other until the crow tapped once on the window pane.

"I'll be back in about a half hour." As he stepped toward the door, the crow took flight.

Laura watched Andrews move to the door connecting his outer office to the main hall on the second floor of the headquarters building. She was close to tears and even closer to letting out a scream to demonstrate her anger and frustration with Fleming Andrews, Colonel, U.S. Army.

Laura often wondered if her negative feelings toward Colonel Andrews in some way reflected poorly on her professionalism. She didn't like the fact that she felt uncomfortable around him almost from the day he arrived. His behavior this summer toward Marie gave her distrust a new focus. She had become particularly sensitive to the callousness of his comments, and read something distasteful and even sinister into nearly everything Andrews said. Maybe it was her conversations with Lieutenant Decker about Marie's disappearance.

With Andrews out of the office, Laura sat quietly at her desk staring into a void. She had been in this job for many years and had been a civilian government employee even longer. This was the first time she could recall actually considering submitting her resignation.

Laura was already eligible to retire from the civil service, but rightly considered herself far too young and healthy to stop working. She wondered if she would be able to remain on the job until Andrews' anticipated change of command and departure from Cameron Station nearly a year away.

28

No more than thirty minutes after Jack Ewing had returned to his office, there was a single, sharp knock on his partially open door, followed quickly by the appearance of Major Todd Miller, the Deputy Provost Marshal.

"Hey, boss. Sorry to bother you, but I wanted you to know that Detective Birch and the dog teams just passed through the front gate. I'm going to meet them in the theater's parking lot."

"They're a little ahead of schedule," Ewing said.

"Yes, sir. Do you want me to delay them in the lot or should we start early?"

"No. As soon as you have our folks teamed with them and you're convinced everybody knows what to do, get started. I'll call the tenant commands so their people can be in place when the dogs get there."

"Roger that. I plan to ride with one of the teams. I'll let you know how it goes," Miller said as he turned to leave.

29

"Hey, ain't you the same guy was here over the weekend? You gots to stop parking under that tree, man. There's some big birds got their asses zeroed in on your vehicle, my man."

Andrews gave the car wash attendant no more than half a smile. That was the only acknowledgment he was willing to give the wise crack.

"Give me the most thorough wash you've got. What do you call it—the deluxe wash?"

"No, boss, the top of the line is the Supreme Wash. I call it *The Diana Ross*."

"Oh? Why's that?" Andrews asked.

"Shit, brother, never mind." The attendant shook his head and smiled. *Some things are better left unexplained.* "Eight dollars, my man. Drive forward."

"Eight dollars for the Supreme Wash?" Andrews asked.

"No. Eight dollars for the Deluxe. The Supreme is ten bucks."

"The Deluxe is fine for now," Andrews said.

As the car wash progressed, Andrews grumbled to himself about the price and the fact that he had now spent more money in three days than he would routinely spend in a month for two car washes made necessary by the birds of Cameron Station.

30

"Colonel, Chaplain Hughes called while you were gone," Laura said when Andrews returned. She stood and followed him into his office, skillfully avoiding the smoke from his pipe. "He wanted you to know that there will be a prayer service for Marie Garrett this evening and he asked if you and Mrs. Andrews would be attending."

"Who told him to organize a prayer service?"

"No, sir. The prayer service…"

"Jesus H. Christ! The guy works one day a week and suddenly, he thinks he's the Pope or the Dalai Lama? I don't believe him," Andrews said. "Get him on the phone for me, would you?"

"Colonel Andrews, Chaplain Hughes didn't organize the prayer service. It's being conducted by the Garrett family's church in Alexandria. Her pastor called Chaplain Hughes to invite him, you, and anyone else you think should attend from the installation." Laura had no idea how she continued to maintain her composure with this man.

"Oh. That's different. It's awfully short notice."

"I imagine they were hoping Marie would be found by now." Laura took some offense at having to state the obvious to him.

"Let me check with my wife and I will let you know."

"Certainly, sir," Laura said and turned to leave his office. She found an odd comfort in the coldness and the terse cadence of those two words when addressing Andrews.

"Close the door behind you, Laura."

"Certainly, sir. You have just about an hour before your meeting with the FBI."

"Yes. I expect Jack Ewing to be early to set up the overhead projector in the conference room," Andrews said.

"Colonel Ewing already sent someone to do that. I will ensure there are notepads and coffee cups for everyone."

"No. No notepads and no coffee. They can bring their own paper and I hope they aren't here long enough to finish a cup of coffee."

"Certainly, sir."

"Don't forget the door on your way out."

"Certainly, sir."

31

When she returned to her desk, Laura saw a light on her phone console indicating Andrews was on a call. She concluded he was talking to his wife, likely trying to develop a reason for not attending the prayer service.

Laura had written the details of the service on an index card to give to Andrews, confident Nancy would tell her husband it would be inappropriate to be absent from the service. Laura also noted the details for her own reference.

Marie's mother asked her pastor to extend the invitation to Laura as well. Mrs. Garrett wanted Laura to know that Marie spoke about her all the time in very complimentary terms. Laura was touched.

Several minutes passed before Andrews emerged from his office. After opening the door, he stepped into the outer office while simultaneously lighting a freshly packed pipe. Laura hoped her face didn't show how little she enjoyed the prospect of going home at the end of the day with her hair and her clothes smelling of tobacco smoke.

She watched him finish the lighting process, wondering why he appeared to be staring out the window behind her. She didn't turn around, but waited for him to speak as the cloud of smoke dissipated.

"My wife and I will attend the service." He hadn't finished the sentence before Laura held out the index card, which he took mid-sentence, without a pause in his speech pattern.

"I'll need all the details about the service," he continued. "What's this?" he said, looking at the card for the first time.

"All the details about the service, Colonel," Laura said.

"Perfect," he said. "I have you well trained, Miss Bennett."

He returned to his office and, for the first time in decades of federal civil service, Laura Bennett broke the pencil she was holding in her right hand.

32

Major Todd Miller had seen military drug detection dogs at work many times both in the United States and when he was assigned overseas. He knew the high quality of their training and the singular purpose with which they did their work. This was his first exposure to cadaver dogs. Their proficiency and reaction to the telltale odor of death impressed him.

At every stop along the way, the operation went efficiently. They progressed more quickly than expected. There was no scent of a dead body. The dog handlers asked if their search authority included the dumpsters outside the specific buildings designated for searches. Major Miller said yes without hesitation, feeling no need to check with LTC Ewing.

A dead mouse inside one building, a dead squirrel in the road outside another, and evidence of rat droppings by a few dumpsters was the extent of the search results—an operation that took just under two hours.

"That's one hell of a dog you've got there," Miller said to Officer Tony Gregory (the Fairfax County police dog handler) as they began to drive from their final stop to the post theater. The plan was for the dog teams to reassemble in the theater's parking lot to report on the results of each search.

"Thanks, Todd. All of our dogs are great, but I'm partial to Patches here. She and I have been together for four years now. She's a pro," Gregory said.

"That's obvious. Really impressive."

They were stopped at the traffic light at a three-way

intersection. Straight ahead about a quarter mile was the theater. To their left was a road that curved out of sight after a short distance.

"Say, what's down this road, Todd?"

"Not much. Mostly empty tracks of land where old World War II era buildings used to be."

"They aren't there anymore?" Gregory asked.

"No. Razed years ago. The road winds around and eventually dead ends at the rail yard. The place was a lot more active when the war in 'Nam was going hot and heavy, but it's pretty quiet now. You can hear a train go by in the distance every now and then, but I bet most people don't even know we have a rail yard on post."

"Did a team check it out today?"

"I'm sure it was checked over the weekend, but, no, it isn't on the list for the dogs to check," Miller answered.

"I'm surprised. Rail yards are a great place to hide a body. In my experience, there's a lot of mischief that can go on in a rail yard—especially one that isn't used very often. Want to give it a quick once-over?" Gregory asked.

"Well, I don't have a key to the yard gate, but if someone is there today, we ought to be able to check out the place."

They turned and drove down the road to the rail yard. The gate appeared to be locked, but Miller got out of the vehicle because he thought he saw some movement inside the fence. He tried the small gate; it was locked. He started to return to the vehicle, giving a casual push to the larger, vehicle gate. It moved enough to cause Miller to stop and confirm it was unlocked.

He pushed the gate open and waved for Gregory to drive forward. When Miller let go of the gate to reenter the vehicle, he noticed that the gate slid closed on its own.

"You folks need something?" The man in work overalls asked as he walked from behind the shed, cleaning his hands on a rag. His name was Bob Cardello. He worked on the staff of the installation facilities engineer. After brief introductions, Miller spoke.

"Mr. Cardello, my colleague from the county police and I are conducting an informal inspection of various locations on post and the rail yard is on the list for today."

"What list? What kind of inspection?" Cardello asked.

"It's totally routine," Miller said.

"Well, nobody told me about an inspection of the yard today. You're lucky you caught me here. I come by once a week or so is all," Cardello said.

"It really isn't the kind of inspection you need to worry about, Mr. Cardello..."

"Call me Bob."

"All right, Bob. This is more of a cooperative agreement we have with the county police. We're not here to evaluate your work in any way. It's more like we're here to evaluate our own work." Miller hoped Cardello would yield and stop asking questions.

"You say this is routine?"

"For sure."

"Well, if this is so routine, why haven't we bumped into each other before now? Is this some kind of a new routine?"

Miller had just about enough of the cross-examination, but he wanted to avoid a standoff with Cardello because he didn't want to have to tell him the true purpose of the visit or mention that Officer Gregory thinks rail yards are a good place to hide a dead body. Besides, he couldn't tell if Cardello was really annoyed or if he was screwing with him. If Cardello said he would have to call his supervisor, Miller was prepared to call off the search and leave the rail yard.

"Mr. Card…, Bob, you're right. This is a new program which is why you haven't seen us or heard of it before. It's convenient that you are here, but we could actually do what we have to do even if you weren't here. In fact, if we're keeping you from something, feel free to break away. No need to stay with us," Miller said.

They all began walking around the perimeter of the yard. Sometimes, they were between a boxcar and the fence. Other times, they were closer to the center with a boxcar between them and the fence line.

"Nah. I'm just yanking your chain. Unless you're doing something I'm not cleared to know about, I'd just as soon stick with you fellas. You see, even if I'm not here, I'm supposed to know when anyone from on post uses, visits, or walks through the rail yard. That's part of my job—to monitor activity which is why I'm still trying to figure out why I didn't get word you was coming by today."

"You know, that's actually great to hear, Mr. Cardello," Officer Gregory finally spoke. "Do you have a record of anyone being in the yard in the last—oh, say, three or four days or so?"

"The last time anyone from Cameron Station was in the yard was last Monday. That's a week ago today," Cardello said.

"You said 'anyone from Cameron Station'. Do people from outside the installation have access?" Miller asked.

"Not supposed to. At least not through my gate. Now, I have to admit that I've come in here every now and again and I just know some boxcars have been repositioned and nobody told me in advanced or after the fact, for that matter," Cardello said. "Sometimes, I find the lock on the gate between my yard and the commercial side—we'll pass it when we get to the far side—sometimes I find the gate unlocked or the lock's gone missing. When that happens, there's no telling who's been tromping through here. A while back, we had kids climbing the fence from the commercial side to spray paint graffiti on some of the boxcars. Climbed right over the barbed wire. And sometimes, kids or whoever just throw shit over the fence. Trash mostly, but sometimes it's a dead animal. Keeps them from having to deal with something a train hit, I suppose."

"Or just trying to piss you off," Miller said.

"You got that right, Major," Cardello added.

"There are no alarms or surveillance systems?" Gregory asked.

Cardello gave him a half-laugh. "You kidding? This ain't Fort Knox, officer. During the war, when ammo or some other sensitive shit was here overnight, there would be a security detail. If there's no security detail—and there hasn't been one for years—there really isn't anything worth stealing in the yard. I'm pretty sure those enterprising Americans who make their living by taking shit that ain't theirs know our routine."

"I'm sure you're right," Miller said. "So, let me get this straight, Bob. You're the keeper of the keys for the yard as far as Cameron Station is concerned, right? And until you came through the gate this morning, no one has been in here since last Monday."

"Yeah, that's what I said. But, of course, I'm not the only one with a key. I can't control when they come through, but even they're supposed to tell me," Cardello said.

"After the fact?" Miller said.

"Yeah. Like I said, before or after the fact, if at all."

"Well, who else has a key to the yard?"

"Oh, let's see. The Post Engineer, of course. He's actually pretty good about letting me know. Then, there's the fire department. And you folks at the Provost Marshal's office."

"So, emergency personnel can gain access in the event there's an incident or a fire," Miller said.

"Right. Of course, when we had any issues here, your folks just as soon cut the lock, rather than bring the key."

"Probably faster," Gregory said.

"Imagine so. They probably don't even know where their key is. I can tell you the colonel knows where his key is, though," Cardello said.

"Well, you said he's pretty good about letting you know when he uses his key," Miller said.

"Who you talking about?" Cardello said. "I'm not talking about the Post Engineer. I'm talking about the colonel—the Post Commander. Colonel Fleming Andrews his royal self and he ain't about to report anything to little old Bob Cardello. Besides, he loves this goddamn place. Comes here on those inspection tours of his when he drives around the post. You know what I mean, right, Major?"

"For sure. We're familiar with Colonel Andrews' driving inspection tours. I didn't know he included the rail yard, but I know there isn't much on post that's off limits to him," Miller said.

"Oh, yeah. I bumped into him here a couple or three times. He told me he calls this place his refuge from the stress of his job. He gets pissed whenever a car with graffiti on it is in the yard. Like it's my fault. Says it's almost a sacrilege to do that to a boxcar. Hell, I remember when he first got here, he told my boss that he wanted to have more keys to more locks than anyone else on post. I always figured the post commander had better things to do, but who knows, right?"

Shortly into the walk through the yard, Patches paused briefly at the spot where Andrews had parked and transferred Marie's body from the boxcar to the trunk of his car. It might have been coincidence. Maybe it was the lingering scent from the spot where the rock that killed Marie sat briefly on the ground. Whether it was because Marie's body hadn't been outside the boxcar long enough for Patches to sense her, or because there was no odor of death escaping from the nearest boxcar—the one with a graffiti rainbow painted on its side, Patches did not give Gregory an alert signal. The boxcar doors were open. Had it been allowed to air out sufficiently? The dog only paused a few seconds to sniff the ground before moving along.

About halfway through the rail yard and just beyond the gate that connected the military and commercial tracks, Patches stopped and signaled to Officer Gregory that something dead was nearby.

"Let's stop here for a minute," Gregory said. His voice was calm and soft spoken. He wanted Miller and Cardello to be still to allow Patches to focus without distractions. "What is it, girl?"

Patches began to move toward a parked boxcar. Nearly every one of the boxcars looked alike. The older ones were faded from exposure to sunlight. Some were dirtier than others. The one on which Patches appeared to focus was another with a rainbow spray-painted on its side.

Gregory stayed even with Patches. Her head was down. Her pace had picked up, but she was not running. She was all business. Miller and Cardello trailed only slightly. They could see that the dog was headed straight for the center of the boxcar.

As she pushed through a patch of overgrown crabgrass, Patches' motion startled a small group of crows on the ground nearby. They lifted into the sky and joined a group of ten or more crows circling above.

Patches now appeared to want to go under the boxcar. Gregory briefly held the dog back. He unhooked the leash from her collar, allowing her to go forward on her own. Gregory led the others around the far end of the boxcar where they found Patches seated, focused on an unidentified mound about three feet away.

"Please stay here," Gregory said to Miller and Cardello, motioning with one hand for them to stand still. Gregory moved forward, hooked the leash to Patches's collar, and patted her side without really looking at the dog. Instead, Gregory stretched his neck to try to get a clear view of whatever it was that caused Patches to alert. For her part, Patches's focus remained on the object.

"Mr. Cardello," Gregory eventually said. "I'm afraid this one is for you, sir."

Cardello and Miller moved forward. They could soon see the outline of a dog lying on the ground near the base of the chain link fence. It was early in the decomposition process.

"Son of a bitch," Cardello said. "If it isn't the kids, it's the damn train jockeys."

"My guess is kids and probably over the weekend from the look of the dog," Gregory said, as he crouched down to pet Patches and refocus her for the walk through of the remainder of the rail yard. "I can see some of the dog's fur stuck in the barbed wire there at the top of the fence. I guess they didn't quite have enough strength to throw it clear of the fence when they tossed it over."

"You gentlemen feel free to keep going. I'm going to get my wheelbarrow from the shed and take care of the poor thing," Cardello said.

At that point, Major Miller got a call on the portable radio he was carrying. One of his MP sergeants asked about his delay returning to the theater parking lot. Miller responded that all was okay and that he and Officer Gregory would be there shortly.

"It's nice to know they miss you," Gregory joked.

Just as he said this, one of the other Fairfax County

officers radioed Gregory to ask about his delay returning.

"See. They love you, too," Miller said as Gregory gave a response similar to Miller's.

Gregory led Patches back around the boxcar, again putting distance between the dog and the fence line. They resumed their walk through the yard. They had nearly returned to their vehicle with no additional alerts when Cardello rejoined them.

"We're about done here, Bob. Thanks for your help," Miller said.

"No problem, Major. I'm just glad I was here when you showed up."

They shook hands. Cardello held open the gate as they drove out of the rail yard. Just as they cleared the fence's outer border, he signaled for them to stop.

"Say, Major, you really are welcome to come back any time you want, but I'd be grateful for a little heads up next time," Cardello said through the open passenger's side window.

"You got it, Bob. I'm sorry I didn't follow SOP this time. No reflection on you. I'll be sure to let the Provost Marshal and the Post Engineer know how cooperative you've been," Miller said.

"We may have something," Gregory said, as he put the vehicle in Park and stepped out of the vehicle.

"What's up, Tony? Patches have to pee?" Miller asked.

"No. Something's got her attention. I think it's the dumpster. She must have picked up something through the open windows just now."

Gregory attached the dog's working collar and spoke to her so quietly that Miller and Cardello could not understand a word. He stood and the dog moved purposefully to the dumpster.

"Say…officer. I can…," Cardello seemed reluctant to speak up. When he did, he took a step forward.

"Hold on, Mr. Cardello. I'll be with you in a minute," Gregory said as he and Patches moved forward.

Patches sat, alerted on the dumpster.

"Want me to look?" Miller asked.

"Sure, if you want," Gregory said.

Miller removed the flashlight from his service belt as he stepped to the dumpster. He slid open the door and shined the light inside. The hairs on his arms were raised in anticipation of what he might find. The mood was made worse by the metal-on-metal sound of the dumpster door sliding open. It sounded less like a squeak and more like someone moaning. The sound caused crows perched unnoticed on the barbed wire atop the rail yard fence to caw loudly and fly away.

"Hey, Mr. Cardello." Miller's voice had a cavernous quality thanks to the fact that his head was still in the dumpster when he spoke. "Mr. Cardello. Bob," he said.

"Yeah?" There was a tone of resignation in Cardello's voice.

"I wouldn't happen to be looking at the same dog carcass that we found a few minutes ago, would I?"

"Well, I…," Cardello said.

"Because I'm sure you know to call Animal Control to dispose of a dead animal any larger than a squirrel."

"Well, I…"

"And I know you would never throw an animal carcass in this or any other dumpster, right?" Miller continued.

"Well, you see, Major, Animal Control takes forever to get out here and I'm due back at the office."

"Mr. Cardello," Miller began.

"Okay. All right. I'll call 'em and fish the damn dog out of the dumpster. I have to tell you, though, the garbage men don't give a shit what's in the dumpster."

"Thanks, Bob. You have a good day," Miller said as he joined Gregory and Patches in the vehicle. They drove away.

"I've got a dollar says he's never going to call Animal Control," Gregory said.

"No bet. He's probably never called before and isn't going to start now. He'll let that thing cook in the dumpster and, if the smell gets too bad, he just won't come back until after the trash gets picked up."

"I just wish he hadn't tossed the dog in the dumpster."

"They do it all the time here and other places on post. We get a lot of calls if the smell reaches a housing area or an office building with the windows open," Miller said.

"I suppose, but that dog could be masking other odors. I'm not crazy about the way Patches acted. It was different. I can't say if it was the dead dog again, a combination of dead animals that have been in that dumpster, or something else."

Miller lit a cigarette. "Is it something you think we should report?"

"Not a chance. There isn't enough there for me to say officially that there was an anomaly. But I know my dog and her reaction was different. In fact, when you slid the door closed, I swear she reacted as though she heard something."

"It did have an odd sound. What do you think she heard?"

"Shit if I know. All I can tell you is that her head cocked and her ears moved as though someone called her. Then, it was as though whatever she heard spooked her a bit. I can't put my finger on it, though."

They drove the rest of the short distance to the movie theater parking lot in silence.

33

"Colonel Andrews," Laura Bennett said. "The FBI team is assembled in the conference room.

"How many of them are there?" Andrews asked.

"Three from the FBI. Special Agent Steve King is the lead agent. He's accompanied by Agent Charles Morrison and Agent Scott McGinn. Lieutenant Decker is also in the conference room, along with Captain McGrath from the SJA's office and Dan Grady from Public Affairs," Laura said.

"Did you invite Decker?" Andrews asked Jack Ewing.

"Yes, sir. Frankly, I thought it would look bad if we told the FBI that we're collaborating with the local authorities, but then we excluded them from this meeting."

"You're probably right, but Chief What's-his-Face from Alexandria didn't invite us to his meeting with the Feds, did he?"

"No, he didn't, sir. But that could play to our advantage. I don't really care what the FBI thinks of Alexandria's willingness to collaborate with us. I wanted to be sure they can't paint you in a bad light, Colonel."

"Once again, Jack, you're watching out for our flank. Good thinking," Andrews said.

"Colonel Ewing," Laura said. "You have a call, sir. It's Major Miller."

"Let me take this before we go into the conference room. Todd Miller is probably calling about the cadaver dogs. Maybe there's been a development," Ewing said to Andrews.

While Ewing was on the phone, Andrews packed tobacco into a pipe he had not yet smoked today, but left it unlit. He picked up his matches and pipe tool to carry to the meeting.

"The cadaver dogs came up empty, boss," Ewing said.

"Of course they did, Jack," Andrews said. "She's not on Cameron Station. That's what I've been saying all along. It wouldn't surprise me if she showed up at home today. Laura, we'll be in the conference room. Feel free to interrupt the meeting when you hear from Marie Garrett."

"Gentlemen," Andrews said as he strode into the conference room. They made introductions. As everyone returned to their seats, with Andrews assuming his position at the head of the table, Ewing stopped to whisper in Lieutenant Decker's ear, advising him of the results of the cadaver dog searches.

Andrews took a quick survey of the room. He routinely sized up people before a meeting started: the wise guy who was already doodling, the know-it-all who didn't bring anything to write on or with, the teacher's pet who was overly interested in the subject at hand and was likely to be a pain in the ass throughout, and most importantly, the person who might be a threat to his desired outcome.

At the far end of the table, McGrath looked as though he wanted to be a thousand miles away. Andrews didn't care much for the young attorney or for his disdain for the Army. Andrews appreciated McGrath's willingness to be transparent about his attitude toward the military, but he could not understand the lawyer's complete lack of ambition for an Army career. He was six months away from the six-year mark (his obligation in return for the Army's tuition assistance in college and law school) and his request for discharge was already submitted.

Next to McGrath were two men in gray suits—one Caucasian and the other African American. Both were in their early- to mid-thirties and, by their dress and grooming, fit the stereotypical image of an FBI agent. Dan Grady sat across from one agent; Lieutenant Decker sat across from the other. Next to Decker and closest to Andrews' left was Jack Ewing. Across from Ewing sat FBI Special Agent Steve King. As close to form as the other two agents were, Special Agent King was not what Andrews expected.

Andrews had no doubt King was a competent agent, but he was closer to retirement age than Andrews would have predicted for an agent working on a mere missing person case. Slim and trim he was not. King reminded Andrews more of J. Edgar Hoover—a much different look than the image presented by the other agents sitting at the table.

Though he had no facts to support his concerns, Andrews was worried the presence of an agent with so much apparent seniority sent an early, ominous message that the FBI was not only taking this case seriously, it was already focusing on him as the prime suspect. *How could they possibly know? What have I done to cause them to suspect me?* At this point, though, he had to put this paranoia aside or, at least, to the back of his mind.

Andrews wanted to own the beginning of the meeting. In his role as host, he knew this should be easy to achieve if he spoke first—especially before Special Agent King. Andrews' primary goal was to direct attention away from Cameron Station and toward the city of Alexandria. He had no way of knowing his effort was unnecessary.

"So, why don't we start?" Andrews began. "We are always happy to welcome our brothers in federal service from the FBI. We know your focus is the missing Alexandria girl, Marie Garrett, who is completing her second summer with us on a paid internship program for kids from underprivileged neighborhoods. We can get you information on the program if you need it.

"Now, I'm confident the Alexandria police are leaving no stone unturned investigating her disappearance. As you may have already learned, my staff and I are helping turn over those few stones that happen to be on Cameron Station. We have been cooperating fully with the Alexandria police department. We actually hosted a small contingent on post over the weekend to facilitate this and, moments ago, we completed a cooperative cadaver dog search of a number of on-post locations selected by the Alexandria PD."

This clearly captured Agent King's attention. He gave a brief glance to the other two agents, both of whom nodded and made notes.

"Not surprisingly, at least to me," Andrews continued, now staring directly at Decker as he spoke, "the search found no human remains."

Andrews paused here, not long enough for anyone to interrupt, but sufficiently to enjoy what he considered an "I told you so" moment at Decker's expense.

"I'm glad Lieutenant Decker has joined us today. His presence is another sign of our cooperation with the city. While I remain hopeful that Marie will soon walk through the front door of her home—safe and sound, my goal is and has been to do all we can in anticipation of Lieutenant Decker concluding that whatever transpired regarding Marie, happened off this installation, after she left work Friday afternoon, maybe on her way home. Once this is done, Lieutenant Decker and his team should be able to confidently narrow their focus to the confines of the city. As I said, my hope remains that it isn't too late to avoid a tragedy."

"Thank you, Colonel," Special Agent King said. "I..."

"Let me just say one more thing, Agent King," Andrews interrupted. "One more thing and then the floor will be yours for as long as you want and I promise I will not interrupt again."

King smiled and waved a hand to show he willingly yielded to Andrews.

"Lieutenant Colonel Jack Ewing here has prepared a short deck of slides to bring you and your team up to speed on the situation from our perspective. We have an overhead projector set up; so, he can brief now or whenever you prefer. Now, Special Agent King, the floor is yours. Please tell us what you can about your mission here and how we can help you achieve it."

Andrews had given a good bit of consideration to what he wanted to say and what he hoped to achieve with his opening comments. Now, having finished, he thought the remarks could not have gone better. His not-so-subtle digs at Decker and the Alexandria police were not specifically planned, but they came easily and felt very good. Andrews now had to wait to see if Ewing, Grady, and McGrath would comply with his pre-meeting guidance: SPEAK ONLY IF I ASK YOU A QUESTION. IF ANYONE ELSE IN THE ROOM ASKS YOU A DIRECT QUESTION, I WILL RESPOND AND I MAY OR MAY NOT INVITE YOU TO COMMENT FURTHER.

Here's where being a son of a bitch pays dividends, he thought. *They each know the price of going against my direction.*

Andrews had total confidence in Jack Ewing, but he thought McGrath might open his mouth just to be contrary. He could never be sure about Dan Grady. The newspaper reporter who resided inside Grady might not be able to resist the urge to ask a question—solicited or not.

Andrews remained apprehensive about the role the FBI would play in all of this, but he reminded himself that his paranoia wasn't fully justified. He came to the session knowing much more about Marie's disappearance than anyone else in the room. The knowledge he had could not be shared and that caused him to be more concerned than was warranted.

Only he and God knew Marie Garrett was dead. Andrews accepted that he took the action that killed her, though he continued to believe she bore the bulk of the responsibility for her own demise. He was also pretty sure Decker suspected him either of being responsible for her disappearance or of obstructing the investigation to protect the person who was to blame.

Andrews felt he had made the most of his chance to tee up the meeting. He believed he presented a calm, confident opening, but he fully expected to have to spend the remainder of the meeting (and who knew how much time beyond that) on the defensive from an onslaught of questions and accusations from the FBI and, if he was given the chance, Lieutenant Bob Decker of the Alexandria PD.

Conscious of the importance of his demeanor at this critical moment, Andrews now sat back in his chair and puffed easily as he put a match to the unlit tobacco in the bowl of his pipe. He shook the match to extinguish the flame and glanced casually to his left, the side of the room with windows. There on the outside sill stood two crows, looking in as though they were attending the meeting.

"Thank you, Colonel Andrews," King began. The formality of his voice and his almost British accent increased Andrews' anxiety. "Allow me to begin where you concluded. I appreciate the offer of the briefing, but I think it would be a better use of our time if one of my team members meets later with Colonel Ewing, one-on-one, to go over the details of the slides. I fully appreciate that it represents only the Army's view of the situation to this point, but I'm confident it will be valuable as we move forward.

"Listening to your introduction, however, I'm afraid I was less than clear when I had my office schedule this meeting. In fact, our being here is more of a courtesy to the Army. As you may be aware, we met with the Alexandria police chief earlier today and we are scheduled to meet again in a couple of hours. He assured me—more than once, in fact—that you and especially Lieutenant Colonel Ewing have been completely open, welcoming, and collaborative from the moment this investigation began. While I wasn't sure we needed a meeting with you, I decided to keep it on the schedule in the interest of thoroughness and to ensure the hand-off goes as smoothly as possible," King said.

"Hand-off?" Andrews asked. "I guess I'm not following you on the hand-off reference."

"Well, this is increasingly looking like an abduction and we can't dismiss the possibility of a racial connotation, since Miss Garrett is a Negro. As a result, we will be working with the Alexandria Police Department to see if this pans out. As with all investigations, we will follow the facts wherever they lead us. This investigation could go in any number of directions. Most of which will allow Alexandria to retain the lead, but there may be times when the FBI will step in.

"Colonel, you made clear allusions in your opening comments to your belief that this is a local issue. I am inclined to agree with you insofar as Cameron Station is concerned. My hunch—but it is only a hunch—is that Miss Garrett's relationship with Cameron Station and the U.S. Army is an unfortunate coincidence that has nothing to do with her disappearance. My mind is not closed to the possibility of the installation's involvement, of course, but I think it far more likely that, upon leaving the base for the weekend, she either decided not to go home directly and/ or that she encountered something unfortunate when she emerged from the bus in her neighborhood."

Andrews almost couldn't believe his ears. If he had written a script, it would not have differed significantly from the words Special Agent King had just uttered. Andrews couldn't help but note with satisfaction the unmistakable look of discomfort on Decker's face. And from the way Decker moved in his chair while King was talking, Andrews was sure Decker wanted to break in on more than one occasion to question King's suppositions.

King's delivery was so polished there was no sufficient rhetorical pause that would have allowed Decker to interrupt.

Andrews again shifted his focus to the window. The same two crows were looking into the room. Not aimlessly, he thought. No. They were staring at him. If they could read his mind, they would know that he just told them to fuck off. And maybe they *could* read his mind because, at that moment, one bird tapped its beak once on the window before they flew off.

They probably flew away to go shit on my windshield, he thought. And so they had.

When he consciously turned his attention from the window to the business at the table, King was still speaking. Andrews was pretty sure he hadn't missed any of King's remarks in the few seconds he had been looking at the crows.

"And also, Colonel Andrews, unless there are any questions from anyone in the room, I think my team should shift our attention and our location to Alexandria PD headquarters. Lieutenant Decker, I assume you will be meeting with us there. Feel free to bring along any detectives who have been engaged to date. They are certainly welcome," King said.

"Special Agent King," Decker spoke up. "I have a number of points I'd like to raise with you that touch on your comments here…"

"Sure," King interrupted, "but why don't you save them for later and we'll let the colonel and his staff get back to their work."

"Well, it's just that," Decker paused. He seemed to be reconsidering what he was about to say. "You know, that's a great idea. We can discuss all this later."

"Colonel Andrews," King turned again to Andrews.

"Agent Charles Morrison here will be my point of contact for Cameron Station."

The African-American agent lifted his hand slightly to acknowledge that he was Morrison.

"Charles will get with you later today, Colonel Ewing, on the slides you prepared. Thank you for doing that, by the way. Additionally, the FBI will do the federal/local liaison, assuming you don't have a problem with that, Colonel Andrews."

"None at all," Andrews said.

"We'll coordinate any media we plan to do. That doesn't preclude you from talking to the press, of course, but, if you do, please make it clear that you are doing so either for Cameron Station or the Army. I can see from your branch insignia, Colonel, that you are a military policeman; so, I know I don't have to go into any depth about staying within our respective lanes, as I think you say in the Army."

"Believe me, Agent King, I am very happy to let the FBI have the lead and I have no problem working through you and Agent Morrison when dealing with the Alexandria PD on this case." A rare moment of total sincerity from Fleming Andrews.

"Well, then, Colonel, we'll get out of your hair and let you get back to the defense of the nation. If you need me or my team, we will be a mere fifteen minutes away at the Alexandria Police headquarters. Don't hesitate to call."

Andrews and King stood, as did the rest of the attendees. There were handshakes all around. As the visitors moved to the door, Andrews made a point to pump Decker's hand with false enthusiasm, squeezing as hard as he could, hoping to see pain in Decker's face. What he saw was closer to anger and dislike.

"Lieutenant Decker—Bob—I won't say I found our collaboration difficult, but I am happy it's pretty much over.

I hope our future engagements are few and far between," Andrews said in a voice no one but Decker could hear.

"That suits me just fine,...*Fleming*." Decker enjoyed seeing Andrews flinch at the use of his first name. "Let me paraphrase Special Agent King, we will go wherever the evidence takes us. To me, that means I'll be seeing you again," Decker said.

34

Andrews asked Ewing, Grady, and McGrath to stay behind as he escorted Decker and the FBI team from the conference room and out of the building. He reentered the room, shut the door, and slapped his hands together.

"Well, I'll be damned. If I had any idea the meeting was going to go that well, I would have invited the FBI in myself. Hell, now I almost feel bad about not offering them coffee and pastries," Andrews said.

"Colonel Andrews," McGrath spoke up.

Andrews instantly thought, *Here comes my dark cloud to rain on the parade.*

"Sir, I have to admit I would not have predicted that outcome. I thought you came on a little strong at the beginning, but that proved to be a good approach," McGrath continued. "You had it right."

"So, I'm not as stupid as you thought I was?" Andrews said.

"I never thought or said you were stupid, sir," McGrath replied.

Turning to Grady, Andrews said, "Dan, I hope you are comfortable letting the FBI have the limelight."

"Believe me, Colonel, nothing makes me happier than to have the media focused somewhere else when the story is about a missing teenage African-American girl," Grady said.

"It went well, sir," Ewing added.

"You know what I enjoyed most about the meeting?" Andrews said to no one in particular. "I enjoyed watching that son of a bitch Decker squirm in his seat. Given the chance, I think he would have accused me, and maybe even the rest of you, of kidnapping or worse.

"Jack, you're going to have to have some contact with him through the FBI on this and maybe directly on other things that'll come up, but I don't ever want to have to deal with that bastard again. I'll talk to the police chief or the mayor, but that pissant is all yours."

"I read you loud and clear, sir," Ewing said.

"I know that bothers you, counselor," Andrews said to McGrath. "But that's just the kind of SOB I am."

"No, sir. It may surprise you, but I agree totally. Based on what Special Agent King said, I see absolutely no reason for you to interact with Decker. In fact, I would advise against initiating direct contact with him in the future."

"Now, that's good advice," Andrews said.

"Does that mean I'm not as stupid as you thought I was, sir?" McGrath said.

Ewing and Grady shot the young lawyer a look of disbelief as they prepared for Andrews to erupt.

"You know, Captain McGrath, I'll let you get away with that little bit of insubordination this time. For the record, though, I never thought you were stupid. You're naïve and a wise guy, but you're not stupid. Frankly, your attitude won't serve you well for the few months you have left in uniform and it will haunt you when you practice law in the civilian world."

"I didn't mean to offend you, sir. I was just…"

"You were just trying to take advantage of my good mood and, at the same time, get in a cynical dig at the old, dumb colonel," Andrews finished McGrath's thought.

"No sir, I…" McGrath tried again, but Andrews cut him off again.

"Captain McGrath, I'm sure you know the old saying that silence is golden. Well, this is your opportunity to get rich. I suggest you stop talking and get out of my face before my mood sours. You're dismissed."

"Of course, sir. Have a good day, gentlemen." McGrath picked up his hat and notebook and exited the room.

"I'll talk to him, Colonel," Jack Ewing said.

"Don't waste your time, Jack. I could have ripped him another asshole, but he thrives on the attention his attitude gets him. He's not worth your time. The biggest contribution he'll make to the Army comes in a few months or so when he gets out," Andrews said.

"I call that addition by subtraction," Ewing said.

"For sure, Jack. For sure. Okay, gents," Andrews said. "Let's get back to work." Andrews went upstairs to his office as Ewing and Grady returned to their respective offices.

35

The FBI meeting had dominated Andrews' day. He was almost euphoric about the outcome and was reluctant to let anything waiting in his in-box ruin his good mood.

He called his boss, the commanding general in charge of the Army Materiel Command, to bring him up to date and to reassure him that the FBI session went well. The general was pleased and thanked Andrews for his excellent handling of the situation. Translation: "Thanks for keeping me out of it." That done, Andrews made a note to update Generals Abell, Schwab, and Macri in the morning.

Sitting at his desk, Andrews realized how tired he was. It had been a long weekend—physically and emotionally draining. Now, at 4:15 on a Monday afternoon, the thought of reviewing an action sent to him from somewhere on post or from a higher headquarters had no appeal to him. He gave the few papers in his in-box a quick look to reassure himself nothing needed his immediate attention.

Andrews got up from his desk and walked slowly into the outer office. His hands were buried deep in his pockets—an uncharacteristic pose for a soldier and especially for Andrews. His head was down. He appeared to be consumed by heavy thoughts, which enabled Laura to go unnoticed when she reflexively frowned as he came into view.

"You know, Laura, unless you slipped something into my in-box that needs my immediate attention, I'm thinking about going home, putting my feet up, and enjoying a long smoke and an even longer cocktail."

"Certainly, sir," Laura said.

"Yep, that sounds like a great idea to me," he added.

She waited until he turned to walk back into his office at a pace only slightly faster than before.

"The prayer service begins at 7:00 tonight," she said.

"The wha…?" He stopped sharply. "Oh, shit. I forgot about the damn memorial service. Nineteen hundred hours. Right. Where is it? Never mind. I have the card you gave me. Nancy and I will be there."

Back in his office, he wasn't pleased his relaxing evening would be delayed because of the prayer service for Marie. That alone wasn't enough to dampen his mood in view of the positive outcome of the FBI meeting. As he fingered the index card Laura had given him with the details of the service, Andrews realized he had referred to it as a memorial service when he was talking to her. Had she noticed the slip-up? He doubted it.

Stay sharp, Fleming. Stay sharp, he told himself.

36

The three FBI agents rode together; Decker drove his unmarked city car. Although they parked on opposite ends of the lot, they reached the back door at the same time and entered the building together.

"Lieutenant Decker, as soon as you're ready, I'd like to sit down with you, and whomever you want to discuss the case, and get a feel for your planned next steps," King said as they walked into Alexandria Police headquarters.

"I'm ready now. I have a couple of uniform guys coming in to bring both of us up to speed on their canvassing efforts. The two detectives who have been working this case with me will join us any minute now," Decker said. "Let me get you a cup of coffee, then I'd like a word with you before they join us, if you don't mind."

"Absolutely. I'll walk with you."

"Nah, I'll get it for you. If you go right through that door, you'll be able to set up. That room will be yours for as long as you need it. How do you take your coffee?"

"Black. Thanks," King said.

Decker waved for the other two agents to follow him.

"Come on, fellas. I'll show you where we keep our coffee. And, by the way, it's a lot better than the poison they serve at Cameron Station."

"Can't prove it by us," one of the agents said. "They never even offered us a cup."

"Must be because Andrews didn't want to risk pissing you off," Decker said without looking back.

Decker and the agents returned to the small conference room with the coffee. Special Agent King sat with his leather portfolio opened on the table in from of him. Decker sat across from King. The other agents joined King on his side of the table.

"Can I be completely frank with you?" Decker asked.

"You want to know why I didn't let you speak up at the last meeting," King said.

"Yes, and…"

"You think I let Colonel Andrews off the hook without knowing all the facts," King said.

"Do they teach Advanced Mind Reading at the FBI Academy?" Decker said.

"Among other skills, Detective," King replied with a knowing smile.

"You gave him a pass and, I have to tell you, I think it was a mistake. I don't know how, but I think he's dirty. I can't prove it yet, but I'm convinced he's involved directly or indirectly with Marie Garrett's disappearance and her likely murder. Wait until you see the notes from the interviews I've done. The nicest thing anyone called him was a creep. Even his wife seemed reluctant to say anything that would imply he was up for Husband of the Year."

"I'd hate to think what my wife would say about me in that situation," Agent McGinn added as a side thought. King threw him a look. McGinn couldn't decide if he was signaling that he was out of line or that King wished he had said it first.

"Slow down, Lieutenant. I didn't give him a pass. Oh, I'm sure he thinks I did and apparently so do you, but, if you listened carefully to what I said, I think you would agree that I did no such thing. At this point, I do think it likely whatever happened to that poor girl, happened off base, but I have not ruled anything out. And that includes an abduction and possibly a murder by someone who lives and/or works on Cameron Station. Earlier today, Colonel Andrews was guilty of selective listening. He heard only what he wanted to hear."

"Well, I'm relieved to hear you say that," Decker said.

"Lieutenant Decker, it was obvious to me and my two colleagues that you do not care for Colonel Andrews," King began.

"That's an understatement," Decker chirped in.

"It's also pretty easy to see that he really doesn't think much of you, either. On top of that and despite the military rank that he has achieved, he has all the characteristics of an insecure person. It's no surprise to me that he did all the talking. I'm willing to bet he told the three men he brought into the room that he would cut off their manhood if they said a word without an invitation from him. And I'm sure he had no intention of inviting them to say anything."

"So, why didn't you press him?" Decker asked.

"To what end? There's time for me to home in on him, if that's where the investigation leads us. He's not going anywhere. He's in a very visible position. He's on active duty *and* he's a cop. He knows well that I can reach out and touch him anywhere on earth. I hardly think he's a threat to go AWOL.

"If I had let you go after him, the two of you would have pissed on each other's legs, if you'll pardon the expression, and, frankly, I would have wasted my time. Does that make sense to you?" King asked.

"I suppose," Decker answered.

"Now, Lieutenant Decker, let's talk about what you have learned so far. I'd like to hear what you know and what you think it all means."

Decker walked over to the closed door of the conference

room. He opened it and invited in his two detectives and the pair of uniformed patrol officers who were waiting in the hall, consistent with the instructions he had radioed in on his way back from Cameron Station.

He introduced the policemen to the FBI agents.

"Okay, folks, let's start with what you have learned from the neighborhood canvassing and then we'll discuss the interviews we've conducted with Marie Garrett's family members, friends, and, finally, the Cameron Station interviews," Decker said.

That sounds like a great plan, but only if your Chief agrees to postpone our meeting scheduled for five-o'clock," King said.

Detective Birch spoke up, indicating he would make a phone call. He stepped out of the room and returned promptly, giving Decker a "thumbs up" hand signal.

The canvassing had produced nothing new. No one had seen or heard from Marie. Her friends all denied any late night social activity and everyone promised to call the police if they heard from her or if they thought of anything that might be helpful to the investigation. The two uniformed officers briefed them on their report and participated actively in the discussion it prompted. After about thirty minutes, Decker thanked and dismissed them.

Decker, King, and Morrison went to refill their coffee cups while the two detectives and McGinn stood in the conference room, making small talk, smoking cigarettes. Ten minutes into the break and they were back in their chairs discussing the case at length. Time passed unnoticed.

"Look, it's pushing five o'clock. We can stop now, if you want, or I can call for a couple of pizzas and we can get to where I would like to leave it for the night. I'm guessing we can easily wrap up about 6:00 or 6:15," Decker said.

"Let's keep going, Bob. I have a couple of ideas I'm

working on, but I'd like to hear everything the three of you have to say before I impress you with my insight or embarrass myself by voicing an idea you've already discounted," King replied. "Let's stop at 6:00, though. I want to attend the prayer service that starts at 7:00."

"I'm going to be there, too. You're welcome to ride with me," Decker said.

"That would be great. Charles and Scott can take the car to the hotel, if you don't mind dropping me there when it's over," King replied.

The pace of the discussion slowed when the pizzas arrived, but the forward progress never stopped. At five minutes before six, Decker said he had only one more observation to make.

"For the record, Special Agent King, I don't know how you can drink that shit," Decker said, eliciting laughs from the others, including King himself.

"Ah, Lieutenant, only a mature and refined pallet can appreciate the rich flavor of Tab. It has only one calorie, you know," King said.

"You do know that it's made by filtering water through dirty, old rusted cans—oil cans, probably," Decker countered.

"Oh, that's very funny," King said, as he poured the last of the contents of his Tab into the glass. "Since you've resorted to humor at my expense, I take it we have reached the conclusion of the material you want to present this evening."

King was enjoying the banter. It had been a long day, it wasn't over yet, but he was pleased Decker had warmed to the FBI's participation in the case.

"I might have just said, 'we're done', but your sentence sounded so...so..."

"Refined?" King interrupted.

"No, I was trying to decide between bureaucratic and bullshit, but we'll go with refined if you'd prefer," Decker said. "We are done and I hope you found it useful. We're working this hard and I'm frustrated. I'm not sure why the chief kicked off a formal investigation so soon after Marie was reported missing, but I think it's because of the possible racial angle and not wanting this to aggravate the tensions between the police and the Negroes in Alexandria."

"I think it was wise," King said. "Asking us to come in so early is also a smart strategic move, in my opinion."

"Yeah, I'm fine with all that now. I've told the chief and I'll tell you, but I would never tell the Garretts. I'm convinced the girl is dead and we are never going to find her body," Decker concluded.

"Well, Bob, I guess I'm with you on half of that. I agree that she is almost certainly dead and I agree that we cannot say that to the family—at least not yet. I'm not so sure the body won't be found, but you could be right about that as well. From what you've told us, it's going to be hard to nail someone for this without a body," King added.

"Okay, guys. I suggest we call it a night. Steve, I'm going to throw some cold water on my face before we head to the church. I could use a shower and a fresh shirt, but that's not going to happen. It's a short drive, but I'd like to be early so we can scout the crowd as people arrive," Decker said.

"Sounds good. You know, I just had an idea that I'd like to share with you on the way."

King turned to Morrison and McGinn. "You guys go have a drink at the hotel bar and call it a night. We'll meet in the lobby at 7:30 a.m. See if these two fine detectives can recommend a decent place for breakfast."

"Oh, that reminds me," Decker said. He reached

into the side pocket of his suit jacket and withdrew a key. "There's a deadbolt on the door. Here's the key. The watch commander has the only duplicate. Everyone knows the room is off limits while you're here. No one will be in here until you unlock it in the morning." He handed the key to King who passed it to Morrison who handed it to McGinn, the most junior agent.

"Everything rolls downhill," McGinn smiled.

37

Nancy Andrews was upstairs when she heard the front door. She pushed aside the curtain on one of the front windows and saw Andrews' car in the driveway.

"Fleming, is that you?"

"Yes, it's me. Were you expecting someone else?" He placed his hat on the hall table near the foot of the stairs and put his briefcase on the floor next to the table. Nancy kept a small ashtray, always spotlessly clean, on the table into which Andrews placed his pipe each day when he returned from the office.

While Andrews' day had been a whirlwind of activity, Nancy had plenty of time to reflect on her morning encounter with her husband. Hurt by his words and actions, she sat silently at the dining room table for nearly a half hour after he left for the office, after which she broke down in tears. Her on-and-off crying spells lasted most of the morning.

She found the strength to stifle her tears and hide her pain during a few phone calls from friends in the Officers' Wives' Club to coordinate upcoming events, and one to invite her to a Tupperware party. Soon after each call, she went through a short period of anger and then another round of tears.

After Andrews called her about the prayer service, she showered quickly and drove to the Post Exchange where she bought a simple navy blue dress to wear to the church. She decided not to wear black because of the message it might send; yet, something in a bright summer color seemed even more inappropriate.

By the time she heard the front door, she had convinced herself her lingering doubts about the soundness of her marriage were not fully justified. She attributed her husband's unwarranted behavior that morning to the pressure on him as a result of Marie Garrett's disappearance and the looming uncertainty of the meeting with the FBI.

Yet, as she walked down the stairs, she was filled with a level of anxiety that no wife should feel just because her husband had come home from work an hour or so earlier than usual.

"Fleming, I've been thinking about you all day. How did the meeting go with the FBI?" She asked the question out of her sincere interest, but she braced herself for a powerfully nasty response.

"How did it go? I'll tell you how it went, Nancy. It was the best damn meeting I've been to in a very long time."

"Oh, Fleming, that's wonderful. I'm so happy for you." She moved forward and laid her hands on his chest. He put his arms around her. They kissed.

"Nance, I guess I'm supposed to apologize for being a bit of a jerk this morning. It's just that you took me totally off guard and…"

"I know, honey. I should have realized the pressure you are under. I was only trying to take your mind off the terrible situation with that poor girl. It has to be driving you crazy, but I am so glad the meeting went well. Can you tell me anything about it?"

Nancy was then subjected to the Fleming Andrews version of the meeting.

"I knew my opening would be critical. I had to ensure the FBI agents knew the truth before they heard that fool Decker's twisted version of the situation, which is totally biased against the Army in general, Cameron Station in particular, and me individually."

"Fleming, that sounds awful. Why would he be that way? He seemed like a nice man when I spoke to him."

Andrews had forgotten Decker had already spoken to his wife. He decided it would not be in his best interest to continue to bad mouth Decker.

"That's not important, Nance. He just wants any blame to fall on Cameron Station, so Alexandria can look better. He is angry with me because I haven't been buying into any of that crap and, I am happy to report, the FBI didn't buy into it either. The lead agent understood what I was saying, agreed with my logic, and said he thought that whatever happened to Marie Garrett almost certainly had nothing to do with Cameron Station or the Army."

"Or you?" She asked.

"What's that?"

"Or you. I assume he also exonerated you."

"Well, of course." Andrews could feel his face flush. "Why would you even ask that question?"

"You said Lieutenant Decker was after the Army, Cameron Station, and you. Then you said that the FBI agent exonerated the Army and Cameron Station, but you didn't mention yourself. I was just trying to…"

"Oh, right. No, of course he exonerated me. In fact, the meeting didn't last very long. Once the lead FBI agent told me he only asked for the meeting as a courtesy to the Army, I knew we were in a good place. Then he said that their investigation should be moved to the Alexandria PD headquarters because—and this is the best part—because I had better things to do."

"Fleming, I'm so relieved and so happy for you. I bet you and Jack Ewing feel as though a heavy weight has been lifted off your shoulders."

"Even our wise guy JAG had to admit I handled

the meeting well. Must have broken his heart to say it," Andrews said.

"I can't believe Mike Connelly would be unhappy that the meeting went well." Nancy was referring to Lieutenant Colonel Michael Connelly, the installation Staff Judge Advocate—the senior lawyer on Cameron Station.

"What? No, not Mike Connelly. Mike is on emergency leave and his deputy was reassigned two weeks ago. So, I was stuck with Captain McGrath," Andrews told her.

"I don't think I've met him."

"Probably not. He's a bright guy, but he has an attitude. He's getting out of the Army when his commitment is up in about six months and it's affected his approach to anything having to do with the Army."

"Well, that's his problem. I'm glad the meeting went well. I guess the only thing that could make the situation better would be for Marie to be found safe and sound."

"Nance, I'm going to have a gin and tonic. Can I make one for you?"

"Do you think that's a good idea, honey? We have the prayer service tonight."

"I know, but I'm going to make it weak, with a lot of ice. I'll be sure to brush my teeth and gargle before we go. No worries."

"I'll pass. I haven't felt like eating all day and I shouldn't put alcohol on an empty stomach. I can get you some cheese and crackers, if you want. Do you want to eat dinner before we go? I have leftovers."

They agreed the cheese and crackers would hold them through the prayer service. They would grab something on the way home.

"By the way, let's take your car tonight, Nancy. My car is covered in bird shit."

"Still? Didn't you have time to have it washed?"

"Oh, I did have it washed right after lunch, but the damn birds ambushed me again this afternoon."

"Oh, my. What did you ever do to make them angry?"

"There's no telling, Nance. Maybe they work for Lieutenant Decker."

They sat in their usual chairs in the den. Nancy ate a few crackers with cheese; Andrews never touched the food. He sat back in his chair with his gin and tonic in one hand. The other held the bowl of his pipe as he drew deeply on its burning tobacco.

"Fleming, I'm going upstairs to do my hair now. That'll free the bathroom if you want to shower before the service."

"Yeah, I guess I ought to shower and shave for a second time today. I really don't want to go to the damn thing at all, but I certainly don't want to show up with a five-o'clock shadow."

Nancy walked to the stairs, but returned to the den with the pipe Andrews had placed in the hall table's ashtray. She put it in the large ceramic ashtray Andrews kept next to his chair. She routinely did this if Andrews hadn't retrieved it from the hall to clean out the spent tobacco and place the pipe on the rack.

"Oh, thanks, Nance," Andrews said.

"You're welcome. I meant to mention this the other day, but so much has happened in the last few days…"

"Mention what?" He said.

"Last Friday was the first time I can remember that you didn't put a pipe in the ashtray when you got home from work."

"Really? Are you sure? I'm pretty sure I had a pipe in the ashtray last Friday," he lied. I can't imagine why I wouldn't have smoked a pipe on my way home."

"I can't remember for sure, but I suppose you could have cleaned it before I noticed it was there," she said, more to placate him and avoid a confrontation.

"That's probably it," he said.

"I'm going to do my hair."

"I'll be up in a few minutes."

38

"Bob, I'm going to be painfully honest with you," King said almost as soon as they pulled out of the police department parking lot. Because of the Monday rush hour and the many traffic lights, the ride to the church would take longer than Decker had predicted, but they would still be among the first to arrive.

"Steve, I've known you less than a day, but I already have a lot of respect for you. I can't say I welcome the presence of the FBI in the middle of one of my cases, but I understand why it was smart for my chief to ask you to be here. You also clearly understand the cop's perspective," Decker said.

"So, I'm not as big an ass as you thought I would be. Is that what you're saying?" King asked, tongue in cheek.

"Hey, I thought *I* was the plain-spoken cop and you were the DC bureaucrat," Decker responded. "I welcome honesty—even if you think it will be painful. What's on your mind?"

"Well, I'm trying to separate your suspicions about Colonel Andrews from your clear dislike of him. I'm trying to decide if there's a good reason to look deeper or if I have to throw the bullshit flag and conclude that you're barking up the wrong tree."

"Steve, you've been an agent for a long time, right?"

"And a cop in a small town outside Boston before I went to the Academy," King added.

"I knew you had a cop's mind. So, you have to understand when something just gnaws at you. I admit, I didn't like Andrews from jump street. He's a pompous ass.

Everything everyone told me about him confirms my view."

"I can see that," King said.

"But, honest to God, I think I can put all of that aside and there is still a voice in my head and a feeling in my gut that says he's got something to hide. You can tell me I'm full of shit, but that's the way I feel."

They drove the rest of the way in silence. Decker didn't like the image of the cops getting the prime parking space at the expense of a relative or close friend. There were spaces close to the church, but he turned the corner and went far down the street before pulling into a spot. He also knew that no cop was going to ticket a police lieutenant's car if it encroached on a bus stop or a fire hydrant. That wasn't really Decker's style and he was happy he didn't have to exercise that option, especially since he had a seasoned FBI agent riding shotgun.

"Bob, there are a couple of ways I think we can play it with Andrews," King said as they walked from the car to the church. "Generally, I tend to favor more subtle approaches, but I get the impression you don't think subtlety will work with Andrews."

"I can tell you his defenses are up from the minute I engage with him. I've seen it more than once. He chooses his words carefully. I get the impression he's playing chess with me and he stands out because everyone else—and I mean everyone else I've talked to on Cameron Station— seems to be open, honest, and fully cooperative. He's the only holdout."

"What about Lieutenant Colonel Ewing?" King asked.

"Jack's top notch. He and I have actually worked together before. To be perfectly honest with you, I think he suspects Andrews of something, as well, but he's too loyal to his commander to say so."

"Do you think he's hiding something?"

"No. Jack is a pro. I know him well enough to know he can barely stomach Andrews. If he had anything beyond a suspicion, he would share it or find a way to ensure we found it. I'm convinced of that," Decker said.

"Well, Bob, even the toughest nut can be cracked if the pressure is applied properly."

They walked into the Old Town AME Church. A handful of people were scattered in pews close to the rear. King signaled to Decker that they should walk to the front and introduce themselves to the man in the sanctuary who was obviously getting things organized for the service.

"That's Reverend Clarence Johnson," Decker whispered to King as they walked down a side aisle. As they reached the edge of the sanctuary, members of the church choir began to assemble in the raised area directly behind the pulpit. Decker got the pastor's attention.

After brief introductions, Johnson led them through the sanctuary to the vesting area behind it. Johnson fully understood why they were there and suggested that, after they observed people arrive from a position outside the church, King and Decker might want to use the stairs at the rear of the church and observe the service from the choir loft.

"Some preachers hide their choirs in a loft. That never made sense to me. I like to have them right up front. I tell them that I have spies in the congregation who will rat on them if they make faces at me behind my back. Anyway, the choir stopped using the loft years ago. We mostly use it to store seasonal decorations and things like that, but it's quite safe and will give you a commanding view. Unfortunately, it will be of the back of nearly everyone's head," Johnson said.

"No, that'll be fine, Reverend. Thanks so much," King said.

"Please. Feel free to call me Clarence."

"Yeah, I can't do that, Reverend."

Pastor Johnson had a broad smile and a welcoming approach. Decker knew him to be a mainstay in the community. On more than one occasion, Johnson spoke publicly to ease tensions with the police in Alexandria's African-American neighborhoods. He could be the ultimate showman when he thought it was what he needed to be. When meeting one-on-one with Decker, the chief, or the mayor, however, he was a strong advocate for the Black community. The conversations were often contentious, but the city's leaders knew Johnson only spoke what he believed to be the truth. They were especially appreciative that he did so without grandstanding in front of the television cameras at police expense.

"Bob. Special Agent King. What else can I do to help you?"

"This will be great, Reverend," King said.

"Yeah. Thanks, Clarence," Decker added.

"I will offer this to you. I know Marie and her mother. Her father is almost always on the road; so, I don't see a lot of him. And her uncle Henry is like a second father to her. Whatever happened to her, happened *to* her. She didn't stray. She didn't go looking for any trouble. I know that in my heart and in my head. It pains me to say this, but I believe she was betrayed by someone she trusted. That's the only way I can imagine Marie falling into trouble," Johnson said.

"Sounds like you've given this a good bit of thought," Decker said.

"It has consumed my weekend. I'm sickened by it. Gentlemen, my unending hope is in our Lord and Savior, Jesus Christ. But don't be mistaken—I'm not naïve. I fear I may never see Marie alive again. It also pains me to think the person or persons responsible for whatever happened to her may well be in tonight's congregation masquerading as a concerned friend," he paused. "I'm sure that's why you are here this evening."

They stood in silence until Pastor Johnson spoke again.

"Well, I have things to do and I know you do, as well. May I offer a suggestion? If you exit through the door right there and follow the brick path alongside the church to the sidewalk, you'll find a spot that offers a good view of those arriving while allowing you to be somewhat inconspicuous. I've done the same thing myself some Sundays. It's amazing how differently some people behave inside and outside church or when they don't know the pastor is watching."

Decker and King agreed and thanked him for his help. Decker took one last look at the main church from the area behind the sanctuary. The church was still almost empty.

"He seems like quite a man," King said as they walked outside.

"He's a real asset to the community, but I never let myself forget that he is constantly working his agenda. Fortunately, it hasn't conflicted with ours so far," Decker said.

"Well, Bob, everybody has an agenda and most people are working it all the time. If it's healthy, there's really nothing wrong with it."

"Oh, I'm not saying there's anything wrong with it. I just don't let myself forget it," Decker replied.

"Say, have you noticed all those black birds in the trees over there? There must be a thousand of them," King said.

"Yep, and there are more heading this way," Decker said, pointing to a small cloud of crows flying in their direction.

39

"I hate these things," Andrews said as he and Nancy drove east along Duke Street into Old Town Alexandria.

"I know, Fleming, but it's important for us to be there tonight. You always criticize the city for being against the Army. This might go a long way toward showing the community that you care."

"I suppose so, but I still hate these things," Andrews said. He turned onto a cross street and made another turn when he reached King Street.

The Old Town AME Church was located on King. It had been a part of the Alexandria community since 1949. As they approached the church, it was obvious that the congregation would be very large and, to Andrews' frustration, parking would be at a premium.

"Damn, I knew we should have used a motor pool car and driver," Andrews said. The small parking lot adjoining the church was already full. He slowed and was now scanning both sides of the road, hoping to find an open space.

"Oh, look," he said to Nancy. "Some inconsiderate bastard has reserved spots by putting orange cones in the street. Must be for the holier than thou. Parking ought to be first come first served, as far as I am concerned. And I say that knowing those spaces would have been taken long before we arrived, but still..." he didn't finish the thought. Nancy had no intention of saying anything that would cause him to rant some more.

"Fleming, stop!" Nancy was uncharacteristically emphatic. As a result, Andrews hit the brakes hard out of concern and surprise. Since they were moving slowly, there was no skid.

"What? What's the matter?"

"Can you back up a little bit?" She asked. "I'm sure the paper attached to that cone has your name on it."

He got out of the car long enough to confirm what Nancy had seen and to move the cone to the sidewalk.

"Yes indeed. Now, that's what I like to see. I'll have to get Chaplain Hughes promoted for this."

After he had successfully parallel parked, Andrews put the car into Park and turned off the engine.

"I guess you won't be able to say all the people in Alexandria hate you from now on," Nancy said before they got out of the car.

"Didn't Jackie Kennedy say something close to that about Dallas, minutes before Oswald blew JFK's head apart?" Andrews replied.

Andrews stepped out of the car just as someone opened the passenger door.

"Why, Father Hughes, thank you very much. That's very gentlemanly of you," Nancy said. She extended her hand to the Cameron Station chaplain who had obviously been waiting on the sidewalk for their arrival. He saluted Andrews who, after returning the salute, shook the chaplain's hand.

"Thanks for arranging the parking, Chaplain. I was certainly willing to find my own parking space, but I appreciate your effort," Andrews said, avoiding direct eye contact with Nancy, who was looking at him in disbelief.

"Well, I can't take the credit, Colonel. Before I could even mention parking, Reverend Johnson told me he was saving a spot for you. He was sincerely flattered when he heard you and Mrs. Andrews would attend the service."

Andrews didn't respond, but his eyes finally met Nancy's. She was now giving him a "See, I told you so" grin. He hated when anyone gave him that look.

Hughes continued. "The pastor's name is Reverend Clarence Johnson. He's a wonderful spiritual leader and a great guy. He'll probably tell you to call him Clarence."

"It sounds like you know him fairly well," Andrews said.

"I do. I've come to know him very well," Hughes responded.

"Have you participated in inter-denominational and inter-faith services together?" Nancy asked.

"Oh, sure. In fact, that's how I first met him. Now we're primarily poker buddies."

"Poker buddies?" Andrews asked.

"Yes, sir. We play nearly every week. It's a friendly game. Nobody loses their shirt or their soul," Hughes smiled.

"Who wins? You or him?"

"Ha! We probably each win our share of the time, but Father Jim Curry from Saint Francis Xavier Church routinely takes us all to the cleaners," Hughes responded.

"Oh, I expected you to say it was the local rabbi. I understand they're good with money."

"Fleming, really." Nancy's annoyance was genuine.

"No, it's Curry. He's got our number, but Rabbi Jeremy Hersch is a real good poker player, as well. Have you ever met him? Wonderful man."

"No. I haven't had the pleasure. And I was only joking, of course. Nancy just doesn't get it. Well, I am now looking forward to meeting the good Reverend Johnson, although I would have thought his focus would be on the family tonight."

"Oh, you'll meet him, sir. No doubt in my mind. He

will be great with the Garrett family, but he wouldn't miss the chance to meet you, as well. Now, here's the lay of the land inside the church. The family is sitting in the first rows on the right as you walk in. They are already in the church. Clarence wants you and the civic leaders to sit in the front pew on the left. Naturally, that includes you as well, Mrs. Andrews."

"Jeez, I wasn't expecting that," Andrews said. In his mind he was thinking, *Great. There is no way I'll be able to sneak out as soon as this is over.*

"Who else will be in the front row with me?" Andrews asked.

"The mayor and his wife, Congressman Simpson and his wife, and the city chief of police."

"Father," Nancy said to Hughes. "It's just about 7:00, maybe we should move inside."

The church was packed and, while he routinely loved being the center of attention, Andrews wished he could have slipped in and out unnoticed. He had never before been in a room with so many black faces and he sensed every one was staring at him. Shortly before he and Nancy reached the end of the center aisle, they were met by Reverend Johnson who gave Andrews a firm, long-lasting handshake.

"Colonel Andrews, thank you so much for joining us this evening. It means a great deal to me and to the community. I am sure it will mean a tremendous amount to the family."

Johnson greeted Nancy and gave a brief man hug to Chaplain Hughes, who then retreated to his seat at the end of the fourth pew. He was one of the few white faces not in the first pew on the left.

"I want to introduce you to Marie's immediate family. You may get to chat with them after the service, but the family asked that there be no reception afterward. That celebration will take place when Marie is home," Johnson said.

"No reception? Too bad. I was looking forward to getting to know the family better," Andrews said. Nancy gave him an elbow in the side that went unnoticed by anyone else in the church.

The pastor led Andrews and his wife down the remaining few feet of the center aisle and turned them to the right to an open space between the church's sanctuary and the first pew. It was a short distance, but provided enough time for Andrews to dread the coming encounter.

"Colonel, this is Cecilia Garrett, Marie's mother and Marie's dad, James," Reverend Johnson said.

Instantly, Andrews felt a sinking feeling in his stomach. It was as though he was in a dreamlike state. Everything suddenly shifted into slow motion. He knew Marie's parents would be at the service, of course, and he pretty much expected he would meet them, but he hadn't grasped what it would be like to look into the eyes of the woman who gave Marie the very life he had taken away.

These were the parents of the girl he had murdered. His conviction that Marie was somehow responsible for her own death escaped him for the moment. They were here to pray and hope for her safe return. He knew otherwise.

There was a vacant look in Marie's mother's eyes. It was obvious she had been crying—probably for much of the last three days and she looked as though she had not been sleeping well, or at all.

"Mrs. Garrett, I'm so sorry," Andrews said as he shook her hand. *Sorry? You ass! Nobody is supposed to be sorry here. Not yet*, he thought. "I'm sorry you are going through this. I know the police will find Marie soon and that she'll be fine," he added.

It really didn't matter what he said or what he added. Cecilia Garrett was numb. She knew who he was, but hadn't processed a word he said. She nodded and dabbed a tissue to one of her eyes.

Andrews moved slowly along, allowing Nancy to greet Mrs. Garrett with a warm hug. Though they had never met before, Marie's mother seemed to welcome the sign of affection from this white woman with whom she had nothing in common. She returned the embrace and held it for a full thirty seconds. When they separated, both women were unsuccessfully holding back tears.

Andrews shook James Garrett's hand, but said nothing to him. Instead, he put his left hand on Mr. Garrett's shoulder and gave him what he hoped would be received as a reassuring nod. In return, James Garrett gave Andrews a hard, unblinking stare that Andrews found unnerving.

Cecilia Garrett's sister and her husband were next. Andrews sensed coldness in their faces as he silently shook their hands. He assumed it was either due to his uniform or the color of his skin. He couldn't get to the end of the family pew fast enough. Next to last in the pew was the Garrett's sister, who was to the left of her husband.

Andrews was happy to have finally reached the last family member he would have to greet personally. There were additional relatives in the second, third, and fourth pews, but there was only one more black face in the first pew he would have to encounter directly.

He extended his hand before he looked up at the man's face. No one took his hand and he realized the two black hands firmly grabbing the pew's wood frontal were not moving. When he looked up, Andrews was stunned. The shiver in his spine and the sweat forming on his torso were real. He remembered feeling this way only twice before. The first, when the crows appeared ready to attack him at the rail yard and the other when he was about to drop Marie's body into the dumpster and found himself looking directly into the dead girl's open eyes. Both images appeared before him in a frightening flash.

"Put your hand down, Colonel, there is no chance of me shaking it."

"Mr. Henry, I had no idea…" In fact, Andrews had completely forgotten Laura had told him Henry Washington was Marie's uncle.

"My name is Washington—Henry Washington. It's about time you got it right. I guarantee you don't want to hear anything I have a mind to say to you," Washington said in a soft, but firm voice, ripe with anger. "I know this is your fault."

That said, Henry Washington reached past Andrews to introduce himself to Nancy and to thank her for attending. Washington made no reference to the brief exchange with Andrews which Nancy only partially heard.

When Andrews turned from Henry Washington, Pastor Johnson was there to escort them to their pew where the mayor, his wife, and the chief of police were already seated. The timing was fortunate because Reverend Johnson was able to meet Congressman Steve Simpson and his wife who had just reached the end of the center aisle. The Simpsons met the family and joined Andrews and the others in their shared pew. Johnson moved to the pulpit to begin the prayer service.

40

"Did you pick up on that? That was interesting," Agent King said, as he and Decker watched the congregation from their perch in the choir loft.

"What?" Decker replied.

"Your friend, the colonel, clearly doesn't want to be here. You can read it in his body language, but whoever the last guy in the front pew is, he must have said something to Andrews that he did not like."

"What makes you say that?"

"Well, Andrews stood in front of him longer than he did anyone else. When Andrews did turn away from the guy, he looked as though he wanted to punch somebody. I wish we could have heard their exchange."

"Maybe the Rev heard it."

"I doubt he was close enough, but we can ask. Look at Andrews now. He still looks like he's in a daze," King said. "Do you know who that guy is? Here see if these help." King handed Decker a pair of collapsible binoculars from the inside pocket of his suit jacket.

Decker popped them open and looked at King. "Did you think we were going to the opera or something?"

"Just tell me if you know who the guy is at the end of the first pew, wise-ass."

Decker looked through the glasses just as Congressman Simpson reached out to shake hands with the man in question. Henry Washington's movement gave Decker a brief look at his face in profile.

"Oh, yeah, I know who that is and I have a pretty good idea what he said to Andrews. That's the girl's uncle, Henry Washington. I interviewed him Saturday morning."

"Oh, you told me about him at police headquarters."

"Yep. He worked at Cameron Station for a hundred years. Left the job last week when his niece went missing. Said he couldn't go back to work. He used to drive His Nibs around the base on his inspection tours. Blames Andrews for his niece's disappearance."

"Really? Why's that?" King asked.

"Said he never liked the way Andrews looked at his niece. Hates himself for not protecting her from him. He said he hasn't told his sister, but he is convinced Andrews did something to the girl. Maybe raped her and even killed her in the process."

"Do you think that's his heart or his head talking?"

"Don't know. Maybe it's both," Decker said as the organ music increased in volume signifying the beginning of the service.

Despite the congregation's active participation, the service had the air of a memorial. In fact, during reverend Johnson's sermon and each time a song concluded and the musical accompaniment stopped, the sound of subdued crying was audible.

Reverend Johnson must have anticipated the mood because he kept the service to forty minutes.

"I ask everyone to respect the Garrett family's need for privacy at this time," Johnson said at the conclusion of the service. "Please depart in peace and prayerfulness. Go home and ask the Lord for Marie's safe return." The clear message was that the family wasn't prepared to meet everyone who had gathered in the church.

With that, people began moving out of their pews and

to the rear exits of the church. Johnson stepped out of the sanctuary and signaled for the family and the civic leaders to remain seated.

"Do you want to go back outside?" Decker asked.

"No. Let's watch the family and the big wigs a bit longer," King said.

Standing directly in front of the mayor and without aid of a microphone, Johnson told the pew's occupants that he was going to spend some time with the family in the fellowship hall.

"There will be light refreshments and you are certainly welcome to join us, but I will understand if your schedules do not permit it," Johnson concluded.

"Reverend Johnson," the mayor spoke first. "This was a wonderful service and I know I speak for all of us when we say how much we hope and pray Marie is found soon—safe and sound. I also think it best if we go our separate ways and allow you to provide the spiritual support the family can most benefit from without our presence."

You silver-tongued bastard, Andrews thought. *How the hell does someone think that quickly and sound so sincere?*

"The mayor is right," Andrews blurted out in a voice that was a bit too loud for the setting. He wanted to be sure no one tried to change the mayor's mind and screw up his escape from the church.

"Well, in that case, ladies and gentlemen," Johnson said, maintaining the soft, low-key voice he used when he began this exchange, "let me thank you again on behalf of the Garrett family for being here this evening. Our doors are always open to you and I hope you will join us soon when, God willing, we will gather to celebrate Marie's safe return," Johnson said.

As they exited the pews, they shook hands and said subdued goodbyes. Most nodded to Marie's mother and father or held up an open palm as a silent goodbye. They began to walk slowly up the center aisle of the now nearly empty church. Nancy intentionally let the group get ahead of her so that she could cross the aisle and again hug Cecilia Garrett without making a show of it. Nancy then took her husband's hand and began to walk with him up the aisle.

Andrews had been focused on Nancy. He didn't know if his face showed his level of annoyance at the delay his wife was causing. At this point, he didn't care if it did. Throughout the service, Henry Washington's words echoed in his mind. Each time they did, he became angrier that anyone—especially someone of Washington's status—would speak to him so disrespectfully.

His anger at Washington and annoyance with his wife also kept him from noticing that Henry Washington had stepped out of the first pew, walked in front of his relatives, and moved toward Andrews.

"Henry, no," Cecilia Garrett said in a low voice, but one that was loud enough to cause Andrews to turn back toward the sanctuary. Andrews did this just as Washington grabbed his shoulder.

"Hey, this could get interesting," Decker said to King. They both leaned forward and strained to hear the exchange that was about to take place between Andrews and Henry Washington.

"Mrs. Andrews, may I have a word with your husband?"

"Why, yes. Yes, of course. Fleming I will be at the back of the church." She turned and began walking up the aisle struck by the loss of color she had just observed in her husband's face.

"I want you to know one thing…" Washington began in a low voice that was firm with anger. He stared directly into Andrews eyes.

"Now, listen to me, Mr. Hen…Mr. Washington. I

resent what you said to me earlier and I don't like your tone of voice right now."

"Oh, *do you*? You must be shittin' me, Andrews. I saw the way you looked at my niece. I saw the way you watched her. I told the police and I hope they lock your ass up for a long time," Washington said.

By that time, Reverend Johnson, realizing what was going on, joined them and, from behind, put his hands lightly, but firmly on Washington's shoulders, trying to gently turn him away from Andrews.

"You're out of your mind, Mr. Washington," Andrews waved a hand at Washington and began to walk up the aisle. Washington reacted by grabbing Andrews forearm.

"Where do you think you're going, Andrews? I'm not finished talking to you."

"Henry, come with me, please," Reverend Johnson said softly.

Andrews shook Washington's hand free and kept walking. Reverend Johnson now put an arm around Washington who put his head in his hands and began to sob as he repeated Marie's name.

"Son of a bitch," Decker said in a very soft voice, laced with amazement.

"I think you and Colonel Andrews will have a lot to talk about tomorrow, Bob."

"You know it," Decker replied. "I'll do my best to break him tomorrow. He's hiding something. I just know it."

"If I can make a suggestion: don't show up unannounced. Call in the morning to get on his calendar. Let him stew about the fact that you are going to see him again. Now, let's get downstairs and make sure he sees we are here before he drives away."

"You can be a devious bastard, Special Agent King. I knew there was something I really liked about you."

230

41

"What was that all about?" Nancy asked as they walked from the church. Andrews ignored her question.

"Do you know Marie's uncle?" she persisted.

"Not really," he lied. "I understand he's a former government employee. I've been told he drove for me once or twice."

"He certainly seems to know you."

"A lot of people I don't know recognize me and think I remember them from a chance meeting somewhere. It happens all the time. I know I've told you that before."

They walked the remaining short distance to the car in silence. A few small clusters of people remained on the sidewalk outside the church, but none took much notice of Andrews or his wife.

Chaplain Hughes had lingered at the rear of the church, intending to walk Colonel and Mrs. Andrews to their car. When he saw the confrontation between Andrews and Washington, he decided it would be best to give the colonel some space. Hughes knew Andrews well enough to know that he would be upset and embarrassed to realize that a military subordinate had witnessed the encounter.

Nancy stiffened in the passenger seat when her husband slammed the car door after he got in and started the engine.

"Son of a bitch!" Andrews began very soon after they pulled away from the curb. "I knew coming to this thing was a bad idea. A total set-up."

"Fleming, it was something you had to do…"

"Bullshit. Jack Hughes could have represented me. Did you see the way they looked at me?"

"The family is under a lot of stress."

"Not just the goddamn family. The whole crowd. Every one of those animals. As we walked in, they stared at me with daggers in their eyes, the bastards. I think the family—especially the uncle—has poisoned the whole community against me and the uniform I wear. And they're making a saint out of that little whore. Those people are very tribal. When one goes after you, they all do."

"Fleming, that isn't fair. I love you, but the last few days you haven't been yourself. I don't think you realize how much Marie Garrett's disappearance has affected you. It's as though you are seeing things that aren't there. Imagining plots against you that, frankly, don't exist."

"Oh, you think so, do you?"

"Fleming, I'm very worried about you. I think you should consider seeing someone about all this. Maybe you should talk it through with Father Hughes."

"Nancy, I see someone—anyone—and I will never get promoted. My career will be over."

"I don't care about any promotion, Fleming. I care about you...about us."

"Of course you don't. You've never been fully invested in my career. Never really supported me. I was your ticket out of Augusta is all."

"Fleming, stop it."

"That's probably how I ended up in this God-forsaken assignment. I had a bright future and now I'm doing bullshit work on a bullshit installation."

For years, Nancy absorbed the pains of his demeaning talk, believing the person within was a loving man who considered her a partner for life. These words hurt her terribly. Rather than respond, she sat silently, hoping he would realize the pain his words caused and apologize. She would, of course, accept.

Silence.

During the ride home, his driving became aggressive. Lane changes were too sudden. Stops were abrupt. He hit the horn several times—none were necessary. Nancy didn't know why, but she felt compelled to break the cold silence to console him.

"Fleming, you know I'm here to listen if you…"

"If I have something to say, I'll let you know, goddamn it. And I have nothing to say to you or anyone else."

For the second time that night, Nancy was unable to hold back her tears.

42

Tuesday morning was not very different from other weekday mornings in the Andrews' house. There was a lot less conversation than usual, but the routine was the same.

While he moved into the bathroom to shave and shower, Nancy slipped into a pair of jeans and a tee shirt, walked downstairs to brew coffee, and retrieve the newspaper from the driveway. She would wait precisely ten minutes after she heard the shower turn off before dropping two pieces of bread into the toaster.

Andrews came downstairs dressed for work just as the toaster completed its cycle. He sat at the table, but only scanned the front page of the paper. He would read the copy that was delivered to the office more closely.

As he finished his first sip of coffee, Nancy placed the plate of toast and a jar of jam in front of him.

"Thanks, Nance."

"Welcome," she said softly and unenthusiastically.

"Aren't you eating anything?" He asked.

"I'm not very hungry this morning."

"Really? I'm starving," he said. "We never ate dinner last night. Look, even if you aren't going to eat, come sit with me anyway."

"I've got things to clean up in the kitchen."

"Sit with me, Nancy. Please."

She entered the dining room with her coffee cup and sat down.

"Nancy, about last night."

She started crying.

"You hurt me, Fleming. You've said nasty things to me before, but the words you used last night cut very deep." She struggled to get out the words between her tears.

"I'm not sure I know what you're referring to. I certainly never meant to hurt you. I want you to know that I thought about what you said and I think you're right. I'm going to consider talking to someone about all the stress I'm feeling in the face of the pressure the community is bringing on me."

Nancy knew this was his way of admitting he was wrong. He couldn't come out and say it. Not Fleming Andrews. She couldn't help but think his words sounded rehearsed and she doubted seriously if he had any real intention of talking to anyone. In his own way, throughout their marriage, this was as close as he could come to apologizing and admitting fault.

There was no sincerity in her voice as she said, "That's wonderful, Fleming." She blew her nose into a tissue.

43

"Good morning, Laura," Andrews said through the clenched teeth that held a pipe in place in his mouth. "Come in with my calendar as soon as I get settled."

"Certainly, Colonel."

Laura knew Andrews' morning routine. He quickly removed papers from his briefcase and then placed it on the floor behind his desk. Next, he placed his pipe in an ashtray to burn out just before he packed and lit another pipe to start the work day. By that time, Laura would deliver coffee in his favorite cup and return to her desk without either of them saying a word.

After a brief check to ensure nothing new had been added to his in-box, Andrews would settle into an easy chair near the coffee table to enjoy his pipe, coffee, and the morning paper.

Today, when he was seated, Laura returned with her steno pad and Andrews' appointment calendar.

"I thought it was a wonderful service last night, Colonel," Laura said.

"What? Oh, yes. Yes it was. I didn't realize you were there."

"Mrs. Garrett was kind enough to invite me."

"Really? How nice. I'm glad you were able to make it. So, what's on the calendar for me today?"

"Right now, the only thing scheduled is your inspection ride, which I have scheduled for 10:00."

"Do you know what time the car wash opens?"

"The car wash? I think it opens at 9:00, but I will confirm that."

"I'll shoot to be there when it opens and be back well before ten hundred hours. The damn birds did another bombing run on my car yesterday. I don't know why they targeted my car, but they're going to ruin the paint job if I let that stuff sit on the car in the hot sun."

"Certainly, Colonel. By the way, Corporal Fields will be your driver this morning."

"Good. I don't know Corporal Fields, but I'm glad it's a soldier and not a civilian. Thanks, Laura."

"One other thing, Colonel. Just before you walked in this morning, Lieutenant Decker called. He wants to get on your calendar today."

"Call him back. Tell him I can't get to him until much later in the week—Thursday or Friday."

"Certainly, Colonel." Laura turned to walk out of Andrews' office.

"See if you can schedule a call with Jack Ewing today. I should talk to him before I do anything with Decker."

"Certainly."

Andrews rushed through his coffee and the national news in the paper. He stood, picked up his hat and car keys. He walked out of his office leaving a trail of pipe smoke behind him.

He paused briefly at Laura's desk. He could tell she was wrapping up a phone conversation.

"Yes, Lieutenant, I will advise Colonel Andrews, but I cannot guarantee something today will be possible. Yes. Yes, I will give him your message. Goodbye."

As soon as she hung up, Andrews said, "I'll be back in a flash. If I leave now, I'll be at the car wash when it opens. I ought to be first in line."

"Colonel, Lieutenant Decker said he must meet with you today, whether in your office, at police headquarters, or in your quarters tonight. I think you heard me tell him I couldn't guarantee anything today."

"Boy, he is really a first class pain in the ass. Okay, wait about fifteen minutes and then call him back. Tell him you've had to do some major adjusting to my calendar, but you can squeeze him in. Make it late in the day. Not before 3:30."

"Certainly, Colonel. By the way, he would not tell me what specifically he wants to talk about or why it has to be today."

"I didn't expect him to volunteer that information."

"I asked him directly, but he wouldn't say."

"He's an idiot." Andrews looked at his watch. "I'll be right back."

44

"I have got to get your name and address, my man. I am sure my boss is gonna want to send you a Christmas card or some shit," the car wash attendant said to Andrews. "What is this, the fourth time you've been here in the last five days?"

"Something like that. I'm in kind of a hurry. I need your best wash. What do you call it again? The Super?"

"No, no, no, my brother. It's the Supreme. Like Diana Ross and the Supremes. Know what I mean?"

"Whatever. That's what I need."

"I'm about to open. Don't usually have anybody waiting on a weekday. You're the only one waiting. Shit, I think I'd move you to the front of the line, if there was a line. The sooner I get you through, the sooner you'll be back."

"If I didn't know better, I'd think the birds were working for your boss," Andrews said.

"It's all good, my man. Ten dollars, please. Just roll forward and I will have you cleansed."

"Really? Just like that?" Andrews said.

"You know it, baby. Just like that."

45

"I'm back, with plenty of time to spare before Corporal Fielding shows up," Andrews said.

"It's Fields, Colonel. Corporal Fields, not Fielding," Laura said.

"Whatever."

Laura followed him into his office.

"While you were gone, Colonel Madison called from Colonel's Division. He would like you to return his call. I told him it could be a few hours before you'd have an opportunity to call. He said anytime today would be fine."

"Hmm. I wonder what the hell he wants," Andrews said. "Not my priority."

"Lieutenant Decker will be here at 4:00 this afternoon, Colonel," Laura said.

"Sixteen hundred hours. Well done," Andrews said, but he was clearly more focused than he would want to admit on the upcoming phone conversation with Colonel Madison.

Colonel's Division was the element of the Army's personnel agency that managed the assignments of colonels, with the exception of lawyers, medical professionals, and chaplains. Andrews knew a call to tell him he will be on a soon-to-be-released selection list for promotion to brigadier general would come from his boss—a senior general officer. A call from Colonel's Division likely meant a conversation about his next assignment, and unofficial notification that he was not going to get the general's star he coveted—at least not this year.

Andrews thought about the rest of his day and couldn't decide which he dreaded more: the meeting with Decker or the call to Madison. It was beginning to look like a shitty day across the board.

"Colonel Andrews, Corporal Fields is in the parking lot. He's driving a Chevy Blazer."

"Great. I'm on the way."

46

As Andrews walked through the rear doors of the headquarters building, he saw the Blazer idling at the curb at the bottom of the steps. A soldier in starched fatigues opened the right rear door as soon as he spotted Andrews and rendered a crisp salute.

It was a far cry from the casual way in which Henry Washington routinely greeted him, never budging from behind the steering wheel as Andrews got in the car. While Andrews was pleased by the treatment, he thought Corporal Fields was overdoing it a bit. Fields didn't look the spit and polish type. Andrews didn't think Fields made it a habit to render crisp salutes. This was an obvious effort to impress the post commander and possibly secure the driving duties on a regular basis which, although it meant listening to Andrews' bluster, was among the softer assignments in the motor pool.

"Good morning, sir," Corporal Fields said.

"You must be Corporal Fields," Andrews replied. He shifted his ring of keys from his right hand to his left, returned the salute, and climbed into the backseat.

Fields responded in the affirmative, closed the Blazer door, and trotted around to the driver's seat.

"Is the A/C about right, Colonel? I'm happy to adjust it," Fields said.

"No, it's fine, Corporal."

"Roger that, sir. Where would you like to go this morning, sir?"

The only place Andrews wanted to go today was the

rail yard. He was betting there would be no activity there. If that was the case, he was confident he would be able to identify the boxcar where Marie died and hopeful he would find his missing pipe.

Andrews was concerned the requested meeting from Decker meant he had not abandoned his investigation of Cameron Station's involvement in Marie's disappearance, despite the FBI assurances. He was willing to bet Henry Washington had bad-mouthed him to Decker and King. Andrews didn't want Corporal Fields, if asked, to say that the first place they went was the rail yard.

"Let's drive through the old warehouse area. The MPs and local police did some work there this past weekend and I want to be sure they didn't leave the place any worse than they found it. After that, we'll see how much time I have and possibly go somewhere else."

"You got it, Colonel. I'm yours until you release me back to the motor pool."

"Excellent. By the way, I was pleasantly surprised by the greeting you gave me when I came out of the headquarters."

"Why's that, sir?"

"Well, my last driver sat on his ass behind the wheel like some cab driver in downtown DC and I was a fare he was picking up off the street."

"That ain't right, sir. Colonel, Mr. Washington is a great guy and I'm really sorry about his niece and all, but, in my book, that's no way to treat the post commander. No way."

"I appreciate that. Fields, let me ask you a question. You seem a bit older than most of the corporals I've encountered in more than twenty years in uniform. Did you enlist when you were older?"

"No, sir. I was drafted right out of high school. Sir, I hope you won't hold it against me because, sir, I've done a lot of growing up since I've been in the Army. But, you see,

I've made my share of mistakes and, as a result, I've made corporal more than once in my military career."

Andrews knew what Fields was telling him. Fields had been promoted to corporal and then demoted for actions in violation of the Uniform Code of Military Justice. Fields made it sound as though this may have happened more than once. He had almost certainly never been convicted by a court martial, which likely would have meant the end of his time in uniform. However, demotions and fines could come as the result of something the military called non-judicial punishment. Soldiers routinely remained on active duty after this. Andrews disagreed with the Army's policy. He firmly believed soldiers showing this degree of recalcitrance should be discharged because, as he often put it, "they are no good for the Army and are unworthy of consuming good oxygen."

"So, you've made a mistake in the past."

"Colonel, I've made more than one mistake in the past but, like I said, I've done a lot of growing up and that kind of thing is behind me now. I may never get promoted again, but I'm fixing to stay in for twenty," Fields said.

"It takes a man to admit he's made mistakes, Fields. I admire that characteristic in a soldier." Fields' hypocritical passenger said this with a straight face as he lit his pipe in the back seat of the Blazer.

"Do you want me to stop anywhere special, sir?" Fields asked as he turned into the part of Cameron Station where the warehouses were located and where the cadaver dogs had searched.

"I don't think so. Just drop to a slow speed and go up and down the streets. I'll give you a shout if I want you to stop."

Andrews pretended to be observing the area and looking closely at the buildings from the Blazer. He even asked Fields to stop briefly once or twice to make the charade more believable.

"Look okay to you, Colonel? Do you want to go through the area again?"

"No. I've seen enough. Let's head back to headquarters," Andrews responded.

"Roger that, sir."

After they drove a few blocks, Andrews said, "I'll tell you what, Corporal Fields, I've got some time. Let's swing by the rail yard."

"Yes, sir. Mr. Washington told us drivers that you like to go there to watch when the trains are being moved around and, when they aren't, you like to go there just to think."

"I don't know what else he told you about me, Fields, but he got that part right."

Fields stopped the vehicle outside the rail yard gate, just short of the dumpster.

"I assume you'll want to go on foot on your own from here, sir."

"Well, yes, but is that also something Mr. Washington told you about me?"

"No, sir. I just figured if you come here to think, you don't come here to have me walking behind you, watching you think," Fields said.

"Good for you, Corporal Fields. I don't know what you did to run afoul of the UCMJ, but you strike me as a man who is more perceptive than many senior NCOs I've known," Andrews said.

"Let me get the door for you, sir." Fields hopped out of the car before Andrews could decline his offer.

"Thanks, Fields. I don't mind opening my own door to get out of the vehicle. I won't be very long. Why don't you turn the Blazer around while I'm in the yard?"

"Will do, Colonel." Fields saluted Andrews and returned to the driver's seat.

47

Andrews had no trouble identifying the key to the lock that secured the rail yard's pedestrian gate. Soon after he assumed command of Cameron Station and realized his affection for the rail yard, he put a dab of red paint on either side of the key's bow. The paint had worn considerably over the past two years, but there was still enough remaining for it to stand out among the many keys on the ring.

As he closed the gate behind him, he noticed that Fields was already backing up the Blazer to reposition it for their return trip. Andrews took advantage of the situation not only to close the gate, but to lock it, guaranteeing that Fields could not wander into the rail yard and disturb him.

Andrews knew what he was looking for and, if no one had disturbed the boxcars, was confident where it would be. After only a few steps, he picked up his pace. The boxcar with the rainbow on its side was in sight. The side door was open.

He stopped steps from the boxcar and turned to survey the entire yard. In the distance, about halfway around the track-work, he spotted a rainbow painted on a second boxcar. *This could become problematic*, he thought, but the first car was right where he remembered it being on Friday. He turned again and approached the closest boxcar with the graffiti rainbow on its side.

After he climbed in, he waited for his eyes to adjust to the shadows in the car. He was encouraged when he saw the stack of cardboard against the wall and withdrew a small flashlight from his trouser pocket.

Andrews was relieved when the pipe was not lying at

the foot of the cardboard stack where it could be seen by anyone doing the most cursory search. He knew he had acted quickly last Friday, but was convinced he would have seen the pipe had it been in the center of the floor. He must have placed it somewhere or maybe he put it in his pocket when the bowl cooled, only to have it slip out when he was on top of Marie.

His relief faded to concern when his ongoing search met with no success.

"It has to be here," he said aloud to himself. "Where the hell else could it be?"

Then he stopped, convinced he heard a scratching sound. He presumed it was field mice that managed to enter the boxcar. He moved the light across the floor and then to the ceiling when he realized the sounds were coming from above. He saw no movement and concluded whatever was causing the scratching noise was outside on the roof of the car.

After he shined the flashlight into the empty corners of the boxcar and along the bare parts of the floor, he looked into the narrow space between the cardboard and the wall. The pipe was definitely not in the boxcar.

He had no option but to put the flashlight in his pocket and step down out of the car.

Andrews tried to recall his positioning from Friday afternoon, looking closely at the ground for any sign of the missing pipe.

Nothing.

He checked his watch and decided to invest the few minutes more it would take to check out the other boxcar with a rainbow on its side. The closer he got, the more convinced he became that he had been in the right car already. This was a rainbow, but it did not look like the one he remembered when he pointed it out to Marie.

The door to this car was closed. Andrews managed to slide it open and shine his flashlight into the dark space. It was totally empty. He climbed in anyway, but was soon convinced he was in the wrong car.

"Well, shit!" He said, standing in the dark space with his hands on his hips. He stepped down to the ground and began walking toward the front gate of the yard. The caw of the crows was unmistakable. When he reacted by looking around for the source, he spotted at least a dozen black birds standing atop the boxcar he initially inspected—the boxcar with the graffiti rainbow on its side.

"Bastards," he said, staring at the birds.

They cawed again, even louder.

Andrews approached the gate with his head down, searching the ground with the fading hope he would spot his missing pipe.

Where the hell can it be?

48

"I was watching you in the rearview, sir," Fields said as they began the drive back to headquarters.

"You were? How could you?"

"Like I said, I was looking in the rearview so I'd be ready when you came through the gate. I can see what Mr. Washington was talking about. You looked pretty deep in thought, the way you was walking with your head down and all."

"Yeah. Got a lot on my mind, Corporal Fields. "Not many people understand the burdens of a military command."

"I don't doubt it, Colonel."

They drove in silence until they were a block from the headquarters building.

"Colonel, the Army is not likely to move me any time soon. And I just want you to know I would consider it a privilege and an honor to serve as your driver anytime you want—to include weekends," Fields volunteered.

"I appreciate that, Fields. I really do."

He really didn't.

49

"Colonel Madison," the voice on the other end of the phone said.

"Fleming Andrews here, returning your call."

"Fleming, Don Madison. Thanks for the call back."

"What's up?" Andrews asked.

"Well, my friend, I'm looking out into the future. Oh, six, nine, and twelve months and I'm reaching out to those colonels who will be ready to move about that time. I'm trying to identify preferences and to get a feel for any plans you might have looking ahead," Madison said.

Throughout his career, Andrews was on edge when he spoke to the individual who controlled his next assignment. Often, his anxiety was manifest by an arrogance that was only partially unintentional. He remembered specifically how quickly the conversation went downhill when he was told he would be moving to Cameron Station. Only the fact that he was going to be the installation commander made it bearable, but he suspected there was a red flag in his file indicating he could be hard to deal with.

He was right.

The moment Madison used the phrase *my friend*, Andrews became defensive. He knew a bullshit line when he heard one. He used them all the time himself.

"Well, Don, why don't you tell me what you're thinking about," Andrews said.

"Fleming, my friend, I don't have anything definite in mind right now…"

Bullshit, Andrews thought.

"…and your preferences will have a great deal to do with anything we decide on together."

More bullshit.

"But, let's look at late spring or early summer next year. You complete a successful command at Cameron Station and then maybe we turn your talents to the formation of future leaders of tomorrow's Army."

"Really?" Andrews said. *This guy ought to be selling used cars*, he thought.

"Yes, Fleming. The Chief of Staff has made it very clear that he wants only the best officers sent to ROTC duty…"

The bullshit is getting deeper.

"…I'm not sure there's anything better than a successful installation commander serving as the professor of military science at a major college or university."

"Don, I'm guessing you have in front of you a listing of major colleges and universities that will be looking for a new PMS next year—say, late spring or early summer." The cynicism was unmistakable in Andrews' voice.

"Funny you should mention that, Fleming. I do and, while it is extremely premature, let me tell you where I think you would excel and could best serve the Army, as well."

"Somewhere south of the Mason-Dixon line, I hope," Andrews said.

"Too soon to rule that out, of course, but right now, I can pencil you in as the next PMS at Fordham University," Madison replied.

"I said the south, Don, not the South Bronx."

"Fordham is a great university, Fleming. It's a Jesuit school. They want a Catholic PMS. Vince Lombardi went there. He was one of the Seven Blocks of Granite, you know. He's a legend there and in professional football. He came out of retirement to coach the Redskins last year. Of course, he was just diagnosed with cancer; so, I don't know how much help he could be recruiting ROTC cadets. Nonetheless, the school is…"

"Don. Don. Stop for a minute. You must be able to see in my file that I have already turned down an assignment in New York once in my career. And my wife is from Georgia. So, while I am inspired by the fact that Vince Lombardi went to the school, let me tell you what I think you are really telling me."

"Okay," Madison said.

"What I just heard you say is that I am not going to be on the next promotion list to BG and…"

"Whoa, Fleming! That is not what I am saying at all. This has happened before with no complications. If you pop on the BG's list, your file shifts over to General Officer division and I find…"

"You find another son of a bitch to take the PMS job," Andrews said.

"Fleming, maybe we should have this conversation some other time," Madison said.

"No need for that, Don, my friend. I've got the message loud and clear: I'm not going to be on the BG's list and you're offering me a job in a part of the country where I don't want to go as a way of ensuring I retire."

"You know, Fleming, retirement is always an option for you whether it's next summer or next month." Madison's tone was no longer that of an enthusiastic salesman. "I'll talk to you some other time, Colonel Andrews." Madison hung up the phone.

"Don't hang up on me, you son of a bitch! Who the fuck do you think you're talking to, asshole?" Andrews said all this into a dead phone line before he slammed the receiver into its cradle.

He was glad he had shut his office door before placing the call to Madison, sparing himself the embarrassment of being overheard by Laura.

50

Andrews kept Decker waiting in the outer office while he called Jack Ewing to find out if he had heard any more from the Alexandria police about the Marie Garrett investigation. Ewing had no new information.

Andrews made small talk with Ewing, feigning interest in his family and the overall morale of the MPs assigned to Cameron Station. Ewing thought it unusual, but he was unaware Andrews was using him as a foil to keep Decker waiting even longer.

For his part, Decker had a pleasant conversation with Laura Bennett, during which she acknowledged that it had been a rough day for Andrews. Decker welcomed the information, hoping Andrews would be even more on edge than usual and that he might be prone to a slip up.

When the light went out on Laura's phone, indicating Andrews' call had ended, she escorted Decker into Andrews' office. Andrews did not get up from behind his desk when Decker approached. Instead, he put a flame to a newly packed pipe and blew out a large cloud of smoke.

"Sorry we couldn't get you in any earlier in the day," Andrews began with a lie. "Laura tried her best, but it's been a very busy day. I'm sure I've kept you on the job well beyond your usual quitting time."

"No, not at all. I'm not heading home any time soon. When I'm this close to closing a case, I find it tough to call it a day."

"So, you're close to finding the girl?"

"I think we're close to wrapping this thing up." Decker enjoyed the discomfort his words obviously gave Andrews.

"That's great news. So, what brings you back here to Cameron Station and to me? I don't want to sound rude, but I still have a shitload of work ahead of me today. So, I would appreciate it if you got right to the point."

"We shouldn't be too long. I was going over my notes and there are a few loose ends I want to tie together. I'm sure you understand," Decker said.

"Not really. I make it a habit to get it right the first time. Then, there's no need to clean up after myself. You ought to try it sometime." It was Andrews' turn to enjoy scoring a rhetorical point.

"Hey, great tip," Decker said. *Asshole*, he added in his mind. "Let's get right to it, then."

Andrews remained seated behind his desk, never suggesting that Decker should take a chair.

"Fire away, Detective."

You don't know how much I'd love to, Decker thought.

"Colonel Andrews, you indicated that you stayed at your desk for some time after Marie Garrett left for the day on Friday, but…"

"That's right," Andrews said.

"…but you can't recall exactly when you left the office."

"Right again."

"And you also indicated," Decker consulted his notes or appeared to check them. "You also indicated you went to the Post Exchange on your way home."

"Yep."

"What was the occasion?"

"What do you mean?"

"For the flowers. You said you went to the PX to buy flowers for your wife. What was the occasion?"

"Detective, it doesn't have to be a special occasion for me to bring home flowers. My wife is a damn fine woman."

"No doubt, Colonel, but she told me she can't remember the last time you brought home flowers when it wasn't a special occasion."

"So, you've talked to my wife?"

"Yes, of course. I mentioned it to you the other day. It's fairly routine, as I'm sure you know from your time as a military policeman." The digs kept coming. "She also said she couldn't remember the exact time you got home, but she said it was later than usual—especially for a Friday."

"Well, I've never known my wife to keep a clock on me, but she will also tell you that the post commander often works outside normal duty hours and the length of my work day is not very predictable. In fact, I'm pretty sure I got home much closer to my usual time than your question implies. Stopping by the Exchange doesn't take all that long."

"Okay, but she mentioned that you routinely try to get home early on Fridays—earlier than on other days of the week, if possible."

"If possible," Andrews said.

"Sure, but she said you make it a habit to call when you're going to be much later than usual. She admitted it was a bit odd that you didn't call on Friday."

"Well, she's right. I didn't call because, as I've said, it wasn't that much later than usual."

Decker flipped a couple of pages in his notebook. "Well, I figure you didn't get home until 6:30 or later."

"You figure? That doesn't sound right to me, but it does sound like you're calling me a liar."

"Not me," Decker said.

"That's the way I see it and I don't like the way this

conversation is going, Detective. You're making leaps in logic and I don't like what you're implying."

"Don't know that I'm implying anything, Colonel. I'm just asking questions and following the facts."

"Well, your facts are wrong."

"It's not so much me, but Mrs. Wax said the two of you spoke in the parking lot sometime after 6:00 PM. She's sure of that because she remembers checking her watch before she left the Exchange. She said it was 6:10 and she met you after that."

Andrews' growing anger was visible on his face. Decker continued.

"Mrs. Wax also indicated you appeared to be a bit preoccupied. She said she startled you in the parking lot."

"Startled me? She scared the shit out of me. Did she mention that she snuck up to my car on the passenger side and appeared out of nowhere in the goddamn window?"

"Actually, she said she walked toward your car waving her hand, but it didn't look like you saw her until she was right at your car."

"She wasn't waving. You know, you sure have done a lot of checking up on me, Detective. Is there anyone I interacted with last Friday who you haven't interviewed?"

"You mean, other than Marie Garrett?"

"That's not very funny," Andrews said.

"I'm not trying to be funny, Colonel."

"Then, what are you saying?"

"Colonel, I'm trying to find a missing girl. More and more, I think I'm really close to solving a murder. There is any number of possibilities for what might have happened. I'm trying to figure out if you should be eliminated from a list of suspects, but you're not making it easy."

"Oh, really? I'm not here to make it easy for you to do what the city is paying you to do, Detective. You ask me questions, I give you truthful answers. I can't help it if the facts don't fit with your preconceived notions."

"I don't know what preconceived notions you're talking about, but you were in the parking lot at the PX somewhere around 6:15 and you also mentioned that you ran from this building to your car because it had started to rain."

"So what?"

"The weather service said it rained from 5:05 to 5:15 and the manager of the convenience store on Duke Street said the same thing. I need your help accounting for the hour or more between the time you ran to your car and when you met Mrs. Wax."

"Maybe I took a shit at the Exchange."

"Did you?"

"I don't recall," Andrews said.

"Hmm."

"Do you want to know what I think? I think you and your bosses would like nothing more than to pin this on a soldier. Nobody likes the Army these days. There's still a lot of hatred because of Vietnam. It's only been a few years. If you're convinced a soldier committed a crime, why not cast doubt on the installation commander himself?"

"That's bullshit," Decker interrupted, but Andrews didn't stop.

"Go for the big fish, Detective. It'll make your career. I'm a middle-aged white guy. She's a young, attractive Negro woman. Plays right into a sick scenario and shifts attention away from the poor job the police are doing cleaning up the cesspool of crime in Alexandria."

Decker stood looking at Andrews without any show of emotion. Andrews was visibly angry. The contrast between him and Decker could not have been more extreme. When Andrews stopped talking, Decker showed a slight grin and said, "Did you rehearse that little display?"

"Oh, fuck you, Decker," Andrews said.

Nonplussed, Decker knew it would be best not to say anything else, but Andrews was clearly upset and Decker was enjoying the situation too much to stop now.

"Colonel, since you were so generous in telling me what you think is motivating me from your completely paranoid view of the world, let me tell you what I think."

"I think I got it about right, Detective." Andrews drew deeply on his pipe.

Decker stepped forward, placing both hands on Andrews desk. Andrews was clearly uncomfortable with this invasion of the space he had intentionally kept between them. He sat back in his chair, but refused to show any of the fear he was feeling.

"You couldn't be more wrong, Colonel. I don't think Marie's ever coming home. I think she's dead and I think you killed her. I don't know why—but I have my suspicions—and I don't know how, but I am not giving up. If you made any mistakes, Andrews, I'll find them and I will throw your ass in jail for the rest of your self-righteous, self-centered life."

"Careful, Detective. Talk like that could cost you your badge. Instead of harassing me with absolutely no evidence to back you up, you ought to get your ass on the street and do some police work."

"I don't need you to tell me how to do my job," Decker said.

"And I don't think you need me to show you the way out of my office and off my installation."

51

The heavy duty vehicles arrived on site early Wednesday morning. Capping an area of a landfill was a routine task for Mike Rosario and his crew. It wasn't something they did every day, but they were veteran enough to have done it many times in the past.

When they arrived with trucks and land movers, the drivers were met with a sight they had never experienced before.

"Hey, Mike, you better come up here, man," Jimmy Berkhardt said into his radio. Berkhart had more time on the job than anyone else on the crew.

"Yeah, I'll be there in about fifteen, Jimmy. Go ahead and start without me."

"We'll give it a shot, Mike, but I'm not sure it'll work out. I'll let you know."

"Is everything okay? Has anything happened? Somebody get hurt?" Rosario asked.

"Nothing like that. It's hard to explain. We'll get moving. I'll keep you posted."

"See you in a few."

It was not uncommon to see hundreds of birds picking around the garbage in the landfill. What the crew saw this morning was a first. They couldn't count the number of crows covering a part of the area to be capped. Jimmy Berkhardt was sure there were thousands on the ground. Together they looked like a black blanket covering the trash. Above them, hundreds more circled slowly in a small cloud.

The crew closed in with a half dozen dump trucks

filled with dirt and a front-loader—its plow face elevated. The black birds didn't fly away. They barely moved. Jimmy signaled for the vehicles to stop. He then inched forward in his open jeep to see if he would have more luck, but four crows began diving at him when he stopped the jeep. Two landed on the frame of his windshield taking turns cawing at him.

"Okay, okay, I got the message," he said to the birds as he threw the jeep in reverse and retreated to a point even with the heavier equipment.

Mike Rosario cut short what he was doing in the admin trailer and joined Jimmy and the crew just as Berkhardt stopped backing up.

"What's the hold up, Jimmy?"

"It's the damnedest thing, Mike. The birds won't move—even when the vehicles roll toward the cap site."

"And?" Rosario still didn't understand why this had stopped the capping.

"And they won't expose the area so we can dump the dirt and cap the site."

"Look, Jimmy, I don't know if these birds are crazy or stupid, but I guarantee they'll move when you start dumping dirt. If not, they are about to become a permanent part of a capped landfill. Let's rock and roll."

"You heard the man," Jimmy said to his team members who had moved in to hear the conversation. "Let's cap the site."

They got back in their vehicles, started the engines, and began moving forward.

"What the hell?" Rosario said. He had been walking back to his pickup truck when he heard the sudden sounds of thousands of crows cawing in unison. He felt a drop in the air temperature. The sky darkened when an enormous black cloud of crows filled the sky. They weren't just circling above. They appeared to be diving at Rosario and the vehicles.

The cawing only got louder as the birds got closer. Some birds flew into the vehicle cabs: attacking the crew with their beaks and talons, crapping everywhere. Most flew through quickly without inflicting more than superficial cuts and scratches on the men. Eddie Mills, who was riding shotgun in the front-loader was not as fortunate. A crow caught him in the left cheek with its beak. By the time Eddie realized what had happened, he was bleeding pretty badly. He applied pressure with his handkerchief, but it was quickly changing from bright white to blood red.

Not all the birds exited the cabs cleanly. In addition to leaving a generous supply of droppings on the interior and the crew, three birds had miscalculated their exits. Two were bleeding badly on the floor of Berkhardt's jeep; the third lay dead with a broken neck on Rosario's dashboard.

Rosario sounded his pickup's horn. Others had done the same thing instinctively, but the sound of the birds was so loud the horns were not heard. And they did nothing to change the crows' behavior or attitude except possibly piss them off even more.

One by one, the six dump trucks and one front-loader braked and turned off their engines. Berkhardt was the last to cut his engine, but the first to exit a vehicle. As the vehicle engines were shut down, the attacking birds seemed to disappear. Some returned to their role as ground cover over the cap site, while others simply lifted higher into the sky.

The silence was welcome, but, at the same time, eerie.

"What the hell was that?" Rosario said to Berkhardt.

"I told you it was hard to explain when we couldn't get them to move, but this was un-fucking believable," Berkhardt said. "I don't think the crew is going to want to do anything until we figure this out."

"I don't blame them and that's why we get paid the big bucks, Jimmy," Rosario said. "I'm going to get my gun out of the pickup. Have one of the men take Eddie to the admin building in my truck. He's going to need stitches in that cut. Then, you and me, we're going to try to figure out just what the hell is so special about that part of the landfill."

Rosario and Berkhardt stepped carefully as they walked toward the blanket of crows.

"Those crows look like they're guarding the area, don't they? Do you really think you're going to need the gun, Mike?" Berkhardt asked, motioning toward the pistol Rosario had stuck in his belt.

"Shit, I hope not. I think the last time I fired this thing was ten years ago, maybe."

Rosario's comment broke the tension of the situation only slightly. The crew members were standing by their respective vehicles, watching Rosario and Berkhardt approach the birds. Each man wanted to see what was about to happen, but none was willing to get any closer.

"I guess that's a good sign," Berkhardt said, their pace slowing slightly.

"What's that?" Rosario asked.

"They haven't pecked out our eyeballs or covered us in any more shit yet," Berkhardt responded, hoping to ease his anxiety with a little humor.

"That's what I like about you, Jimmy. You always see the bright side of a situation."

"I don't know about that, Mike. I did say 'yet' remember," Berkhardt added.

They both stopped and sensed the same unspoken feeling of fear come over them.

"What the…?" Rosario said.

Absent any sense of urgency or anger, the birds lifted slightly, less than a foot off the ground. Many of them had repositioned laterally when they settled back down, exposing some of the area previously covered. This movement startled Rosario and Berkhardt until both realized the birds were not threatening. Both men stood still for a moment, trying to assess the situation. There was no turning back now.

They took a couple of cautious steps forward and the birds shifted again, this time exposing more of the area previously covered.

"There's something there," Berkhardt said. "It looks like a rolled up carpet or a small rug."

"Yeah, I see it, too," Rosario said.

"Do you believe the size of that rat?" Berkhardt pointed with a mix of excitement and fear in his voice.

The rat could have easily been confused with a squirrel because of its size, but its movements were definitely not those of a squirrel. It darted quickly, heading directly for the rolled up object.

"I'll shoot the son of a bitch," Rosario said, as he reached for the pistol in his belt.

Before he could grab the gun, however, a crow swooped down, and in one motion carried the screaming rat away in its talons.

"Do you think they'll go after us when we get too close?" Berkhardt asked.

"I actually think they've cleared the way for us. I'm beginning to think they *want* us to find whatever that rug or blanket is covering," Rosario said. "And, if that's the case, I don't like what I think we're going to find."

"Hold it, Mike," Berkhardt said as he put a hand out as if to stop Rosario's forward movement.

"What?"

"We need to call the cops. I see feet sticking out this end of the thing."

They continued to walk forward until they were standing over the blanket.

"It's a body all right," Rosario said. "We ain't capping this place today, Jimmy."

52

Dr. John Benson worked nearly twenty years for the Washington, DC, Medical Examiner before moving to the country a decade ago to be a small town doc. *The country*, at the time, was Woodbridge, Virginia.

Dr. Benson told his former colleagues he would be separated from them by only two rivers—the Potomac and the Occoquan—but that he was hopeful of leaving the grittiness of the city behind. Memories of the riots in the wake of the assassination of Martin Luther King Jr. soured Benson's view of DC and spurred his decision to leave.

In the years that had passed, Woodbridge was no longer considered as far away as Benson suggested when he said goodbye to the District. Government workers in ever-increasing numbers, both military and civilian, commuted daily to the Pentagon and DC from locations even farther south.

Though ready to leave Washington, Benson knew he was too young and too healthy to retire fully. When he learned that Prince William County was establishing an expanded coroner's office, he applied for a position and made the move. Benson found what he was looking for. He and his wife were close enough to make the drive to DC for an evening, but, day-to-day, the pace was slower, the workload was reasonable, and the deaths he saw were routinely far less violent than the bodies brought to the DC morgue.

Today brought back bad memories. The body on his table was a young, African-American female. Murdered and literally thrown away like a piece of trash. There was a nasty wound to the back of her head that was certainly enough to have killed her. The absence of an exit wound and the fact that the skull was intact ruled out a gunshot.

She was wrapped in a blanket, bloody in several places. Dr. Benson believed she was already dead when she was put in the trash and that she lost additional blood and other fluids in her body as she was compressed and mangled to some extent in the trash truck that brought her to the landfill.

He was pleased the police had not removed the blanket and that the body was delivered to him still wrapped. As he drew back the cloth, he could see a match between the stains from pooled body fluids and locations on her body where bone had broken through the skin.

Dr. Benson carefully removed her clothing, drained what little fluid remained in her body, and washed off the remaining surface dirt.

"Who does this to another human being?" Benson said aloud as he looked down on the body.

In addition to the wound to her skull, he noted a hole in her side. She had definitely been stabbed either pre- or post-mortem. No weapon was visible on the surface, but by shining a light into the wound, he could see an object. He concluded it was probably the wooden handle of a knife. He also assumed she had been stabbed by her assailant and that the knife was driven deeper into her body by the compression she experienced in the trash truck.

Benson decided to X-ray the body before he went probing into her side or began extracting the knife. He wanted to know exactly what he was dealing with.

53

"Lieutenant," Detective Birch said to Decker, who was sitting with his elbows on his desk and his face buried in his hands.

"What?" he said, without looking at Birch.

"There's a guy on the phone named Short on the blinking line. He says you're gonna want to talk to him."

"Tell him I'm too short on time to talk to him and that he should call back when he grows taller."

Every detective who overheard the exchange between Decker and Birch groaned at the weak play on words. Decker played along and gave all of them the finger. That got a laugh.

"Seriously, boss, he said he's going to make your day."

"Okay, I'll talk to Mr. Short, but it isn't going to be a lengthy conversation."

"Jesus, Lieutenant, you're killing us," an unseen voice said after the second round of groans subsided.

"Decker," he said, after picking up the receiver and pushing the blinking button on the phone.

"Lieutenant Decker, my name is Short." Decker had to smile as a half dozen additional smart-ass retorts ran through his mind. "Sergeant Dick Short from the Prince William County Police." The list of possible snarky comments just got much larger.

"Hey, Sarge. What can I do for you?"

"I'll get right to the point. I think we found her—the Negro girl you've been looking for."

Decker felt his pulse quicken. He sat up in his chair and waved to Agent King to move closer. The other cops in the room sensed that the mood had gone from joking to serious.

"What do you mean, you *think*?" Decker asked.

"Well, the coroner's got the body of a female Negro. Appears to be a teenager. He's trying to do an ID and get a cause of death. I haven't seen the body, but I understand it's in pretty bad shape."

"It's been less than a week, Sergeant. There shouldn't be that much decomp," Decker said.

"It's not so much the decomp, Lieutenant, although the summer heat has done a number on her. The detectives on the scene said the body was beat up pretty bad. Kinda mangled, you know? You see, we found her in the county dump—I mean landfill. I got a lecture from the lady in charge that the facility is a landfill and not a dump."

"Why do you think a body found in a landfill in Prince William County could be my missing girl?"

"Well, you guys in Alexandria are kind enough to send us your trash. Looks like she got here in the back of a trash truck that dumped its load sometime in the last week, based on the location where it was found. Those trucks compact the trash as they collect it. Everything in the back gets pretty rough treatment."

Decker had attracted a small crowd around his desk. They were trying to piece together the conversation based only on the side they could hear.

"How in the hell was someone able to see the body after it had been there for almost a week?"

"That, Lieutenant, is the damnedest thing. The crew at the landfill was scheduled to cap that area this morning," Short began.

"What does that mean?" Decker asked.

"Like I said, I got an education on landfills today from the lady who is in charge for the county. I'll spare you the nitty-gritty of landfill management and skip the small stuff."

Decker couldn't help but smile again. Despite the fact that Sergeant Short had his undivided attention and Decker wanted nothing more than to learn that the body found was indeed Marie Garrett's, he had to smile at the thought that a guy named Short just told him he was going to leave out the small stuff.

"Landfills are filled in sections, over time. When one area is determined to be full, crews come in and cap the area by covering the trash in a thick layer of dirt. Trucks start dumping their loads in another area and the process goes on for years. If that area wasn't scheduled to be capped today, who knows how much trash would have covered the body. She might never have been found."

"Okay, but that doesn't tell me how they found the body. Did somebody see it from one of the trucks? That sounds like a real long shot to me, Short," Decker said, hoping the sergeant didn't catch Decker's unintentional play on his name.

"No, you're right. That really *would* be a long shot." Decker's remark went unnoticed. "And God knows what actually gets buried in landfills," Short said. "In this case, the crews couldn't do their job because of the damn birds."

"Birds?"

"Thousands of them. They said it was like out of a Hitchcock movie or a Stephen King novel. There were too many birds to count and these tough guys admitted they were scared shitless."

"Hmm. I would think a dump...er...landfill always attracts birds. What made this different?" Decker asked.

"Oh, yeah. These guys always encounter all kinds of

scavengers. Birds you see every day, as well as vultures, and eagles. Rats and mice, of course. Raccoons and coyotes, too. But when the trucks get near, they scatter. Not this time."

"What did they do? Attack?"

"When you get down here, I'll let you read their statements, but bring an extra pair of boxers, because what they wrote will make you go in your pants."

"I'll keep that in mind, Sergeant. Give me your address. I'm going to bring along one of my guys and Special Agent Steve King from the FBI, since we've been collaborating on this case. We'll be there ASAP."

"Tell you what, Lieutenant. Why don't we meet at the county coroner's office?"

54

Decker, King, and Detective Birch arrived at the Prince William County coroner's office in just under thirty minutes.

"My brother-in-law commutes to DC from Woodbridge and he always bitches about the tough drive. This wasn't that bad," Birch said.

"Right and I bet he doesn't use lights and sirens when he drives home," Decker responded.

"You Lieutenant Decker?" The man getting out of the county police cruiser asked.

"That's me."

"I'm Short," the man said extending his hand that was connected by a long arm to a frame that was at least six foot five inches tall.

"No you're not. Not by a long shot," Decker replied, shaking the tall man's hand.

"Not the first time I've heard that, Lieutenant. You must have burned up the highway getting here as fast as you did. Appreciate the radio transmission to my HQ when you crossed into our county. I got here less than five minutes ago. I figured I'd wait for you in the lot before going in. I admire what these guys do, but I don't like hanging around their place of business, if you know what I mean," Sergeant Short said.

"I feel the same way," Decker said.

After they made introductions, they moved inside. The admin person at the front desk showed them to a waiting room modestly equipped with a couch, two chairs, and a coffee table. They declined her offer of coffee and waited for Dr. Benson to join them.

"Sergeant Short, I've got to tell you, your story about the birds is the damnedest thing I've ever heard," King said.

"Please call me Dick, sir, and you're right. I had a hard time believing it, but every one of the workers at the land fill told the same story. It's something out of the movies."

"Nah," Decker said. "It's too weird for a movie. Nobody would believe it."

The four of them turned to the door as it opened. Dr. Benson introduced himself. They shook hands and retook their seats. Benson carried two thin folders and a small, lunch-size paper bag.

"Well, Doc. Do you have my missing girl?" Decker asked.

"I'm afraid I do, Detective. I suspect you didn't think she would be found alive, but, from the photographs you made available through the media and police channels, I have no doubt it's her. Preliminarily, I can say she died from blunt force trauma to the back of her head. The killer must have wrapped her body in the heavy blanket in which she was found. It is padded—the kind you might see movers use to protect a piece of furniture. Her body was twisted and compressed. So, I'm guessing, he put her into a trash dumpster that was emptied into a trash truck and then unloaded into the land fill. Let's face it, gentlemen, no part of the process is particularly delicate."

"Can we see her?" Decker asked.

"Of course. I was able to position the body in a nearly prone posture—untangling it, if you will. Her face is fine which should bring some comfort to the family if they want an open casket. I have a few photos here. They're of her face. I think they can be used for the family to make a positive identification. I'm afraid her body has experienced a degree of decomposition."

He handed Decker one of the folders.

"I have copies for you, Sergeant Short," handing him the second folder.

"It's Marie, all right," Decker said. There was no sense of satisfaction in his voice. "Was there anything with her body, Doctor? Any signs of abuse?"

"You know, some things are hard to distinguish. Her body sustained injuries post-mortem from the rough treatment. There are early signs of natural decay made worse by the heat, but I saw no indication that scavenging animals had gotten to the body. Frankly, that's unusual even after so little time."

"Has anyone told you about the birds? We think crows protected her body until we recovered it," Short said.

"My field team said something about that, but I really haven't had the time to consider what sounds a bit far-fetched, if you ask me," Benson replied. "I'm nearly certain she was raped. She definitely had sex not long before she died. The trauma and the tearing tells me it was rough."

"The poor kid," Birch said.

"You've got that right, Detective. No person deserves this kind of death, and the treatment she received even after her death is unforgivable. A man named Vitullo who works for the Chicago police department is developing a kind of kit designed to collect physical evidence, especially after a sexual attack. I've read the literature on it and I used a kind of make-shift Vitullo kit to try to capture evidence from Marie's body."

"That could be helpful," King said.

"I'm not so sure," Dr. Benson said. "I can't begin to guess the amount of contamination to which her body was subjected. I don't think anything useful will come of it. I also think even a rookie attorney could cast sufficient doubt on its quality."

"I appreciate the effort, Doc," Decker said.

"There is one other thing I want to share with you before I take you back. When I examined Marie's body, I noticed a gash in her side." As he spoke, Dr. Benson pointed to his side, just above the waist. "Before going further, I X-rayed her body and then extracted a pipe." He began to unroll the top of the paper bag.

"He stabbed her with a piece of pipe?" Decker asked.

"Not a piece of pipe. This." He withdrew a plastic evidence bag containing a straight-stemmed smoker's pipe. "There's still some unburned tobacco in it and I'm guessing you'll be able to pull fingerprints from the bowl and stem with no problem."

They had expected to see a weapon of some kind. Instead, they stared incredulously at the pipe. Decker began to smile.

"The way in which her body was wrapped, my guess is the killer left it behind in the blanket unintentionally. I don't think for a minute that he stabbed her with it. In the course of her body being tossed around while essentially swaddled, I think the pipe stabbed into her side, with the thin, hard plastic mouthpiece entering first. All I could see was the end of the wood bowl when I shined a light in the wound. I thought it was a knife handle, but I X-rayed to be sure."

"Doctor Benson," Decker said. "I'm pretty sure you have just put one arrogant son of a bitch in jail for the rest of his miserable life."

55

Coverage of the Marie Garrett story moved from the Metro section of *The Washington Post* to above the fold on A-1 when the commander of Cameron Station was arrested in connection with her murder. The Virginia Commonwealth Attorney and the Army's Judge Advocate General collaborated to achieve their respective goals.

The Army court-martialed Andrews for dereliction of duty, conduct unbecoming an officer, fraternization with a subordinate, and a few minor charges. Those convictions were enough to reduce Andrews in grade from colonel to private, to sentence him to a lengthy stay in the Fort Leavenworth prison, and to give him a Bad Conduct Discharge. But Andrews would never spend a day in the Fort Leavenworth facility.

The Army ceded jurisdiction for Marie's abduction and murder to the civilian authorities. The murder trial received extensive coverage, but the story was relatively short-lived.

The trial was brief and the dramatic details surfaced almost immediately after the arrest, to include the fact that Nancy Andrews did not plan to be in the courtroom at any time during the trial. In fact, Nancy was so hurt by her husband's betrayal that, while he was consulting with his attorney, she was meeting with a lawyer of her own to discuss divorce.

Andrews' attorney, Bill Cahill, was competent, but he didn't have a lot to work with and he didn't shy away from telling Andrews how weak their case was.

"I don't agree," Andrews told Cahill. "No jury is going to convict me for murdering someone like that."

"Fleming, you're either dreaming or delusional. I am not going to ask you if you are guilty. I don't want to know. But, if you can't give me more than what we've got, you are in trouble—big trouble."

At trial, in the face of the physical evidence the prosecution offered, Andrews demanded his lawyer suggest, what he called, two plausible alternatives that he was convinced would introduce enough reasonable doubt to keep the jury from finding him guilty.

Cahill, initially refused.

"Fleming, no one—and I mean no one—will believe either of your ideas is a possibility," Cahill said.

Andrews insisted.

"Lieutenant Decker," Cahill began his cross-examination. "Tell me about the pipe that was found embedded in Miss Garrett's side."

"Well," Decker said, "the medical examiner concluded it was jammed into Marie's side as a result of the rough treatment the body received by being dumped into the trash truck, mixed in with other trash pickups, and eventually dumped into the landfill."

"And it was Colonel Andrews' pipe, was it not?"

"That's right. The lab found Andrews' prints several places on the pipe. Additionally, it was filled with Andrews' brand of tobacco and a forensic dentist said the teeth marks on the stem were from Andrews' teeth."

"I see," Cahill said, "but we don't know that Colonel Andrews put the pipe there, do we?"

"I don't know what you're asking me, Counselor," Decker responded.

"We'll get back to that, Lieutenant. Tell me about Miss Garrett's purse," Cahill continued.

"Her purse was found in Andrews' briefcase, hidden in a

secret compartment."

"A secret compartment, Lieutenant? Really? Let's not get all James Bond here. Colonel Andrews didn't install this compartment did he?"

"What?"

"The compartment that you unfairly describe as *secret* is, in fact, a standard feature of every briefcase of that make and model. Is it not?"

"Yes, of course, but it is not easily seen when the briefcase is opened."

"Of course it isn't, Lieutenant," Cahill said. "Lieutenant, isn't it possible that Miss Garrett might have taken advantage of an opportunity to take Colonel Andrews' pipe as a souvenir? A souvenir of an officer she idolized and then, as an immature girl capable of making bad decisions, slipped her purse into Colonel Andrews' briefcase to ensure he would reconnect with her outside the workplace in order to return it to her?"

Cahill couldn't believe he actually presented such a ridiculous scenario. Some in the courtroom laughed aloud when he got to the end of his question. Those who did not laugh appeared to grumble disapprovingly in unison. For his part, Andrews nodded his head at Cahill, convinced the defense had scored points with the jury.

The judge gaveled the courtroom back into order. Before Decker could begin to answer, the Commonwealth Attorney, Matt Solomon, objected.

"Your honor," Solomon said, getting to his feet, "just because the defense has absolutely no coherent argument to refute the evidence, it should not be construed as license to make a mockery of the proceedings with ridiculous propositions."

"I'll make the judgment calls, Mr. Solomon, but I'm humbled by your concern for the dignity of the court. Nonetheless, Lieutenant Decker, you were asked a question."

"Yes, your honor. My professional and personal opinion of your theories, Mr. Cahill, is that they are ridiculous. We found nothing to suggest either of your theories is a possibility. Again, they are ridiculous, Mr. Cahill."

More noise from the courtroom was again met with the judge's gavel.

"Enough," the judge said. "Order in my courtroom or I'll throw all of you out. Do you have any other questions or theories you want to offer, Mr. Cahill?"

"No, your honor. No further questions."

Cahill sat down and turned to Andrews.

"Well, that went over like a fart in church. Are you happy now, Fleming?"

"You wait and see," Andrews said to Cahill. "I know people. It went over well with the jury."

Cahill shook his head and looked away.

In their summations, the defense could only assert that there remained a reasonable doubt about Andrews' guilt. Cahill contended that the prosecution had not proven its case. He recounted Andrews' years of service to the nation at a time when it was not popular. He said this was a manifestation of Andrews' good character as it was developed at West Point.

"The fact that Miss Garrett's purse was not discovered in Colonel Andrews' briefcase until it was thoroughly searched after his arrest is compelling evidence that not even Colonel Andrews knew it was there," Cahill appealed to the jury. "If Colonel Andrews is as calculating and cold-blooded as the prosecution would have you believe, he would have most certainly gotten rid of the purse and its contents. He had plenty of time and opportunity to do so."

In fact, as the weekend drew on, Andrews had all he could handle with the stress coming to bear on him. He allowed the need to deal with the purse to slip his mind.

Solomon was tempted to offer the jury a lengthy list of West Point graduates whose service to the nation was anything but honorable, thereby challenging the defense assertion that a diploma from West Point was a guarantee of good character. He decided against this approach, fearing it would deflect the jury's attention from where it should be: the murder of Marie Garrett.

He ridiculed the defense for suggesting that Marie may have stolen the pipe as a memento of a man she idolized.

"I don't think Marie was planning to take up pipe smoking and it's hard for anyone—except Mr. Andrews, of course—to believe that Marie Garrett idolized this man she and so many others have described as a little creepy."

Solomon then went on to list the specific items submitted in evidence. He pointed out that the defense had been unable to successfully refute any of the evidence against Andrews. He recounted the testimony of Laura Bennett, Dan Grady, Susan Braswell, Lieutenant Colonel Jack Ewing, Captain Rick McGrath, Sergeant Major Ed Rodriguez, and several other soldiers and civilian Cameron Station employees, calling into question Andrews' integrity.

"It wasn't easy for some of these dedicated employees to have to admit that there was something off about Colonel Andrews. Sometimes blatant, but usually subtle and always not quite above board. It was hard for people—especially women—to admit that they were uncomfortable around him," Solomon said. "When you find him guilty of this awful crime, do not think for a minute that you are hurting an honorable man. No. You are ensuring that justice is served. You are ensuring the guilty party pays for the terrible murder of Marie Garrett—an innocent young woman who had a bright future ahead of her. Mr. Cahill wants you to think Fleming Andrews is a wonderful American. Fleming

Andrews is a lot of things. He's an egomaniac, a pedophile, a psychopath, a predator, and a pervert. And, at the end of the day, when you have done your work, I am confident he will also be a convicted murderer."

The judge handed the case to the jury at 9:30 in the morning. Three hours later, the lawyers were advised that a verdict had been reached.

"Back already?" Andrews said to Cahill. "That's probably not a good sign."

"You're fucked, Fleming. Start getting used to the fact."

"I should have fired you when I realized I had to come up with my own counterarguments," Andrews said.

"I wish you had. You still can, in fact. Maybe I should walk away. It might be your only chance of being able to claim you were poorly represented. The evidence against you is overwhelming, Fleming. You are not a sympathetic defendant. The jury can't stand you."

"The evidence is bullshit," Andrews countered. "It's all circumstantial and can be explained away any number of ways."

"It didn't work so well in court and, frankly, the fat lady is about to belt out her final tune."

"Maybe I should have testified myself."

"Oh, that would have been entertaining. I've never seen a human being shredded in front of my eyes."

"Screw you," Andrews said.

56

Andrews was convicted and sentenced to death. He was incarcerated in the federal penitentiary in Richmond, Virginia, to be executed after the appeals process was exhausted.

Who Andrews was and why he was there was common knowledge. He found everything about prison life to be below his standards and not at all comfortable. He ridiculed the guards and had disdain for every other prisoner. He had been wrongly convicted of an act he was justified committing. His time alone gave him ample opportunity to convince himself further of his righteousness.

His evening rants in his cell were met with complaints by the other men on death row. The guards thought he was going crazy. Eventually, the doctors began sedating him at night. Each of the other six men awaiting execution offered to kill Andrews if the guards would agree to turn their backs for a few minutes. Tempting as that was, the guards knew they could not allow a fatal assault on Andrews in his cell.

As happens to many prisoners in their initial year behind bars, Andrews' appetite was not great and he fell victim to nearly every germ that floated throughout the institution. The cold he caught after a couple of months in prison, became persistent. It was obvious that he was dehydrated and was suffering from some kind of serious upper respiratory ailment. The doctors thought he would respond better to treatment if he spent a night or two in the dispensary.

After he was moved to a bed in the dispensary, a nurse gave him a sedative and started an IV to rehydrate him. She told him to relax while the IV did its work.

"The doctor will be in shortly, Mr. Andrews," the nurse said. "You're going to be here for the night. Just lay back and try to get some rest." She exited the room and turned off the overhead light.

"It's colonel," he said. "Call me by my rank, damn it." She had already gone down the hall and did not hear him. She turned right at the guard desk and headed to the nurses' station. Andrews quickly fell asleep.

One of the two nurses on duty notified the senior prison guard assigned to death row that Andrews would spend the night in the dispensary. Within minutes, a call was made from the death row guard's phone, directing a change in the two prisoners assigned to the evening's dispensary laundry detail. Two additional prisoners were allowed to accompany the detail, but their names were not recorded.

The face appearing in the window of the locked dispensary door caused the guard to buzz in the two-man laundry detail, as well as the two other prisoners who accompanied them. All four nodded to the guard as they entered and the door locked behind them. Two prisoners pushed the laundry cart filled with clean towels and linens down the hall to the nurses' station. Its wheels squeaked loudly on the dispensary's tile floor. The other two inmates moved quickly down the hall to Andrews' room.

The guard followed the laundry cart. When he passed the open door of the on-duty doctor's office, he reached for the doorknob.

"Want me to shut your door while the cart is here, Doc?" the guard asked.

"Hey, thanks, officer. I appreciate it."

The guard lingered in the hallway, midway between his desk and the nurses' station. He was prepared to delay the doctor in meaningless conversation if the door opened too soon. It did not.

Both nurses on duty were engaged with overseeing the exchange of clean towels, sheets, and other linens for soiled items to be washed. The process took several minutes. When they were done, the two prisoners pushed the cart down the hall to the guard's desk, where they met their two colleagues and were permitted to leave the dispensary.

Fifteen or so minutes later, a nurse tapped on the doctor's office door to see if he had additional instructions regarding Andrews' care. The doctor admitted that he had not yet had an opportunity to look in on Andrews, but he would directly. The nurse left the doctor's office and decided to check on Andrews herself.

When the nurse returned to Andrews' room a short time later, she found Andrews face down on the bed. The coroner would determine the cause of death to be suffocation, but would note that Andrews had also been strangled and struck violently on the head and torso nearly a dozen times. The wounds were consistent with those made by a strong stick, likely a broken mop or broom handle, presumably the same one found protruding from Andrews' rectum at the time he was found by the nurse.

The incident was investigated internally and determined to have been the result of a prisoner-on-prisoner attack with the assailant or assailants not able to be determined. Such a finding almost certainly would not have stood up to close scrutiny had the victim's family protested or raised any doubts.

When the prison authorities contacted Nancy to advise her that her husband had been killed in prison, she let them know she had filed for divorce days after he was sent to prison and had no interest in claiming the body or any of his possessions.

"Throw him and his crap in the garbage…the same way he treated that poor girl. That's what he deserves."

Andrews was buried in a prison graveyard where the

unclaimed bodies of deceased inmates had been interred since the prison went into operation nearly 100 years earlier. The marker on the grave bore his name, the year of his birth, and the year of his death. At the top of the stone, in much smaller type, was Andrews' prisoner serial number, to ease any future effort to research him or his crimes.

57

At the time of Andrews' trial, no one could have foreseen what the future held for Cameron Station. Much had changed since the Army first took possession of the land in 1941. It was the home of the Defense Logistics Agency, provided commissary and exchange services, and several other smaller tenant activities to include a military printing shop and a photo lab.

With the end of the Cold War and the need for the Defense Department to economize and lower its operating overhead, Cameron Station stood out as a military anachronism. In 1990, Congress passed the Base Closure and Realignment Act which established a commission to identify military installations as candidates for closure or a change in mission. The rules of the base closure process permitted the commission to develop a list of military bases to be closed across the United States, sanctioned by an all-or-nothing congressional vote.

Few were surprised when Cameron Station was among the military installations identified by the commission. Cameron Station had outlived its military usefulness. The only fact more obvious was that the real estate that was Cameron Station had enormous value as residential property.

Cameron Station no longer had an active military mission as of September 30, 1995. By the end of 1996, sixty-three acres were ceded to the city of Alexandria as a city park, while 101 acres were sold to a private developer, who quickly got to work building private dwellings. At some point, it was decided the community would retain the name *Cameron Station*.

In 2000, the city built an elementary school on the land where the residential community meets the parkland. The school would be dedicated to the memory of Marie Garrett.

In the thirty years since her death, Marie's parents had died. A year to the day after her death, Marie's father was killed in a massive pile-up on a fog-shrouded interstate in Pennsylvania. Family tradition held that Cecilia Garrett died of a broken heart not long thereafter.

Marie's uncle, Henry Washington, now nearly 80-years old attended the outdoor dedication in front of the school. After the speeches, as attendees queued up to tour the building, Washington shuffled slowly away from the school and toward the concrete spillway that separated the Cameron Station community from the remaining commercial railroad tracks on the other side. At his side, was his service dog, a black lab named Bailey.

Washington suffered from a neuropathy resulting in numbness in his feet that often caused him to lose his balance. He also dealt with anxiety attacks whenever he became disoriented. Bailey was trained to allow Washington literally to lean his lower leg against her. She would push back, providing a counter-weight that allowed him to regain his balance. The dog sensed when Washington's anxiety was increasing. She was able to ease and shorten those periods, again by making contact with him and by being present for him.

When they reached the fence at the edge of the spillway, Washington stopped and looked across to the area that had been the installation's rail yard so many years ago.

"That's it there, Bailey," he said in a soft voice to his dog. "That's where that son of a bitch killed my little girl. I was like a second daddy to her. It's my fault he was able to do that to her." He was struggling to maintain his composure.

Looking up now, he noticed birds coming to rest in the trees across the way, near the tracks. In the tree line that easily stretched a quarter mile, they appeared to select a small set of trees directly across from Washington.

They kept arriving. The trees were filled with leaves, but now their branches were heavy with the black-feathered blossoms that were hundreds of crows.

And they kept arriving. Were there a thousand by now? Who knew? There were too many to count. As they entered the trees and encountered the leaves, they made a rustling noise. Once they chose a branch, the thousands of birds made no sound. Nothing. No annoying caw. Not a feather ruffled.

Above Washington, a large number of crows swooped low, then darted for the same group of trees. Bailey growled softly, looking up and then across the spillway.

"Easy, Bailey," Washington said.

In silent salute, they perched.

Just when it appeared the calm would last forever, the crows—husbands and wives, young and old—sprang from the branches and flew in a black cloud toward Washington. Silently and sharply, they turned in unison to the west, before gradually going their separate ways.

Washington lost the sense of how long the ritual lasted. He also had no idea if anyone else observed it. He had seen this behavior before, but this was somehow different. This was special.

Bailey reacted to the sudden emergence from the trees. She growled deeply—louder than before.

"It's okay, girl," Washington said. "Their work is done."

Epilogue

Harold Jefferson was nearing the end of his tenure as the groundskeeper at the Richmond Penitentiary. Retirement was less than sixty days away. Every two weeks in the summer months for the last twenty-five years he would climb on the small tractor, lower the mowing attachment, and drive up and down the rows of headstones in the prison graveyard.

Today, his replacement, Tyrone Franklin did the mowing. When Franklin was done, the two men walked through the graveyard, with Jefferson critiquing Franklin's work. He pointed to an area where it was necessary to do more trimming, and to others where Franklin hadn't cut a tight enough corner.

Franklin figured the warden would never inspect the graveyard and Jefferson had already told him he couldn't remember the last time anyone visited the graves. Franklin guessed the dead convicts weren't about to complain. Yet, Franklin accepted the evaluation, albeit with a grain of salt.

He sensed Jefferson needed this moment to be the veteran, teaching the new guy the finer points of this part of the job. If it made it easier for Jefferson to hand over the reins, Franklin was okay with it.

"Okay. I got it. I see what you mean. Thanks, man," Franklin said.

"Franklin, now I'm going to show you something that I guarantee will be true no matter how hard you work to keep it from happening."

The men walked together until Jefferson stopped in front of one of the headstones at the end of a row.

"This here is it," Jefferson said.

"This is what?" Franklin asked.

"This. Look."

"I can't hardly read it, there's so much bird crap on it. What's it say? I see a M-I-N-G and a D-R-E-W. Something like that," Franklin said.

"My man, you can clean this headstone every day and when you come back in a couple of hours, it will be covered in bird shit again. It's the damnedest thing," Jefferson said.

"There isn't a tree anywhere near this thing."

"It's got nothing to do with trees. You are standing on the grave of Fleming Andrews. He raped and killed a young black girl in the 70s."

"Do tell."

"He was some big shot in the Army up there in the Pentagon or something."

"No kidding?" Franklin said.

"Uh-uh. No kidding. Court sent him to death row, but some prisoners killed him. Word is the guards let it happen. Not a tear was shed when this guy died. To this day, the birds make sure his headstone is covered in shit," Jefferson added.

"Seems fair to me," Franklin said.

"Yes it does. Seems fair to me, as well."

Acknowledgments

I gratefully acknowledge the constant support of my wife, Eileen, to whom this book is dedicated.

My thanks also go out to Charlie Abell, Dorsey Chescavage, Barbara Dieker, and Ron Maney. This effort may well have been abandoned if not for their continued encouragement and confidence in my ability—a confidence that often exceeded my own.

I am also grateful to my editor, Kathy Garvey, who promised to be thorough and, if necessary, ruthless as she helped ensure there would be a quality end product. Kathy failed to mention how patient she would be with this rookie.

Fredericksburg, Virginia
August 2018

Author's Notes

Cameron Station

Until 1995, when it was closed as a result of a Base Closure and Realignment Commission recommendation, Cameron Station was, in fact, an active military installation in Alexandria, Virginia. Railroad tracks run very close to the property, but I don't think the installation ever had its own rail yard.

An elementary school was constructed where the residential property meets the park land. The school was dedicated to the memory of Samuel W. Tucker, an Alexandria native, attorney, and civil rights activist. It was certainly not my intention to diminish the honor justly paid to Mr. Tucker when, in *Murder Gets Even*, the school is dedicated to Marie Garrett.

Crows...Really?

Crows are smart. Perhaps not as smart as I suggest, but I wouldn't count them out. Scientists consider Corvids (crows, ravens, rooks, jays, and a few others) to be among the smartest animals on earth. Young crows engage in play. Adult crows are monogamous for life. They recognize human faces and can remember good and bad experiences. They have been shown to grieve the loss of other crows.

Crows join humans, elephants, and apes as the only animals that use tools. In fact, crows have been observed in the wild, crafting tools out of sticks to sharpen points and make functional hooks. They have been called "apes with wings" and, yes, a "flock" of crows is called a murder.

I welcome your comments.

I hope you enjoyed the book. If you would like to comment, you can do so by emailing me at *johnmolinobooks@gmail.com*.